MW01134041

THE GHOST
AND THE DOPPELGANGER

HAUNTING DANIELLE

HAUNTING DANIELLE - BOOK 16

THE GHOST
AND THE DOPPELGANGER

BOBBI HOLMES

The Ghost and the Doppelganger
(Haunting Danielle, Book 16)
A Novel
By Bobbi Holmes
Cover Design: Elizabeth Mackey

Copyright © 2018 Bobbi Holmes
Robeth Publishing, LLC
All Rights Reserved.
robeth.net

ROBETH
PUBLISHING, LLC

This novel is a work of fiction.
Any resemblance to places or actual persons,
living or dead, is entirely coincidental.

ISBN-13: 978-1986476942
ISBN-10: 1986476944

To the fans of Haunting Danielle.
Without them this book would not have been written.

ONE

Flames hovered over the rock surface like slender golden fingers waving erratically in the night air. Beneath the fire, the faux stone structure concealed its propane tank. Heat and ambiance generated by the fire pit made the balcony both a romantic and cozy setting. Beyond the balcony's short stucco wall, city lights illuminated March's moonless night. They randomly twinkled while headlights from the traffic provided motion to the evening landscape.

Sitting side by side in patio rockers, the woman propped her stockinged feet up on the footstool separating her from the fire pit, while the man next to her refilled both of their wineglasses. Casually dressed, she wore a long royal blue cashmere sweater over a pair of black leggings, and he wore denim jeans and a long-sleeved burgundy golf shirt. It was chilly enough to need long sleeves, yet not quite cold enough—with the fire pit and night air—to need a jacket. Yet, if the temperature dipped a few more degrees, Stephanie Mountifield might be tempted to go inside and retrieve a throw to toss over her lap. She had left her shoes inside, while he rarely went around in just stockinged feet. When removing his shoes earlier, he had put on a pair of slippers.

When he finished pouring the wine, Stephanie took a sip and said, "Just one more week, Clint. Then we're out of here. Paris. I can't believe we're going to Paris and then Greece!"

"First, we go to Oregon," Clint Marlow reminded her.

Stephanie shrugged. "You know what I mean." She glanced around Clint's condominium balcony. Unlike some of the other balconies in the complex, there was no barbecue. Clint preferred eating out, and so did she. The patio furniture was less than six months old, and they wouldn't be taking it with them. He was selling the condo furnished. Had he known six months ago what he was going to do, he probably wouldn't have bought the new furniture. However, Stephanie knew he didn't regret the purchase. He had told her the condo would sell quicker if it was attractively staged, and the balcony was inviting, especially with its current furniture. He had been right. Within a week of listing the property, he had received multiple offers.

The sound of the evening traffic was partially dulled by the water feature plugged into the patio's corner. A stream of water spilled from one ceramic vase to another before recycling back to the top of the fountain and sent on the same journey, again and again. Like the fire pit, the fountain provided ambiance. Both the fire pit and fountain would be staying with the condo's new owners.

With a sigh, Stephanie asked, "Are you going to miss it here?"

"What's to miss? Irritating clients? Incompetent agents?" Swirling the wine in his glass a moment, Clint paused and studied Stephanie. "What about you, are you going to miss it?"

She shrugged. "I don't know. All I've ever wanted to do is travel. But…I do worry, what if it doesn't work out in Oregon?"

Clint drank some of his wine and then leaned back in his chair, resting his elbows on the rocker's arms. "This is going to work. I'll make it work."

"And when we get to Paris, is it possible she might come after us there?" Leaning back in the rocker, the wineglass in her right hand, Stephanie absently held out her left hand, studying the engagement ring. Wiggling her fingers slightly, she enjoyed the twinkling of the generous diamond while listening to what Clint was saying.

"The art of a con is never letting your mark know they've been taken. She won't have a clue."

Dropping her left hand back onto her lap, she turned to Clint. "I don't like it when you say it like that—it makes you sound like some sort of thief or something."

Clint laughed. "What do you think we're doing?"

"I don't look at it as stealing, exactly. After all, Danielle Boatman doesn't have the right to any of it. She wasn't related to Walt Marlow. You are. She's nothing more than the niece of the house-keeper's illegitimate daughter. And not even a blood niece!"

"And I will be putting some of that to right, won't I?" Clint flashed Stephanie a smile and then finished what was left in his wineglass.

"I'd love to see that necklace I read about. That should be yours too!"

Clint leaned forward and set his empty wineglass on the side table between the two rockers. "Don't get crazy, babe. I've no desire to go to prison, and neither do you. I have a feeling she'd miss the necklace if we took it."

Stephanie let out a sigh and leaned back in her chair. "I suppose...but still...it is a shame."

"Babe, when we're done, I'll buy you your own diamond and emerald necklace." He reached over and patted her knee.

"You would, wouldn't you?"

"I'd do anything for you." His gaze moved over the blonde, admiring her thickly lashed blue eyes, petite turned-up nose, and the most kissable mouth he had ever seen. The rest of her was even better, he thought with a groan.

Smiling, Stephanie stopped rocking for a moment and leaned toward Clint, giving him a brief kiss on his cheek. She then leaned back in her chair and started rocking again.

"Everything is falling into place. The day after escrow closes, we'll be on the plane to Portland." Clint picked up the wine bottle and refilled his glass.

"And after Portland, a Paris wedding." Stephanie sighed.

"It will be perfect."

"I talked to my father today." Stephanie held out her glass for Clint to fill.

"And?" He refilled her wine.

"I told him we're going to be doing some traveling. I didn't give him any specifics."

Clint smiled. "He didn't ask if we were going to Texas to see him?"

"He doesn't ask that anymore. Although he did ask if we set a date for the wedding yet."

"What did you tell him?"

"I told him I'd let him know when we get married. Kind of like he did when he married that woman."

"Ouch." Clint cringed.

Stephanie shrugged. "It's true."

"Well, we're going on an amazing adventure." Clint raised his wineglass in toast. "Here's to my dear cousin, Walt Marlow, who's making all our dreams come true!"

DANIELLE BOATMAN SAT ALONE at the Pearl Cove bar, waiting for her friends to arrive. It was girls' night out. To be precise, it was their first girls' night. Not the bar's, but Danielle's and her friends'. It had been Heather Donovan's idea. Danielle suspected Heather's inspiration came from the fact she didn't have a boyfriend. Neither did Danielle, yet when their informal group went out together, she and Chris always seemed to be a pair—a platonic pair.

Lily was now married, and Melony and Adam were a couple like her and Chris, yet she suspected they weren't exactly platonic. And if Marie had her way, the two would stop avoiding commitment and admit they were boyfriend and girlfriend.

But tonight, it was just the girls: Danielle, Lily, Melony, and Heather. Adam was hosting a poker party at his house. Walt was home alone, reading a book Danielle had checked out for him from the local library, and Marie was off gallivanting with Eva. Gallivanting was Marie's word, not Danielle's.

Danielle sipped her Chardonnay and glanced at her watch, checking the time. Her friends weren't late, she was early. Just as she set her wineglass on the oak bar top, motion to her right caught her attention. Someone was sitting down next to her at the bar. Glancing over to the newcomer, she expected to see one of her friends. After all, until that moment, she was the only one sitting at the bar, why would anyone else choose to sit right next to her when there were at least a dozen empty barstools? But then she had her answer. It was a young man—one she had never seen before—grinning at her as he rested his elbows on the bar top.

Danielle flashed him a weak smile and picked up her wine, taking a sip. Friendly conversation she could deal with, but if he intended to hit on her, that she could do without.

The stranger started the conversation with, "You have really nice hair."

Before Danielle could give a polite thank-you, he added, "I bet you could really fix it nice if you wanted to."

Startled by his comment, Danielle frowned. "Excuse me?"

Before the man could explain, the bartender walked up and asked what he would like to drink. After the stranger ordered a beer and the bartender walked away, he looked back to Danielle and said with a shrug, "I guess a braid is easy. You know, gets you out of the house with minimal effort. But I bet if you spent a little more time on your hair," the man paused a moment, eyed Danielle critically and then added, "maybe experiment a little with some makeup, you could be kind of hot."

"Umm...thanks...I think." Danielle glanced at her watch again and then looked to the doorway leading to the entry.

"Stood up?" he asked.

"What?"

"Ah, come on, it happens to all of us one time or another. I saw you checking out your watch when I sat down, and you just did it again, and your eyes keep looking to the doorway. I hate to see a girl like you get embarrassed when the guy stands her up. It's not right."

"Girl like me?"

"You're cute—in your own way. You have potential there, but some guys just never see it. But don't worry, if he doesn't show up, I'll let the bartender think I was the one you were waiting for so you don't get embarrassed."

Furrowing her brows, Danielle studied the man a moment. He wasn't unattractive. If he had never opened his mouth, she might have described him as pleasant looking. She guessed he was about ten years older than herself, considering his thinning brown hair.

"You really shouldn't do that," he whispered.

"Do what?" Danielle asked.

"Wrinkle your forehead like that. You'll get more wrinkles."

More wrinkles? she thought.

To her relief she spied Lily and Heather entering the restaurant, with Melony close behind them.

Snatching up her drink from the bar, Danielle stood up. "My friends are here. Have a nice evening." Without another word, she turned from the stranger and hurried away.

"I THOUGHT we were going to have a drink in the bar first," Heather grumbled when the four were seated in the dining room.

"I'm sorry, but I met the most obnoxious man in the bar," Danielle explained as she took a seat at the table. "I just wanted to get away from him."

"Someone was hitting on you?" Lily asked as she sat down.

"Not exactly. I thought he was going to, but he ended up insulting me." Danielle shrugged and then picked up a menu.

After the server took their drink order and left the table, Lily asked, "What do you mean he insulted you?"

"I guess he doesn't like braids," Danielle began. She went on and recounted her entire conversation with the stranger.

After Danielle finished her telling, Heather said, "Ahh, the guy was negging you."

"Nagging me?" Danielle asked. "Why do you say that?"

"No, negging," Lily corrected. She looked to Heather and nodded. "Definitely, he was negging her."

"What in the world is negging?" Danielle asked, looking from Lily to Heather and then to Melony, who only shrugged.

"Negging is new to me," Melony said as she picked up her glass of iced water and took a sip.

"It's a pickup technique some guys use," Heather explained.

"Pickup technique?" Danielle choked out. "You can't be serious?"

"On the plus side, it means the guy thinks you're out of his league," Lily said with a grin.

Danielle shook her head. "I don't get it."

"It's a lame strategy some loser concocted to hit on girls. Guys supposedly use it on hot girls in an attempt to undermine their self-confidence, the theory being women will do anything to get the guy's approval after he's made her feel insecure," Heather explained.

"Well, that's the stupidest thing I've ever heard." Danielle looked to Lily. "How is it you knew about this negging and I didn't?"

"I suspect because you were married to Lucas and not really out where guys were hitting on you. Whereas I was single for all that time. And the two guys you did date after Lucas aren't the negging type. I certainly don't see Joe doing something like that; he'd see it as dishonorable. And Chris, well, guys like Chris don't need to stoop to negging."

"I guess that explains why I've never heard of it before now. I haven't really been out to bars alone since my divorce. Yet now I'm curious." Melony stood up.

"Where are you going?" Heather asked.

"I've got to see what this guy looks like," Melony said with a laugh.

"I have to admit his comment about my braid got to me," Danielle said after Melony left the table and headed to the bar. "I've been considering cutting my hair. Trying a new hairstyle."

"Danielle, I can't believe you'd be a pushover for a negging guy!" Heather gasped.

Danielle scrunched up her nose. "Eww, don't be gross! The guy was a jerk. I just meant I've been thinking of cutting my hair, and when he opened with that comment about my braid, it got me to thinking about it again."

"Just as long as you aren't considering cutting your hair because some jerk at the bar made a derogatory remark about it," Lily said.

Danielle rolled her eyes. "Don't be silly."

"I know that guy!" Melony gushed when she hurried back to the table and took her seat. Just as she did, the server arrived with their cocktails.

When the server left the table, Danielle asked, "The annoying guy in the bar?"

Melony nodded as she picked up her cocktail and took a sip. She set the drink back on the table and said, "I went to school with him. I heard he moved back to town. He used to be a good friend of Adam's."

"Why doesn't that surprise me?" Danielle said with a chuckle.

TWO

The next morning Walt found Danielle sitting at her vanity, staring into the mirror, her fingers absently fidgeting with the ends of her long dark hair. She had already dressed for the day, wearing navy blue leggings and a casual dress, her feet bare. So focused on whatever was on her mind, she failed to notice Walt had entered the room and now stood directly behind her. Since he had no reflection, she couldn't see him in the mirror.

Walt stood there a moment watching, and when Danielle continued to twist the ends of her hair while staring at her reflection, he finally asked, "Can't decide to wear it in a braid or down?"

With a gasp, Danielle jerked around in the chair to face Walt. "I didn't hear you come in!"

Walt smiled. "Sorry. I didn't mean to startle you. But you seemed so intent. What were you thinking?"

Releasing hold of her hair, Danielle moved her chair around and fully faced Walt. Folding her hands on her lap, she looked up at him and asked, "I have a question to ask you."

Walt stepped back and sat on the foot of Danielle's bed, his gaze never leaving her. "Go ahead and ask."

"Do you think I should cut my hair?"

Walt arched his brows. "Cut your hair?"

Danielle nodded. "Yes. I've been braiding my hair for a long time, and I really think I need a new look."

"I like your look," Walt told her.

Letting out a disgruntled sigh, she asked, "You don't think I should cut it?"

Instead of answering immediately, Walt studied Danielle a moment, his head tilting slightly to one side and then another. Finally, he said, "I think you've changed me."

"Changed you? What are you talking about?"

"There was a time I wouldn't hesitate telling you exactly what to do."

Danielle frowned. "And now?"

"I think you should do whatever you want to do. I'll admit, I'm partial to long hair, and yours is beautiful. But as I recall, you look rather adorable in a Castle Bob."

Danielle smiled, recalling that long-ago dream hop where Walt had taken her dancing. In the dream, her hair had been cut short like a flapper's. With a cheeky grin she said, "Well, not sure I want to cut it that short."

"It's your hair, Danielle. I'm sure you'll look lovely however you decide to wear it. If you feel you need a change, then that's what you should do."

"I think I'd like to cut it." Danielle stood up. "Melony gave me the name of a hairdresser she likes. I think I'll see if I can get an appointment."

"Today?"

"I doubt she'll be able to get me in today. I probably won't be able to get an appointment for a couple of weeks. That's why I need to call her now."

"DANIELLE'S CUTTING HER HAIR?" Marie said after Walt told her about his recent conversation with Danielle. The two spirits sat alone in the parlor.

"Yes," Walt said dully. "She called a hairdresser Melony suggested. Apparently, there was a last minute cancelation, and she's going down there in about an hour."

"You don't seem too happy about this," Marie noted.

Walt shrugged. "Don't say anything to Danielle. It's something she really wants to do, and it is her hair."

Marie chuckled.

9

"What?"

"You surprise me sometimes, Walt Marlow. You sound quite liberated for a man who was born in the 1800s."

"Almost the 1900s," Walt reminded her. "And the fact is, Danielle is a woman from this time, and even if I told her she shouldn't cut her hair, I don't imagine that would stop her." He chuckled at the thought.

"I certainly hope not!"

Walt grinned.

"I wonder if Danielle would mind if I tag along while she gets her hair cut? I rather miss going to the beauty parlor," Marie wondered aloud.

"THANK you for letting me go with you," Marie told Danielle. She sat in the passenger seat of Danielle's new Ford Flex.

"Nice to have the company," Danielle said as she backed out of the driveway. Glancing over to Marie, she smiled. The spirit looked just slightly younger than Marie had been at death. Instead of portraying herself as the ninety-one-year-old woman who had been smothered at the nursing home, Marie chose to shave off a little more than a decade—a younger version, eighty. Unbeknownst to Danielle, when with Eva, Marie presented herself as an even younger version—not much older than Eva had been at the time of her death. Marie never knew what other spirit she might run into when with Eva, and she was vain enough to want to look her best.

Twenty minutes later, Danielle sat in a chair at the beauty parlor, looking into the mirror, Marie at her side.

"You have beautiful hair," the hairdresser noted as she ran her fingertips through the ends of Danielle's hair. "How short do you want to go?"

"I was thinking above my shoulders, but below my chin. It has some natural curl. I'd like lots of layers. I don't want to spend a lot of time fixing my hair. I'd like something I can wash and comb out with a blow dryer. Maybe use a curling iron if I have to."

Thirty minutes later, the hairstylist had washed and cut Danielle's hair and was just combing it out when Marie walked to the front window. She looked outside. Just down the street was Adam's office. She turned to Danielle and said, "I think I'll pop down to Adam's. If I'm not back when she's done, please meet me there." Marie disappeared.

———

ADAM NICHOLS SAT ALONE in his inner office. His receptionist, Leslie, had left for an early lunch a few minutes earlier, so he decided to take the time to check out a few of his favorite websites. He didn't visit them as much as he used to—but he was a little bored this morning, with time on his hands.

Leaning back in his desk chair, his right hand on the desktop moving the mouse, Adam smiled lazily at the monitor. He watched as a scantily clad blonde appeared on the screen.

The next moment—unbeknownst to Adam—his grandmother's spirit appeared by his side.

"Oh, here you are, always working hard," Marie said to deaf ears. She smiled lovingly at her favorite grandson. "What are you doing, checking out properties for a new buyer?"

Marie stepped closer to the desk and looked at the monitor. The moment she caught a glimpse of what Adam was watching, she began to sputter, "What in the world? Oh my!" Marie's eyes widened.

Adam chuckled and shifted in his seat, his attention on the blonde, who was about to remove what little clothing she had on.

"Adam Nichols, what in the world are you watching?" Marie gasped. With a huff, her hands clenching, she scowled menacingly at the screen, focusing all her energy—not quite sure herself what she hoped to accomplish. In the next minute the electricity went off in the office—and then went on again, causing the computer to reboot.

"What the..." Adam frowned, sitting up in the chair.

"And if you turn that trash back on, young man, I'll do it again!" Marie snapped.

It wasn't Marie's warning that prevented Adam from returning to the website—he could neither see nor hear her—it was the fact he heard the bell ring in the front office, signifying someone had come in. He wondered briefly if Leslie had returned early. Just as he stood up to see who had entered the office, he heard a male voice call out, "Hello, anyone here?"

Still annoyed with her grandson, Marie angrily followed him as he walked to the front office of the property management company. Once there, they were greeted by a young man about Adam's age. Technically speaking, Adam was the only one acknowledged, as the newcomer could no more see or hear Marie than Adam could. Marie thought there was something familiar about the man, but she couldn't quite place him.

"Chet?" Adam asked.

The man laughed and put out his hand to Adam. "You better recognize me, Nichols."

Breaking into a smile, Adam heartily shook the man's hand. "Hey, good to see you, Chet. I heard you'd moved back to town!" The two men shook hands for a moment, and then Adam motioned to the chairs sitting in the waiting area.

"I've been back for almost a month now. Staying with my sister until I can find something more permanent." Chet sat down in one of the chairs.

"Did you just come to say hi, or are you looking for a rental, or maybe something to buy?" Adam sat down.

"Both. I've been meaning to look you up. I'll be needing something of my own if I decide to stay permanent, but I don't need anything right now. Wondered if you could give me a list of available rentals so I can get an idea of what's out there."

"Sure. No problem." Adam stood up and walked to Leslie's desk. He grabbed one of the flyers she had sitting in a rack. When he returned to Chet, he handed him the flyer and asked, "So what brought you back to Frederickport? I thought you were living in Kansas or something."

Chet glanced at the flyer as Adam sat down again. "Kansas City, Missouri. It's a long story."

"Oh, I remember him now," Marie said with disgust. "Never liked that boy. He was more useless than Bill."

"So you aren't sure if you're going to stick around?" Adam asked.

Chet shrugged. Setting the flyer on his lap, he looked up at Adam and grinned. "You know who I saw last night? I wasn't sure it was her or not, but I asked around. Melony Carmichael!"

"You saw Mel?" Adam asked.

"Damn, she looks hot. I remember you two had quite a thing. How long has she been back in town?"

"She moved back last year, after her mother died. Where did you see her?"

"She was at Pearl Cove with some girlfriends. I have to say, Frederickport's looking promising in the women department. Is it true Melony's divorced now?"

"Stay away from Mel," Adam grumbled.

"That's more like it," Marie said with a nod of approval.

Chet laughed. "Not surprised. But no worry. I'm kind of interested in one of her friends. I almost had her going home with me last night, but then Melony and her other friends barged in. I don't think Melony knew who I was; she didn't say anything to me."

"Taking her home to your sister's house?" Adam snorted.

"Well, to her house."

"One of her friends? Which one?" Adam asked.

"We didn't exchange names. Who needs names?" Chet laughed.

"He's delightful," Marie snipped.

"Do you at least know what she looks like?"

"Hot little brunette. She had her hair in a fancy braid."

"Braid? You mean a fishtail braid?" Adam squeaked.

"Heavens, you're the one Danielle told me about!" Marie gasped.

Chet frowned. "You know the name of braids?"

"I know Danielle wears a fishtail braid."

"So her name is Danielle? She doesn't have a boyfriend, does she?"

"I thought she was ready to go home with you?" Adam asked.

Chet shrugged. "You know me. Boyfriends never stop me. But it's nice to be prepared if one shows up at my door the next morning."

"You mean your sister's door," Adam said under his breath before saying, "Danielle's a friend of mine."

Chet arched his brows. "How good a friend? Melony and Danielle?"

"You have a dirty little mind," Marie snapped.

Before Adam could answer Chet's question, the subject of their conversation barged into the office. Danielle came to an abrupt stop when she saw who Adam was with.

"Well, hello again," Chet said from the chair, making no attempt to stand up.

Adam stood up and looked nervously from his old high school friend to Danielle. "You cut your hair?"

"I see you're busy," Danielle told Adam, ignoring Chet. "I'll talk to you later." She turned and headed from the office, Marie trailing after her.

The moment the door closed after Danielle, Chet slapped his knee and started to laugh. "She's mine!"

"What in the world are you talking about?" Adam asked.

"She cut her hair!" Chet laughed again.

THREE

"I love it!" Lily insisted. She stood with Danielle in the Marlow House foyer, gazing into the entry hall mirror, studying the reflection of her best friend and her new shorter hairstyle.

Lily's red hair was now much longer than Danielle's, and for once hers was the one wound into a braid. Of course, it was a traditional braid—nothing like the fishtail style Danielle used to wear or a French braid. Lily called it her *Anne of Green Gables* braid—yet unlike the storybook Anne, who typically wore two braids, Lily wore just one. Her reason for taking to wearing a single braid to work was for practical purposes. It was easier to keep her hair tidy when working with second graders all day; plus, she had a secret aversion to catching lice from one of her students should she wear her hair loose at school.

Lily had arrived at Marlow House five minutes earlier. She had been on her way home from work when she had received Danielle's text message showing a picture of her new haircut. Lily wanted to see it in person, so instead of going straight home, she stopped first at Marlow House, which was just across the street from where she lived with her husband, Ian.

"I think I do too," Danielle said with a grin. Still looking into the mirror, she gave her hair a gentle fluff with the tip of her fingers.

"How does Walt like it?" Lily asked.

"I think it's adorable," Walt said when he appeared the next moment.

Danielle flashed Walt a smile and said, "Thank you, Walt." She turned to Lily and said, "He likes it."

If Lily could see Walt—which she couldn't—she would know he was wearing his gray, three-piece pin-striped suit, minus the jacket and tie, the sleeves of the white shirt unbuttoned and pushed up to his elbows.

Lily turned from the mirror, looking in the direction Danielle had addressed her hello. "Afternoon, Walt."

"Tell her hello, and let her know, that according to Evan, her students love her."

After Danielle conveyed the message, Lily chuckled and said, "I understand Evan and you have been exchanging emails. You have no idea how it's killing that poor kid not to let his friends know he's pen pals with a ghost."

"You know he hates that word," Danielle reminded her.

Lily shrugged. "Get over it."

Together they started walking toward the open parlor door. "Does Ian know you're here?" Danielle asked.

"Ian's not back yet. Remember, he was helping his sister move today," Lily reminded her. "I don't expect him home before four."

"That's what I don't get," Walt said, shaking his head. He followed Lily and Danielle into the parlor.

"What's that?" Danielle asked.

"Before you remind me—*again*—that I lived in what you call the Roaring Twenties—I'm not sure I will ever get used to how everyone now is so—well, blasé about everything."

"Is this about Kelly moving in with Joe?" Danielle asked. "Without being married?"

Lily glanced at Danielle. She had an idea what Danielle and Walt were probably talking about.

"I know people lived together without the benefit of marriage back in my day," Walt began. "But for a brother, like Ian, to actually help his sister pack her bags and move in with a man. In my day, a brother was expected to beat the crap out of the palooka for taking advantage of his sister."

Danielle chuckled. "That's kind of a funny image; Ian beating up Joe."

"Okay, what are you talking about?" Lily asked.

After Danielle recounted Walt's words, Lily rolled her eyes and said, "Kelly doesn't need Ian protecting her honor. She's a grown-up woman."

"But you didn't move in with Ian until you were married," Walt reminded her.

Before Danielle had a chance to repeat Walt's words, the doorbell rang. Lily took a seat on the sofa while Danielle went to answer the door. A few minutes later Danielle returned to the parlor with Adam Nichols by her side.

"Hey, Adam," Lily greeted him. She had removed the band holding her braid and was in the process of untangling her hair with her fingers.

"Hi, Lily. Get any apples today?" Adam teased as he took a seat in one of the chairs across from the sofa. Unfortunately for Walt, it was the seat he was using. With a grumble, Walt moved to the sofa with Lily.

"I wouldn't mind if the kids brought me fresh produce. But I would prefer chocolate," Lily said with a sigh and then added, "But no, nothing. The ungrateful children. So what brings you here?"

"I just stopped by to see if Danielle needed something," Adam explained.

Danielle walked to the empty chair and sat down. She looked at Lily and explained, "I stopped at Adam's office after I got out of the hairdresser. Just to say hi. It was down the street. But he was with someone, so I just left."

"About that…" Adam turned and faced Danielle. "Please tell me he's not the reason you cut your hair."

Lily frowned. "What are you talking about?"

Danielle groaned. "He said something to you, didn't he?"

"I told him he was crazy. Hey, I may be straight, but even I know Chris is a much better catch than Chet."

"Would someone please tell me what you're talking about?" Lily said impatiently.

"I'd like to know that myself," Walt said.

Letting out a sigh, Danielle looked at Lily. "Remember that guy who tried that negging crap with me last night? He was the one with Adam when I stopped by his office."

"Ahh, so you know about negging?" Adam sounded relieved.

"Your generation has such odd dating practices," Walt told Danielle. Before leaving for the beauty shop earlier that day,

Danielle had told Walt and Marie about her experience the night before at the Pearl Cove bar.

"Well, I didn't until I met your friend. Kind of a jerk, by the way," Danielle said.

"Yeah, Chet's not exactly the classiest guy," Adam said with a shrug.

"That's pretty obvious," Walt muttered.

"Melony said he was a friend of Adam's," Lily reminded her.

"Hey, I wouldn't call him a friend exactly. I mean, we were friends in high school, but I haven't seen him for a couple of years, and even before that, we didn't really hang out anymore." Adam paused and looked at Lily. "Ahh, so Mel did recognize him. He didn't think she had."

Lily shrugged.

Adam looked back to Danielle and asked, "So why did you cut your hair?"

"I've been thinking about cutting it for some time, and last night Mel gave me the name of a hairdresser she likes. I called to make an appointment, and she had a cancelation, so I took it." Danielle grinned.

"Just so you know, Chet is convinced you rushed out and got it cut because of what he said to you at the bar."

"Your friend Chet is delusional," Danielle said.

"Maybe." Adam grinned and added, "I like the new hair, by the way. Makes your eyes stand out."

"Why thank you, Adam," Danielle said with prim politeness.

He glanced to the door. "You have any guests?"

Danielle shook her head. "Nope. I decided not to book anyone this week, since my next guests are staying for two weeks—thanks to you."

Adam frowned. "Me?"

"Yeah, you're the one who sent Walt Marlow's cousin the link to our website, where he saw the portraits."

"Ooooohhh…" Adam grimaced. "So when's he going to be here?"

"Next Wednesday. He's staying through Easter and leaving on the thirtieth," Danielle explained.

"The day before Danielle's birthday!" Lily chirped.

"It's your birthday this month?" Adam grinned. "Have anything exciting planned? I bet I could get Chet to take you out."

"Oh, shut up, you jerk," Danielle scoffed.

Adam laughed and then said, "Seriously, are you doing anything special for your birthday?"

Danielle shrugged. "I haven't given it much thought. I just want to get through this visit with Walt's cousin. He's bringing along his fiancée and some artist, who'll be copying the portraits for him."

Adam chuckled.

"What's so funny?" Danielle asked.

"It always cracks me up when you call him Walt, like you're old friends or something, not some guy who's been dead a century."

"I think I should throw another croquet ball at this guy," Walt grumbled.

"Sometimes it feels like Walt's still here," Danielle said sweetly.

"Yeah, right." Adam rolled his eyes. "I can't believe the artist will be able to finish in just two weeks. Those are two big paintings."

Danielle shrugged. "He had me take photographs of the portraits. I emailed him a ton of pictures. He wanted detailed measurements and even wanted pictures of the backs of the paintings."

"Wow, you're a sport," Adam muttered. "And he's staying here for two weeks?"

"Walt's cousin must have some money," Lily suggested. "I know he's in real estate and has flexible hours, but that's a lot of time to be away from work, and then he says they're getting married this summer, so I would assume they'd be going on a honeymoon. Plus, it must be costing a fortune to pay an artist, not to mention the expense of the artist staying here with them."

"I still don't know why you want to keep those monstrosities," Adam said. "I'd sell them."

"I don't want to sell them," Danielle insisted.

"I forgot, you're Ms Money Bags, don't need the money." Adam chuckled.

"No, I don't need it. Plus, I like the portraits. They belong here."

Adam glanced briefly to the ceiling and muttered under his breath, "Yeah, you wouldn't want to screw up your feng shui."

FOUR

T he days had flown by, and it was Wednesday again, the day
Clint Marlow would be arriving at Marlow House with his
bride-to-be and the artist he had commissioned to copy Walt's
portraits. Danielle's housekeeper and cook, Joanne Johnson, was in
the downstairs bedroom putting fresh towels into its bathroom. It
had been decided the artist would stay in the downstairs bedroom,
as it was closer to the library, where he would be painting. Danielle
was in the kitchen frosting a cake she had baked earlier that morning, and Walt and Marie were in the library, chatting. Max dozed on
the sofa next to Marie, his white-fringed black ears occasionally
twitching in his sleep.

Marie glanced around the library, taking in the dark paneling,
antique furniture, and floor-to-ceiling bookcases filled with leather-
bound books. "I'm surprised Danielle's going to let him work in
here. What if he gets paint on something?"

"The man is supposedly a professional; I assume he can manage
to confine the paint to his brushes and canvas. But if not, Danielle is
supplying drop cloths, and I will be supervising." Walt stood by the
portraits, smoking a thin cigar.

"I guess you'll be able to take care of any mishaps." Marie
reached over to pet Max, forgetting for a moment that was impossible. When her hand moved through him, she let out a sigh.
Although his eyes were still closed, the cat began to purr.

"I believe you've become fond of him," Walt said with a chuckle.

"I have to admit he is an interesting fellow. I never imagined a cat could be so opinionated."

"Indeed." Walt flicked an ash off his cigar, only to have it vanish a moment later.

"I have been meaning to tell you something." Marie shifted on the sofa to better face Walt. She folded her hands on her lap.

"Yes?"

"I've been able to harness some energy." She glanced briefly at the cat and then added, "Although apparently not enough to pet Max."

Walt arched his brows. "Do tell."

"I've managed to turn off the electricity at Adam's office. It doesn't stay off. But it goes off for a moment. I've done it about four times now."

"Why would you want to interfere with your grandson's electricity?"

Marie shook her head. "I really don't want to discuss that. But the point is I managed to do it. I thought that as long as I didn't stay in one place, as you do, I wouldn't be able to do any of your tricks."

"They aren't tricks, Marie. As you yourself just said, it's simply a matter of us manipulating energy."

"Whatever it's called…but I thought whatever energy I did have, I was using up by being able to move about. And now this! It's rather exciting."

"Don't get carried away with yourself." Walt chuckled. "It's fairly common for a spirit—even one not restrained to a location, such as myself—to be able to do something, and manipulating electricity is a fairly common one, from what I've come to understand. In fact, even my dear wife Angela, who's confined to the cemetery and virtually stripped of any spiritual powers due to her past indiscretions, was able to interfere with Danielle's cellphone and make her car stall. I'm surprised Eva didn't tell you that."

Marie was just about to respond when she heard the doorbell ring.

Walt glanced at the desk clock. "I wonder if that's my cousin now?"

JOANNE HAD JUST ENTERED the kitchen when the doorbell rang.

"I'll get it," Danielle said as she wiped her hands on a dish towel and removed her apron. "It's probably our guests."

"I have to admit, I'm curious to see this one," Joanne said as she picked up the plate holding the cake Danielle had just frosted and moved it to a covered cake pan. "I want to see if he really looks that much like the portrait."

"I suspect we'll find out in a minute." Danielle tossed her apron onto the counter and headed to the doorway leading to the hallway, while Joanne remained in the kitchen.

By the time Danielle made it to the front door, Walt and Marie were already standing side by side a few feet from the doorway, anxious to get a look at the new guests. Danielle flashed them a grin and then threw open the door. The moment she saw the man standing next to the attractive blonde on her front porch, she froze. While she had expected Clint Marlow to resemble Walt, she hadn't expected him to look exactly like Walt—if you didn't consider his hair, which was cropped much shorter than Walt's, or the modern clothing: new jeans and a long-sleeved blue golf shirt.

"Hello. I assume this is Marlow House? There's no sign." Even the man's voice was Walt's.

"Goodness, he looks and sounds just like you," Marie exclaimed. "How peculiar!"

After a moment of silence, the blonde drawled, "Can we come in?" There was the slightest hint of a Southern accent in her voice.

"Oh, I'm sorry," Danielle sputtered. "It's just so strange." She opened the door wider and stepped aside so they could enter. Still holding onto the doorknob, she looked at Clint and said, "It's just that I didn't expect you to look and sound just like Walt."

"Sound like Walt?" the woman asked with a frown.

Blushing, Danielle said, "I just meant how I imagined Walt might sound."

The man chuckled as he set his suitcase down on the floor and glanced around, his fiancée by his side. "You had me wondering there for a moment."

Danielle shut the front door, and when she turned to the couple, Clint held out his hand to her.

"I assume you're Danielle Boatman? I'm Clint Marlow, and this is my fiancée, Stephanie Mountifield."

Still blushing, Danielle accepted his hand in a perfunctory hand-shake. "Yes, I…" Danielle froze, unable to finish her sentence. She looked down at her hand holding Walt's…no, Clint's, she reminded herself. In all the time Danielle had known Walt, she had never physically touched him. Not flesh on flesh. There had been dream hops and energy that mimicked a physical touch, yet until this moment, she didn't realize how lacking those other times had been.

"Danielle, are you okay?" Walt finally asked.

"Do you think you could return my fiancé's hand now?" Stephanie asked.

As if burned, Danielle snatched back her right hand, clasping it with her left one. She looked up into Clint's blue eyes that could have been Walt's.

"Danielle, snap out of it!" Walt said harshly.

With a shake of her head, Danielle moved out of her haze. Again blushing, she said, "I'm sorry. Yes, I am Danielle Boatman. I'm just a little overwhelmed at how much you look like your cousin. It's bizarre."

"You did look like you just saw a ghost," Clint said with a laugh.

"Nice to meet you, Mr. Marlow." Danielle turned to Stephanie and added, "And nice to meet you, Ms. Mountifield. I hope you both enjoy your stay here."

"Please, it's just Clint and Stephanie," Clint insisted. "I'd like to put our suitcases in our room before we have a look at the portraits."

"Joanne can take you both to your room. It's upstairs."

"This way," came a voice from behind them. The couple turned around and found a middle-aged woman standing in the hallway.

"This is Joanne," Danielle introduced them.

"WHAT HAPPENED IN THERE?" Marie asked when she went into the parlor with Walt and Danielle.

"I don't know. But it was like Walt had suddenly come to life." Danielle plopped down on the office chair and rubbed her forehead.

"I was standing there the entire time," Walt reminded her, sounding almost as annoyed as Stephanie had been when she had demanded Danielle release hold of Clint's hand.

"I know." Danielle stopped rubbing her forehead and looked up at Walt. "I can't explain it. It was surreal. I know he wears his hair differently, and he certainly doesn't dress like you. But dang, he was you—in the flesh."

"But he's not, Danielle," Marie gently reminded her.

DANIELLE'S brief infatuation with Clint Marlow abruptly ended thirty minutes later when she showed him and his fiancée to the library to view the portraits. It didn't take long for her to see the differences between the two Marlow men.

"What did my cousin do, spend all his time with his nose stuck in a book?" Clint asked after learning most of the books in the home library had once belonged to Walt. "No wonder his poor wife wanted to knock him off. If she hadn't died herself, she could have claimed self-defense; he was boring her to death."

"I take it you don't like to read?" Danielle asked.

Clint shrugged. "Why waste your time reading? If it's any good, it'll be made into a movie anyway."

"Your cousin is a shmuck," Marie grumbled from the sidelines.

"I'd have to agree," Walt said as he summoned a cigar.

"He doesn't seem that interested in looking at the portraits," Marie noted.

"I read *Fifty Shades*," Stephanie said with a giggle, her hand reaching for Clint's.

"Yeah, baby, that is my kind of book," Clint said with a raspy chuckle while squeezing Stephanie's hand.

"When is the artist arriving?" Danielle asked.

Clint released Stephanie's hand and wrapped his arm around her shoulders, pulling her closer. She snuggled into his side. "Not until sometime tonight. Before seven, I think he said. Can you tell me where there's a good restaurant? We're starved." Clint's arm dropped briefly from Stephanie's shoulder, and then his hand slapped her backside. "You hungry, baby?"

"YUCK," Danielle said after Clint and Stephanie left to find a restaurant. Joanne had also gone home for the day, leaving Danielle alone with Walt and Marie. The three sat together in the kitchen while Danielle ate a ham sandwich. "I wanted to tell those two to get a room, but then I remembered they had—here!" She laughed and shook her head.

"In a way he reminds me a little of my friend Jack," Walt said as he fiddled absently with his cigar.

"You mean the Jack I met?" Danielle asked.

Walt nodded the affirmative.

"Who's Jack?" Marie asked.

"He's the one who left the gold coins in your house across the street," Walt told her.

"How does Clint remind you of Jack?" Danielle asked.

"Jack was that way with his women. Liked to show off, let everyone know she was his—make tasteless innuendos about their intimacies. I always felt if a man really cared for a woman, why would he want to disrespect her? Put her on display?" Walt shrugged and took a puff off his cigar.

"It's because you're a gentleman," Marie said.

Walt chuckled. "Not so sure about that."

"I have to say I was proud of you, Walt," Danielle said.

He frowned. "Proud, why?"

"He talked about ghosts and then made a tasteless joke about your death, and you didn't smack him with anything."

Walt looked at Danielle and smiled. "Of course not. Now, had he been making those remarks about you…"

THE ARTIST ARRIVED at Marlow House a few minutes past seven that evening. Clint and Stephanie had already returned from dinner and were there to greet him. Danielle was surprised when they brought in the canvases for the reproductions.

"You've already painted them?" Danielle asked in surprise when she saw the paintings almost identical to the ones in the library. Yet, on closer inspection, she realized they were far from complete.

"There was no way I could finish two paintings of this size in just two weeks," the artist explained. "I worked from the pictures you sent me, and I'll work from the originals to finish them."

IAN AND LILY walked over to Marlow House about twenty minutes after the arrival of the artist. While Lily compared the partially completed reproductions with the originals—fascinated by the artist's skill—Ian was more intrigued by the artist himself.

"What's your name again?" Ian asked the man.

"Jim Hill."

With narrowed eyes, Ian studied the man as he walked away to join Clint and Stephanie by the original portraits.

"What's wrong?" Danielle whispered to Ian out of earshot of the other people in the library.

"His name is not Jim Hill," Ian told her.

FIVE

C arla had just finished telling Adam and Bill that Pier Café's Thursday lunch special was corned beef and cabbage, in honor of Saint Patrick's Day, when Ian and Lily Bartley walked into the restaurant, followed by Joe Morelli and Ian's sister, Kelly. The two couples walked by Adam and Bill, said hello, and then headed to a booth.

"I heard Kelly moved in with Joe," Carla whispered to Bill and Adam when the two couples were out of earshot.

"I thought Morelli was still hot for Boatman?" Bill asked.

Order pad in hand, Carla rolled her eyes. "That's old news, Bill. Like last year."

Adam chuckled. "What's wrong with you, Bill? Can't you keep up? I think they've been dating for over a year now."

Bill shrugged. "Like I give a crap about who Morelli is shacking up with? Give me the corned beef and cabbage."

"Me too," Adam added.

After Carla left the table, Adam asked, "Why are you so grouchy?"

"Because I can't figure out what's wrong with your stupid electricity. I'm about to give up. Are you sure the power keeps going out? I've asked around, and none of the other businesses on your street remember the power going off for a minute. I spoke to the electric company, and no one else has reported a problem. It has to be something with your office wiring."

"That's why I have you, to figure out this crap." Adam picked up his coffee and took a drink.

"It's crap alright. So tell me, what are you doing when the power goes off?" Bill asked.

Adam shrugged. "Just working on the computer."

"Does it happen every time you're on the computer?"

"No. Just when…" Adam paused a moment and then took another sip of coffee.

"Just when what?" Bill asked.

"Nothing. No, it doesn't happen every time I'm on the computer."

ON THE OPPOSITE side of the diner from Bill and Adam, the two couples sat in a booth, Kelly and Joe on one side of the table and Ian and Lily on the other side.

As Joe picked up the menus from the end of the table and started handing them out, he asked Lily, "Wasn't there any school today?"

Lily took a menu from Joe and said, "We had early release today."

"Don't think I could teach even if I had early release every day," Ian said, taking a menu from Joe. "I really hated teaching."

Kelly chuckled. "I remember." She then set the menu Joe had handed her on the table and leaned forward to Ian and Lily and asked, "I want to know, does he really look that much like the portrait?"

"Eerily so," Lily told her. *And he even sounds like Walt,* Lily thought. While Lily was unable to see Walt during waking hours, he visited her frequently in dream hops, and she knew what his voice sounded like. Even Ian had met Walt in a dream hop. They both agreed Walt's voice sounded like Clint Marlow's.

"What's he like?" Joe asked.

"I didn't really talk to him much, but overcritical Lily here thought he was a jerk." Ian chuckled. "After seeing the guy for less than thirty minutes."

Lily playfully smacked Ian's arm. "Well, he was! Hey, you're the one who thought the artist was using a fake name."

"I didn't say that," Ian scoffed.

"What's this about a fake name?" Joe asked.

Rolling his eyes, Ian shook his head and then said, "I didn't say he was using a fake name. It's just that when I first saw him, I could swear I knew him. The guy's name was on the tip of my tongue. But when he told me his name, it wasn't the one I was searching for."

"They say we all have a doppelganger," Kelly said. "Walt Marlow obviously does; maybe this artist does too."

"Perhaps I should check him out," Joe suggested.

Kelly turned to Joe and frowned. "Why would you want to do that?"

"Maybe he is using an alias. Maybe your brother's right, and he is this other guy. I've never understood why Danielle wants to run a boardinghouse, bringing strangers under her roof."

"It's a bed and breakfast, not a boardinghouse," Lily reminded him.

"That's worse. New strangers in, week after week. A woman living alone. She's already had problems with some of her guests, and she certainly doesn't need the money," Joe said.

"Joe, Danielle is a grown woman. I'm sure she can take care of herself," Kelly said sharply. Ian and Lily exchanged glances, each thinking the same thing, *the green monster?*

———

BILL AND ADAM had just been served their lunch when Chet walked into Pier Café. He was about to go to the lunch counter when he spied Bill and Adam sitting in a booth.

"Hey, guys!" Chet greeted when he walked up to them.

"Chet?" Bill asked with a frown. "When did you get back in town?"

"About a month ago," Chet said as he sat down next to Bill without being invited, inadvertently shoving the handyman down the bench. With a grumble, Bill grabbed his plate and silverware and slid it down the table to where he was now sitting.

"Gee, Chet, why don't you join us?"

Ignoring Adam's sarcasm, Chet reached over Bill and grabbed a menu. "Thanks, I think I will."

Exchanging brief glances, Bill and Adam continued eating their lunch.

While looking over the menu, Chet said, "I was thinking maybe you could take me over to Marlow House. Tell her I happened to be with you and you had to stop for some reason. You can make up something. I don't want her to think I'm actually interested in her."

"What's he talking about?" Bill asked.

"Chet has gotten it into his head that Danielle Boatman is hot for him," Adam said with a snort between bites.

Bill laughed.

"Don't laugh. She cut her hair for me!"

With a sigh, Adam set his fork on his plate and looked up at Chet. "She didn't cut her hair for you. She had been thinking of cutting it for a while now."

"Yeah, right," Chet scoffed. "That's what she tells you. She's just embarrassed that I know. Trust me, she secretly wants me to tell her how good she looks now. Of course, I won't..." Chet grinned.

"Boatman cut off her braid?" Bill asked Adam.

"Yeah. It looks really cute though. Makes her look kind of sassy."

"Hands off, Adam. You have Melony," Chet warned. "If you were interested in her, you should have moved on her by now."

With a frown, Bill turned to Chet. "I still don't know what you're talking about. But Danielle Boatman? Like you'd have a chance in hell with someone like her."

Adam chuckled. "Actually, I'm kind of surprised hearing you say that, Bill. What is it you used to call Danielle, a space cadet?"

Bill shrugged. "A space cadet that pays well." He glanced over at Chet and added, "Space cadet or not, considering who that girl's dated since she moved here, I don't see Chet in the running."

"Like who?" Chet challenged.

Bill motioned across the room to Joe Morelli's booth. "Like the guy not wearing the Cubs baseball cap."

"Looks like he has a new girl. Which is even better for me. And that one looks younger than Danielle. That must have hurt, dumped for a younger model."

"Danielle didn't get dumped," Adam told him. "It was the other way around. Anyway, her last boyfriend could probably get any girl in town."

"What's so wonderful about this guy?" Chet asked.

"He's not my type." Bill chuckled. "But I have to agree with Adam. Google *pretty boy* and I bet his picture comes up."

"Is he her boyfriend now?" Chet asked.

"They're just good friends," Adam said. "But they did date for a while."

"If they're just friends, he's probably gay," Chet said. "Which again works in my favor. She's probably doubting her femininity about now."

"You're as stupid as you were in high school," Bill muttered.

"So tell me, Bill, you seeing anyone? Maybe I could help you out, give you a few pointers on picking up women," Chet sneered.

"Holy crap!" Adam gasped.

For just a brief moment Chet and Bill assumed Adam's exclamation was in response to their conversation, yet when they looked to him, they both saw he was looking toward the entrance of the diner. Curious, they looked to where Adam was staring. They spied a man and woman walking in their direction, looking for a place to sit down.

"Who is he? He looks familiar," Bill whispered to Adam.

"It has to be Walt Marlow's cousin. Damn, dress the guy up in some vintage clothes, let his hair grow out a little, and you could stick him in the portrait."

Just as the couple was about to pass their table, Adam stood up and put his hand out to the man. "Hello, you must be Clint Marlow."

Coming to an abrupt stop, Clint stared a moment at Adam's hand, yet he made no attempt to take it. Instead, he narrowed his eyes and studied Adam's face. "Who are you?"

Now feeling awkward with his hand reaching for a handshake, Adam immediately dropped it to his side and stammered, "Umm, I'm Adam Nichols. I'm the one who sent you the link to the Marlow House website."

Clint studied Adam for just a moment longer, making no attempt to shake his hand or introduce him to his fiancée. He finally said, "Yeah, well, if you were looking for an agent to do referrals with, I don't do them." Without another word, Clint and Stephanie walked to an empty booth.

Adam sat back down, his eyes still on Clint, who didn't even look back in his direction.

"He seems like a nice guy," Bill said with a chuckle.

LILY AND IAN didn't notice Clint and Stephanie until they sat down two booths away. They hadn't witnessed the exchange between Adam and Clint.

Leaning over the table toward Kelly and Joe, Lily whispered, "There they are. They just sat down."

Joe and Kelly looked over to Clint and Stephanie, who were unaware they were being watched.

"He does look like the portrait," Kelly gasped. "I think he looks nice."

"Kelly's right, he does look nice," Ian teased. "You really should give the poor guy a chance."

Standing up abruptly, Lily tossed her napkin on the table and said, "Fine, I will." She marched over to Clint and Stephanie's table.

"Hello," Lily said cheerfully.

Without a smile, Clint looked up from his menu. By his expression, Lily didn't think he recognized her.

"We met last night. I'm Lily Miller…I mean Bartley. I live across the street from Marlow House." Lily grinned.

Still not smiling, his voice loud and clear, Clint said, "I know who you are. What do you want?"

Taken aback by his rude tone, Lily stammered, "Umm…I just wanted to say hi. See if you were enjoying yourself in Frederickport."

"Why? Are you the Frederickport welcoming committee?"

Stephanie giggled at Clint's comment, yet said nothing.

Lily stared at Clint, not sure what to say next.

"Miss Miller, or whatever your name is, I'm sure you are a nice person. But as you can see, I am here with my lovely fiancée, trying to enjoy our little vacation. I don't really need or want to get all chatty with someone who I will never see again after I leave Frederickport, or even care to. So please, would you go back to your table and give us our privacy."

SIX

J im Hill—assuming that was his real name—liked to sleep in. He was still sleeping when Clint and Stephanie went off for lunch Thursday afternoon. When he did wake up, Joanne offered to make him something to eat, since he had missed breakfast that morning. He declined, insisting he only needed coffee—lots of it—and to organize his impromptu art studio.

In the library he started to set up his easels near the window, to take advantage of the sunlight. When Joanne informed him she needed to first put down the drop cloth, he was insulted, yet begrudgingly moved out of the way while she laid it out. He made no attempt to help her.

When she was done, he set up his easels and then went to his room to retrieve his paints, brushes, and other supplies. Danielle was just coming down the stairs when Jim went into his bedroom. Curious to see if he had set up the easels, she went to the library. There she found Marie and Walt standing by the portraits, comparing the partially completed reproductions to the originals.

"Has he started yet?" Danielle asked with a whisper after she entered the library. She didn't want Joanne or their guest catching her seemingly talking to herself.

"I think he went to get his paints," Walt told her, waving his hand for a cigar.

"He certainly was annoyed when poor Joanne told him they

needed to put down a drop cloth," Marie grumbled. "I don't like that man."

"We don't even know him," Danielle reminded her.

"I don't need to know him," Marie declared. "It was enough watching him stand there, not offering to lift a finger to help Joanne put down the drop cloth. Frankly, if I were her, I would have told him to get off his lazy backside and help, or he could take his painting outside!"

Smiling at Marie, Danielle moved closer to the portraits, her attention on the reproduction of Angela. "I'm a little surprised. It looks like Angela."

"Isn't that the point?" Marie asked.

"Yes…but Clint mentioned in an email that he didn't really have a need for Angela's portrait, but he didn't want to split them up. This was when he first offered to buy the originals. At the time he said something about maybe painting his fiancée's face over Angela's."

Stepping closer to the reproduction, her nose slightly scrunching, Marie studied the partially completed face on the canvas. "It's obviously Angela. Clint must have changed his mind about substituting Stephanie's face for Walt's wife."

Danielle's cellphone began to ring. She pulled it out of her back pocket. "Hello? Lily? Why over there? Sure, I guess." With one finger Danielle tapped the phone's display to end the call.

"Everything okay with Lily?" Walt asked.

"I don't know. She wants me to go over to her house." Danielle tucked the phone back in her jean's back pocket.

"Do you always talk to yourself?" Jim asked from the doorway.

"Um…I was just talking on the phone."

"While you were putting it into your pocket?" He walked into the library carrying a suitcase, its edges smudged with dried oil paint in varying colors.

"I guess I was thinking out loud," she stammered.

"So you do talk to yourself." Had his voice had a lighter tone, Danielle might have assumed he was teasing her. But by his sober expression and clipped words, she suspected he wasn't prone to playful banter.

Setting the suitcase near the easels, he said, "I need total privacy while I work."

"Certainly." Danielle forced a smile.

"I want the door closed and locked when I'm working."

Danielle frowned. "Locked?"

"I don't like interruptions. It interferes with my flow." He leaned down to the suitcase and opened it.

"I don't think we should tell him he's not going to be alone. Even if you lock the door," Walt said with a chuckle.

Jim grabbed several brushes from the suitcase. He paused and looked to Danielle. "Why are you still here?"

"So you're going to start now?" Danielle asked.

"Obviously."

Danielle started to walk away, but then paused a moment and faced the artist. "Can I ask you something?"

"If you promise to leave after you ask your question so I can get to work," he said impatiently.

"Clint mentioned wanting to put Stephanie's face in the portrait instead of Angela's."

Jim frowned. "Who's Angela?"

Danielle pointed to the original portrait of Walt's late wife.

"I'm reproducing these portraits exactly as the original artist created them. I certainly have no intention of doing something tacky like putting another woman's face on one of them."

"I CAN'T COME over to your house while Walt's cousin is there," Lily told Danielle the moment she opened her front door.

"Well, hello to you too." Danielle followed Lily into the entry hall. "What do you mean you can't come over to my house?"

As Lily shut the front door, Sadie came running from down the hall to greet Danielle, her tail wagging.

"It's just too humiliating!" Lily groaned, now heading down the hall.

Danielle paused a moment to greet the golden retriever and then walked with her to the living room. She found Ian sitting on the sofa, a legal pad of paper in one hand and pen in the other, his Cubs baseball cap abandoned on a chair by the window.

"I've never been so embarrassed in my entire life." Lily plopped down on the sofa next to Ian.

"I'm sorry for teasing you, babe." Ian tossed the pad of paper and pen on the coffee table and then patted Lily's knee. "If I hadn't, you wouldn't have gone over to their table."

"What are you guys talking about?" Danielle took a seat on Ian's recliner, facing the sofa.

"We ran into Clint and Stephanie at Pier Café when we were there for lunch," Lily began. She then went on to recount what Clint had said to her.

"What a jerk," Danielle grumbled when Lily finished her story.

"I could have absolutely died. Everyone in the diner heard." Closing her eyes, Lily flopped back dramatically on the sofa, flinging her right wrist over her eyes.

"He really was an ass," Ian said, once again patting Lily's knee.

"Did you say anything to him?" Danielle asked Ian.

He shook his head. "I have to admit, I was…well…speechless. And then when Lily returned to the table, I got up to say something—"

"But I stopped him," Lily interrupted. "That would make it even more awkward, especially for you."

"I'm really sorry, Lily."

"It's not your fault, Dani. But, gee, I wish he would have tried that when we were at Marlow House," Lily grumbled.

"Yeah, I don't think Walt would have contained himself." Danielle chuckled at the thought.

"Thing is," Ian began, "it wasn't Lily who looked bad at the café. It was all Clint. He looked like a major horse's ass."

Uncovering her eyes, Lily sat up on the sofa and smiled. "Yeah, when we were leaving, Carla tried to make me feel better by saying she was going to have the cook spit in his food. But then that just made me wonder if she'd ever done anything to our food!"

"Adam and Bill were there too, with some other guy," Ian told her. "Adam told me outside that Clint said something similar to him, and told Lily not to feel bad."

"It was still embarrassing. I don't want to see that guy ever again!" Lily insisted.

"According to Walt, you were rather taken with him," Ian teased Danielle.

"When did Walt say that?" Danielle asked.

Ian chuckled. "It wasn't in a dream hop. Walt sent me an email last night telling me about his cousin."

"So he wasn't rude to you?" Lily asked.

"He's been polite enough." Danielle shrugged. "I think Walt was talking about the reaction I had when I first met Clint. It was like… well, like Walt had come alive."

"Clint is nothing like Walt!" Lily snapped.

"I agree; his personality is totally different. But when I first met him, aside from the hair and clothes, he was Walt. It was uncanny. Especially when I shook his hand; I can't explain it."

"When I first met him, I didn't get good vibes," Lily told her.

"By the way, the artist he hired is just as charming," Danielle said.

"How so?" Ian asked.

"He told me—told me, he didn't ask—that the door to the library had to remain locked while he was working, and no one was allowed to enter. He only works in complete privacy."

Lily chuckled. "Good luck with that. Did Walt hear him?"

Danielle smiled. "Both Walt and Marie heard it. I imagine one or both of them will be in the library while he's painting. I know Marie was concerned he'll get paint on something."

"I've been meaning to ask you, how's it working out with Marie not moving on?" Ian asked.

"It's different than having Walt sticking around. I always know he'll be there, in the house. Whereas Marie comes and goes, but when she's at the house, she and Walt seem to get along very well. I think she enjoys hearing stories about her parents, and he enjoys talking to someone about his life—someone who knew the same people he did."

Danielle reached down and petted Sadie, who was now curled up by her feet.

"If this Jim Hill guy is going to be locked up in the library, I don't imagine Walt will be able to use the computer," Ian noted.

"He should be able to at night when the guy's sleeping," Danielle said. "You're thinking of Walt's emails?"

"Marie's not the only one who's been enjoying visiting with Walt." Ian smiled.

"You know, Dani, I'm beginning to think there is something funny about all this." Lily said.

"Funny about what?" Danielle asked.

"Walt's cousin. And the artist. Maybe Ian's first hunch was right. Maybe the artist's name really isn't Jim Hill," Lily suggested.

"But maybe it is. People do have doubles, Walt and Clint prove that. And maybe rude people attract rude people. I doubt there is anything covert going on. And I really don't think you need to avoid Marlow House."

Lily shook her head. "Dani, why does Clint want to spend all this money reproducing those paintings?"

Danielle shrugged. "Because they belonged to his distant cousin and namesake, one who happens to look just like him. You know he wanted the originals, but I wouldn't sell them to him."

Lily shook her head again. "That's the thing, Clint doesn't seem like someone interested in genealogy."

"We already knew that," Danielle reminded her. "He told me in an email he was never particularly interested in family history. I think he just wants them because the one of Walt looks just like him. I don't think he'd care about the portrait if the distant cousin in the painting didn't look like him."

"Maybe, but if he came all this way for two weeks and is paying an artist to reproduce the paintings, then I would assume he was interested in the originals. Yet last night, did you see him look twice at those portraits? If I was interested enough in some paintings that I would be willing to commission an artist to reproduce them, the first thing I would do when I got to the originals was look at them! After all, if he just wants a vintage picture of himself, he could simply dress up in old-fashioned clothes and have someone take his picture. Heck, you can even use special effects on a photograph to make it look like an oil painting. It would be a lot cheaper."

Danielle considered Lily's words for a moment before saying, "Hmmm, you have a point. He didn't seem that interested in the portraits last night. And this morning after breakfast they left the house without even going into the library to look at them."

"When I first met the artist, I thought I knew him," Ian said.

"I know, you mentioned that last night. But you didn't know him as Jim Hill," Danielle said.

"No. While I couldn't remember the name, this guy's double is also an artist. I know that," Ian insisted.

"How do you know that? You can't even remember the other guy's name," Danielle asked.

"I just do. It's driving me nuts," Ian said. "Maybe you're right, and it's all a coincidence. But I'm going to try to figure out who the other artist is."

SEVEN

"You having any luck?" Lily asked Ian when she brought him a beer late Thursday evening. He sat on the sofa with his laptop and Sadie curled up by his feet.

Looking up from the computer screen, Ian accepted the beer. "Nothing. I don't have much to go on. I think this is a waste of time."

Lily sat next to Ian, bringing her bare feet up on the sofa. She glanced over his shoulder at the computer. "I'm sorry. I wish I could help."

Ian took a sip of his beer and then said, "If I just had a picture of him, I could do a facial-recognition search."

"Then get one."

Ian chuckled. "I don't think we can just march across the street and take his picture. If he is using an alias, I imagine our artist is camera shy."

"Then take a picture when he's not looking," Lily suggested.

"If we could get him outside at just the right angle, I might be able to get one with my telephoto lens, but that would take some skilled maneuvering, and frankly I don't think I could pull it off. We need a close-up."

They sat in silence for a moment. Finally, Lily said, "How about Walt?"

"How about Walt what?"

"He could take this guy's picture. According to Danielle, Walt intends to stay in the library and keep an eye on him while he's painting. I bet he could manage to catch a close-up of him when he's preoccupied with his painting. Walt could use Dani's cellphone."

Ian chuckled. "You don't think it might freak this guy out a little if he notices an iPhone floating in midair, taking his picture?"

"It's not like Walt would have to shove the phone in his face. There are lots of discreet places in the library he could set the phone where the guy would never notice. And when he's not looking, when he's focused on the painting, Walt could snap his picture."

Ian considered Lily's suggestion a moment before commenting. "I suppose it might be possible." Ian leaned forward and placed his beer on the coffee table. He then turned his attention back to the laptop.

"What are you doing now?" Lily asked.

"Sending Walt an email."

"YOUR ARTIST JUST WENT TO BED," Walt announced when he entered Danielle's bedroom late Thursday evening. He found her already tucked into bed, reading.

Glancing up over her book at Walt, Danielle said, "He's not my artist." Without thought, she scooted to one side, making room for Walt. A moment later he sat on the side of the mattress, kicked off his shoes—which vanished the moment they left his feet—and then lay on the bed next to Danielle, over the blankets and sheets. Leaning back on the headboard, he crossed his arms over his chest and let out a sigh.

"Maybe not, but he is the most peculiar artist. Do you know what he did for the first hour behind locked doors?"

Closing her book and setting it on her lap, she looked to Walt. "Snooped through my desk? Played on the computer?"

Walt shook his head. "No. He examined the original portraits."

Danielle shrugged. "I'd expect him to do that if he wants his reproductions to look like the originals."

"The backs of the paintings? The frames?"

Danielle frowned. "How do you mean?"

"He wasn't examining the painting sides of the canvases, he was meticulously looking over the frames, the backs of the canvases, and then he would look at the backs of his paintings, as if he was comparing them."

"That's odd."

"Didn't I just say he was peculiar?"

"I kind of regret agreeing to all this," Danielle said with a sigh. "Your cousin was such an ass to poor Lily, she doesn't even want to come back over here until they leave. And I know he was rude to Adam too. Although he has been very pleasant to me."

"Of course, he wants something from you," Walt reminded her.

"I know. But wouldn't you then expect him to be at least civil to my friends?"

Walt shrugged. "Sorry. I can't begin to understand how my cousin thinks. And if he didn't look so annoyingly like me, I would insist he wasn't really related to me."

Danielle grinned at Walt. "Having annoying relatives is part of life. I had Cheryl." Danielle glanced upwards and said, "Sorry, Cheryl, you could be annoying."

"Yes, but you loved Cheryl in spite of it—and even missed her after she moved on. I don't see me gaining any affection for my cousin. Nor am I going to miss him when he's gone."

"True. But you never know, had you grown up with Clint, maybe you'd discover a side of him that was somewhat loveable."

"I seriously doubt that. Anyway, you said having annoying relatives is part of life—yet I'm dead, so I shouldn't have to deal with them."

"He's still your cousin."

"He's a stranger with my face."

"I guess this whole thing is pretty weird for you. Not sure how I'd feel if some distant cousin showed up who looked just like me."

"Since I never had children, I might see this as a way of the Marlow line continuing on. Yet I would have preferred a less obnoxious person carrying our torch into the future."

"Let's hope Stephanie and Clint's offspring are less annoying." Danielle tossed the book on the nightstand. "I'm going to go to sleep now. I have to get up early and make breakfast for your not-so-charming cousin and his entourage."

AFTER WALT LEFT Danielle's room, he moved through the second floor of Marlow House and discovered the door to Stephanie and Clint's room closed. There was no light slipping out from under the door, and all was quiet. He assumed they were sleeping.

Downstairs he found the door to Jim Hill's room was also shut, and like the bedrooms upstairs, there was no light coming from under the door. Walt stood a moment outside the downstairs' bedroom and listened. He could hear faint snoring. The artist was asleep.

Walt moved through the rest of the rooms on the first floor, making sure everything was as it should be. Marie had left with Eva earlier that evening, and he didn't expect to see her again until tomorrow. He found Max sleeping on the sofa in the parlor. Instead of waking the cat, Walt went to the library, shut the door, and sat down before the computer to check his email. The room was dark save for the light coming from the monitor. After logging in to his email account, he was pleased to discover several messages waiting for him.

FROM LILY: *Hi Walt. Unless you stop by in a dream hop, you won't see me until after your cousin leaves. I imagine Dani told you what happened. Your cousin is a jerk. Keep an eye on him. I don't trust the guy.*

FROM EVAN: *Dear Walt. I am fine. I hope you are too. It was Saint Patrick's Day today. Dad told me to wear my green shirt to school so I wouldn't get pinched. No one pinched me. We got out early today. Dad says the week after next is spring break. Maybe I can come see you then. Your friend Evan MacDonald.*

FROM IAN: *Walt—I'm sure Danielle told you I recognized the artist your cousin hired. But I don't think his name is Jim Hill. I could be wrong, but I'd like to check this out. I really need a photograph of him to help me do an internet search. Lily said you might be able to take a picture of the guy when he is painting. She thinks you might be able to do it without him noticing by using Danielle's cellphone. Do you think that is possible? I'd need a good clean shot of his face. Thanks. Ian.*

WHEN DANIELLE WOKE up Friday morning, she found Walt sitting in a chair next to her bed, staring at her.

"Well, this is just creepy," Danielle grumbled as she sat up in bed, rubbing the sleep from her eyes with her right hand. She yawned and then asked, "Have you gone voyeur on me? Please don't tell me you do this all the time."

"Not all the time." Walt grinned.

Now sitting up in bed, her dark hair sticking out in all random directions, she glared at Walt.

"Oh, settle down," Walt said with a chuckle. "I just wanted to catch you before you got up and went downstairs. I need you to show me how to use the camera on your iPhone. And I need you to let me borrow it."

Running her fingers through her hair like an impromptu comb, she frowned. "Why?"

UNLIKE THE CAMERAS in his day, Walt thought taking a photograph with Danielle's iPhone was remarkably easy. It took him a few tries to get it right. Several times he accidentally pressed the little camera icon with circular arrows and found the camera pointing at where he was standing. Of course, his image was not present. Danielle showed him how to disarm the flash. Walt might be able to sneak a picture of the artist, yet if the flash suddenly went off, that would complicate matters. After Walt thought about it a few minutes, he figured the only thing that would probably happen would be that the artist would run screaming from the house, never to return. Would that be so bad?

Danielle also showed him how to enlarge the screen before snapping the shot, since he would need to keep some distance between him and the artist.

The guests were all still sleeping when Danielle and Walt went into the library together to look for the ideal place to situate the camera.

"Stand there." Walt pointed to a spot between the easels.

Danielle did as Walt instructed and watched as he literally stepped inside the bookcase behind the portraits. She frowned.

"What are you doing in there?" The back of Walt's head disappeared into a half-dozen books on one of the middle shelves, while his features eerily protruded from the books' spines. His chin rested on the shelf he had placed the iPhone on, right in front of the row of books. The phone tipped upward, the camera lens aiming at Danielle while Walt looked into the glass display. Without moving his hands, he snapped a picture.

"See how this looks," Walt suggested. The phone floated from the shelf to where Danielle stood.

She grabbed the phone in midair and looked at the picture he had just captured. "Hmm, not bad. You can see my face clearly."

"I think I can do this."

"Unless he happens to look up and sees the phone move on its side."

"He won't. I'll make sure to do it when he's focusing on his painting."

"Okay." Danielle muted the phone before handing it back to Walt.

"What did you just do?" he asked.

"I don't want the phone ringing. But as soon as you get his picture, you need to let me know, and I'll come in and get my phone."

EIGHT

It wasn't a perverse sense of humor that inspired Macbeth Bandoni's mother to give her son an unusual name. The actress's love for the theater was the inspiration. Her husband, a portrait painter, had no problem naming his only child Macbeth. The artistic pair had led a bohemian lifestyle, barely eking out a living in their chosen professions. Had it not been for their son, who had taken up the paintbrush like his father, their name would have disappeared into obscurity.

Unlike his parents, Macbeth Bandoni enjoyed money. The suffering-artist gig might have been his parents' thing, it wasn't his.

It wasn't until sites like Google became a thing that he came to resent his name. Google Macbeth Bandoni's name in quotes and over a hundred search results about him came up. Some artists might enjoy the notoriety, yet not Macbeth, considering some of the articles chronicled his past arrests.

When taking this job in Frederickport—one of his more lucrative ones in years—he knew he would need an alias. When testing out the alias Jim Hill in quotes, almost four hundred thousand results came up, including a celebrity on the first page.

There were two reasons for the alias. First, when in Frederickport, the last thing he needed was someone like Danielle Boatman doing a search on his name. If she googled *"Jim Hill,"* she would find nothing on him and then assume if there was anything about him online, it was simply lost in the countless Jim Hills out there, meaning he was just another faceless artist trying to make a living.

The second reason was a precaution should the job not go as planned. When he left Frederickport, he assumed Danielle Boatman would have absolutely no idea what had happened. Yet should she later become suspicious, he didn't need her searching his name online and discovering the colorful life of Macbeth Bandoni. And he certainly didn't need to hand her a name so she could then have him hunted down should their con later be discovered.

After procuring a cup of hot coffee, Macbeth made his way to the library to begin his work. It wasn't quite ten thirty a.m. yet. Upon locking the door behind him, he noticed a distinct scent of cigar smoke. He sniffed the air and glanced around. Yesterday he had noticed the same smell in the room.

Coffee mug in hand, he walked over to his easels and studied his paintings. Sipping the coffee, he mentally plotted the day's work. Still focused on the unfinished canvases, he set his coffee mug on a nearby table. Just as he did, a flash blinded his eyes.

Startled, he looked up to the bookcases behind the paintings and then heard a crash and hissing sound behind him. Abruptly turning to the sound, he found the metal trash can next to the computer table overturned on the floor and a black cat racing across the room to the door leading to the hallway. The moment the cat reached the door, he began frantically pawing against it. Macbeth walked to the cat and let him out of the room.

Macbeth closed and locked the door. He then went to the desk and righted the trash can. From the desk he walked to the bookshelf, searching for the source of the flash.

"YOU MIGHT WANT to get your iPhone out of the library," Walt told Danielle when he found her alone in the kitchen a moment later, rinsing out her coffee cup. "I got the picture."

"That was quick. How did it turn out?" Danielle set her rinsed cup on the counter and turned to Walt.

"I have no idea."

She paused and glanced to the back door; the pet door was moving back and forth, as if someone had recently left through it—

which was what had happened. Looking back to Walt, she asked, "Any idea why Max just tore out of here?"

Walt smiled sheepishly. "It might have something to do with the fact I picked him up and tossed him in the library trash can."

"You what?"

"It was partially your fault," he told her.

"Why would you do something like that? And how is that remotely my fault?"

"The flash went off when I took his picture. I thought you told me it wouldn't."

"Did you turn it off?"

"Turn it off?" Walt frowned.

"I showed you how to turn it off. But what has that to do with poor Max?"

"When I took the picture, it flashed. I had to do something quick to divert his attention so—"

"So you picked up Max and tossed him in the trash can?"

Walt shrugged. "It did work. Hill looked away, which gave me time to move your iPhone to another part of the room so he wouldn't connect it to the flash. And the only reason Max is so upset is because he was sleeping at the time."

Danielle shook her head. "Poor Max."

DANIELLE STOOD at the library door, knocking. She could use her key, but she chose not to. After a few moments, the door opened, and she found herself looking into the disgruntled face of the man she knew as Jim Hill.

He wasn't an attractive man, with a round face, bulbous nose, and black bushy eyebrows. His olive complexion and dark thinning hair made her think he was Hispanic or Italian, yet considering his surname, she didn't think it came from his father's side of the genes. She towered over him by at least three inches, which would make him about five feet two.

"I told you I do not like to be interrupted when I work!" he hissed.

"I'm sorry." She smiled pleasantly. "But I believe I left my cell-phone in here this morning." Without another word, she pushed her way into the room and walked to where Walt had placed the phone.

"You also left your cat in here," he told her when she picked her phone up off the bookshelf—a good distance from where it had been when Walt had snapped the picture. "I think it would be a good idea if you kept your cat out of this room while I'm here. I don't need him knocking over my easels and ruining my work."

Holding her phone, Danielle smiled at the artist. Behind him, Walt leaned casually against the sofa, puffing on a cigar. He winked at Danielle.

"Certainly. I'll make sure Max stays out of here." Danielle smiled sweetly.

SADIE GREETED Danielle at the front door when she walked across the street to Ian and Lily's house ten minutes later. Lily was at school, yet Danielle knew Ian was home, working.

"I emailed you the picture," Danielle told Ian as she followed him inside, the golden retriever trailing behind them.

"I got it. It was a good shot. Let's see if I can find anything."

"I'm not sure how you're going to use the picture to find this person you believe Hill really is."

"There are some websites that use facial recognition to find photographs. I just need to upload this one and see if any matches come up."

"That's assuming our artist has any pictures of himself posted online." Danielle followed Ian to the dining room, where he had his laptop set up on the table. He sat down in front of the computer while Danielle took a seat across from him, and Sadie curled up by his feet.

Danielle watched as Ian focused his attention on the computer's monitor, his fingers moving quickly over the keyboard. "I seriously doubt you'll find anything aside from the fact our artist's name probably is Jim Hill."

A moment later Ian shouted, "Macbeth Bandoni!"

Startled by his outburst, Sadie lifted her head and looked up at Ian.

"Who?" Danielle frowned.

"I knew it! He's not Jim Hill. He's Macbeth Bandoni," Ian told them.

"Who is Macbeth Bandoni?"

Ian looked up at Danielle. "I think we need to go have a talk with the chief."

DANIELLE AND IAN sat with the police chief in his office, the door closed.

"So who is Macbeth Bandoni?" Chief MacDonald asked.

"A number of years ago I did a story on art fraud. It was about wealthy people who had lost millions by investing in art that turned out to be forgeries," Ian explained. "Many of the victims would only talk to me off the record if I promised not to use their real names."

"They were too embarrassed?" the chief asked.

Ian nodded. "Exactly. We're talking very wealthy people who would rather lose a couple of million than look like fools. One of the forgers involved was an artist named Macbeth Bandoni. An extremely talented painter who specializes in recreating master-pieces. His name has also been linked to a number of missing masterpieces that some believe were smuggled out of Europe after first being hidden under other paintings. They were literally painted over."

"And you're saying this is the guy staying with Danielle?" the chief asked.

"I'm certain of it."

The chief looked from Danielle to Ian. "If this guy is a forger and thief, why isn't he in jail?"

"He's been arrested numerous times, but they always dropped the charges for one reason or another," Ian explained. "And it's not illegal to reproduce masterpieces, it's just illegal to pass one off as an original."

"On one hand," Danielle began, "I'd commend Clint for finding such a talented artist to reproduce Walt's portraits—and it wouldn't really bother me if he was this Macbeth fellow—but the fact that—"

"He's using an alias," the chief finished for her.

"Yes. That is troubling. Why would he do that?" Danielle asked.

Leaning back in the chair, Ian let out a sigh and said, "I suppose it's possible he's using an alias simply because he'd rather not have to explain his colorful background should anyone find out who he is. But my gut tells me something else. There's a story here, I know it."

"Any idea what it might be?" the chief asked.

"It has to be connected to those portraits," Ian said.

"Walt told me he spent almost an hour inspecting the back sides of the original paintings and the frames. It seemed a strange thing for him to do," Danielle said.

"I suppose it's possible Walt's portraits were painted over something more valuable," the chief suggested.

"Hmm, that could be a possibility. I wonder if there is a masterpiece hidden under one of Walt's portraits," Ian murmured. "I'd like to take a closer look at those paintings again."

"That's going to be difficult. At least, during the day. Jim—or Macbeth, or whoever he is—insists on privacy while he paints, and he doesn't want anyone in there," Danielle told them.

"I'm assuming Walt's not honoring his request?" the chief asked with a chuckle.

Danielle smiled. "No. Walt's in the library when he is. Marie's usually in there too when she's not out with Eva."

"Eva...that's right...her portrait was painted by the same artist, wasn't it?" Ian asked Danielle.

"Yeah, you know it was. So?" Danielle frowned.

"Who was the artist?" the chief asked.

Danielle shook her head. "I don't know. The signature is illegible; I can't make out the name. Walt might have told me, but I don't remember."

"If we knew something about this artist, then we might be able to figure out if he was ever associated with any art theft. That might explain why someone like Macbeth is using an alias and inspecting the backs of your portraits," Ian said. "Can you ask Walt about the artist?"

"Sure. But I imagine he's going to be in the library all day, watching this Macbeth guy. I can't really go in there and get him. And I haven't seen Marie, so I can't get her to go in and ask Walt," Danielle said.

"Until you talk to Walt, perhaps you might want to head down to the museum and get a closer look at Eva's portrait. Maybe they know something about the original artist," the chief suggested.

NINE

I an went to the museum alone while Danielle returned to Marlow House. She intended to ask Walt about the artist who had painted his portraits. But first, she would have to wait for him to come out of the library.

When Ian arrived at the museum, he found Millie Samson on docent duty. The older woman greeted Ian and asked if there was any special reason for his visit.

"I'm thinking of doing a follow-up story on Eva Thorndike," he lied. "I wanted to have another look at her portrait."

"I just love that painting," Millie told him as she followed Ian into the main section of the museum and to Eva's display.

Now standing before the portrait, he looked up at it. "It's not as large as the Marlow portraits."

"No. We'd never get it up on that display if it were. But you know, it was painted by the same artist."

"What's the history on the portrait?" Ian asked. He already knew some of it, but he wanted to hear what Millie had to say.

"It was painted a few months before she died. I assume she was sick at the time, so I imagine the artist took liberties with the painting so she'd look healthy," Millie suggested.

"It might explain why she looks so much like the Gibson Girl in that painting," Ian mused.

"After Eva died and her parents sold their vacation home here, they donated the portrait to the local theater, where it was prominently displayed for years. The theater eventually closed down, and the portrait was given to the city. By that time, I don't think there was anyone left from the Thorndike family who was interested in taking the painting back. As you know, Eva was an only child."

"And then it was given to the museum?" Ian asked.

"After it sat boxed up in storage for years. It was one of the first items the city turned over to the museum after we opened."

"So what do you know about the artist?" Ian stepped closer to the painting and inspected the artist's signature. It was no more than an illegible scribble.

Millie shrugged. "According to Ben Smith—at least the story his father told him—the artist was a young man who worked with the local theater group, painting settings and doing odd jobs. He wasn't from Frederickport. He needed money, and Eva got her parents to hire him to paint her portrait. I imagine they were pleasantly surprised at how well it turned out."

"Indeed. Any chance you know the artist's name?"

"No. And I know Ben doesn't either. When we were setting up the display, we wanted to include something about the artist, but we couldn't find anything on who he was. Not even a first name. I do know he left the area after he finished Eva's portrait."

"He obviously came back to paint the Marlow portraits."

"Yes, but I don't really know the story on that. Neither does anyone in the Historical Society. We discussed it at a board meeting once, when trying to find out something about the artist. If the newspaper ever wrote an article on it, it was in one of the newspapers lost in the fire. Unfortunately, everyone is gone now. There's no one left to ask."

JOANNE WALKED into the parlor and found Clint Marlow opening one of the drawers of the parlor desk.

"Can I help you find something?" she asked curtly.

Clint shut the drawer and glanced up at the middle-aged woman. The way she clutched the wooden handle of the duster might make a person wonder if she was preparing to smack someone.

"I was just looking at this furniture. Was it here when Danielle inherited the house?"

"Yes. Most of it was." Joanne began running the duster over the furniture.

Folding his arms across his chest, Clint leisurely circled the room, studying the décor and woodwork. "I have to say, I'm a little surprised Danielle decided to stay. If it were me, I would have sold this relic. I certainly wouldn't turn it into a bed and breakfast and let strangers into my home. Not if I had the money she has. In fact, I would have torn it down and had something new built. I bet that would bring in a good profit."

Joanne stopped dusting and turned to Clint. "Then I'm glad Danielle inherited Marlow House and not you!"

Clint studied Joanne a moment. "Are you always so free with your opinions with the guests? I don't imagine Danielle would appreciate it. It could get you fired."

Narrowing her eyes, Joanne glared at Clint. "Go ahead and tell Danielle what I said. I don't care."

"I think I will."

Before Joanne could respond, Danielle walked into the parlor.

"Hello, Clint." Danielle then turned to Joanne and asked, "Have you seen Max? He ran out the pet door earlier today, and I haven't seen him since."

"I saw him going up the attic stairs about half an hour ago," Joanne told her.

"Joanne, I would like to speak to your employer alone. Would you please leave us?" Clint said curtly.

Flashing Clint a look of disgust, Joanne stormed from the parlor.

"Is there a problem?" Danielle asked.

"I just thought you should be aware of your housekeeper's poor attitude."

Danielle frowned. "Joanne?"

"Yes. She was quite rude to me. I don't think that's good business practice. I thought you should be aware of it. If it were me, I'd let her go and find someone more suited for working with the public. Having someone like that around is going to ruin your business."

"THERE YOU ARE, MAX," Danielle said when she found him napping in the attic. The cat lifted his head sleepily and looked at her, his black tail swishing from side to side. He yawned. Leaning over, Danielle scooped up the cat and then sat down on the sofa bed, situating Max on her lap. He began to purr.

"Did mean ol' Walt throw you in the trash can?" Danielle stroked his back. Max closed his eyes and settled down comfortably on Danielle. "You're such a good kitty."

"I don't like that man," Joanne said from the open doorway.

Danielle glanced up at Joanne and smiled. "So what happened down there?"

"What did he say happened?" Joanne walked into the attic, no longer carrying the duster.

"Just that you were rude and I should fire you. I'm sorry, Joanne, the guy is kind of a jerk. I bet if you were rude, he asked for it."

Joanne took a seat on a folding chair facing Danielle. She recounted her conversation with Clint.

Danielle shook her head. "What a tattletale he is. That's why he thought I should fire you? Gosh, I'm going to be glad when these two weeks are over."

"I just wanted to tell you myself what happened."

Danielle smiled at Joanne. "Considering how he treated Lily, I can't think of anything you could say to him that would upset me."

NOT LONG AFTER Joanne left Danielle and Max in the attic, Walt showed up.

"He's taking a break," Walt announced when he appeared. "I am happy to report he hasn't gotten paint on anything—aside from his canvas."

Max looked up at Walt and made a gurgling growling sound.

Startled by the strange noise, Danielle glanced down at the cat on her lap. "Max is not happy with you."

"No. I understand that." Walt looked at the cat; their eyes met. "I'm sorry, Max. But when that flash went off, I knew I had to do something fast to distract him."

Max stopped growling. He continued to look at Walt.

"I understand, Max. Yes…yes…okay…I promise."

"What did you promise him?" Danielle asked.

Max closed his eyes and settled back down to sleep.

Waving his hand for a lit cigar, Walt smiled down at Danielle. "He doesn't appreciate it when I…well, pick him up when he doesn't expect it. I need to stop doing that."

"Yes, you do."

Walt shrugged and took a puff off his cigar.

"I'm glad you're here."

Walt arched his brow. "You are?"

"Yes. It turns out Ian was right. Our artist is not Jim Hill."

Walt frowned. "Who is he?" Walt took a seat on the sofa next to Danielle and Max.

Danielle glanced at the open doorway. It closed, with a little spiritual help from Walt. "Where is our artist? Is he in his room?"

Walt shook his head. "No. He left with Clint and Stephanie. I don't know where they went."

"Well, good." Turning to Walt, Danielle told him about her morning with Ian. When she was finished, she asked, "So what do you know about the artist who painted your portraits?"

Walt shrugged. "Nothing, really. I didn't get that friendly with him. I don't even remember his name. He had a French accent, I remember that—only because Angela found it very charming."

"He's the same artist that painted Eva's portrait."

"I remember when Eva had her portrait done. I ran into the artist once when I went over there, but I don't think we exchanged two words at the time. From what I remember, he moved from the area before Eva passed away, and he didn't come back to Frederick-port until about a week before Angela commissioned him to do our portraits."

"How did Angela happen to hire him?"

"She was at the theater with friends, and he was there. Someone introduced them and mentioned he was the artist who'd painted Eva's portrait. I suspect Angela hired him because she was always a little jealous of Eva."

"Poor Eva was dead."

"True. But it was common knowledge back then that Eva had been my first love."

"Oh, Walt, you're talking about me," Eva gushed when she appeared the next moment—Marie by her side and a flurry of glitter hailing their entrance.

"Eva, hello," Danielle greeted her cheerfully. She looked at

Marie and asked, "What have you two been up to?" From Danielle's lap, Max looked up at the new arrivals. He yawned lazily and then put his head back down, closing his eyes.

"We've been out and about. I told Eva about Walt's cousin, and she's dying to see him," Marie explained.

"I would be dying to see him if I weren't already dead." Eva smiled over at Walt and asked, "So why were you talking about me?"

"I've been asking Walt about the artist who painted your portrait," Danielle answered for Walt.

"Johnny?" Eva asked.

"His name was Johnny?" Danielle asked.

Eva considered the question a moment and then smiled. "Actually, his name was Jacque. He was French. For some reason everyone called him Johnny." Eva shrugged. "As I recall, I think it was because Johnny sounded more American. He wanted to fit in."

"Do you remember his last name?" Danielle asked.

Eva shook her head. "No. Why do you ask?"

"It's kind of a long story. By any chance, when Johnny painted your portraits, did he happen to paint over a used canvas?"

"Used canvas?" Walt frowned.

"Yes. Sometimes artists reuse canvases. Maybe it already had a coat of paint on it when he started painting?"

Eva shook her head. "Not mine. My parents purchased the canvas for my portrait. Johnny was a dear, but he was as poor as a church mouse. In fact, the only reason my parents hired him was because I asked them to. At the time Johnny was working for a little theater group, primarily painting scenery. He was very talented. But the manager of the group skipped town without paying its people, and it really left Johnny in a tight spot. He desperately needed the money."

Danielle looked at Walt. "How about your portraits? Did he supply the canvases?"

Walt shook his head. "No. It was Angela's idea to do life-size portraits. We had to special order the canvases. They were new."

"I would love to find out the artist's full name," Danielle grumbled.

"There is one person who might remember," Walt suggested.

There was a moment of silence and then Danielle groaned. "Angela."

TEN

Alone in her bedroom, Danielle sat on the side of her mattress, talking to Lily on her cellphone.

"I thought you would cancel tonight," Lily told her.

Dressed for company, fresh makeup on, and her hair recently washed and combed, Danielle looked to her closed bedroom door while holding the phone to her ear. "No. I'm not going to cancel just because Walt's cousin is a jerk. I'm just changing tonight's theme, and, Lily, you have to come."

Danielle could hear Lily's sigh through the phone. "I'm coming. Is he going to be there, or are they going out? Please say they're going out."

"I told them I was having a casual dinner party, and they were welcome to stay. I didn't mention I had originally scheduled the party so some of my friends could meet Walt's cousin. But I don't think they're going to be here. He asked me what the best restaurant in town was. I suggested Pearl Cove."

"What about Jim Macbeth?"

Danielle chuckled. "His name's not Jim Macbeth."

"Well, that's what I'm calling him."

"He's not going to be here either," Danielle told her.

"So he's going to Pearl Cove with them?"

"No. He's driving to Astoria. Said he used to know some people there and was going to see if they're still in town. He also told me to keep the library locked while my guests were here, that he didn't want anyone messing with his paintings."

"That's kind of nervy. What did you say to him?"

"I told him he was pretty demanding for a guy using a fake name and with a reputation for art fraud."

Lily gasped. "You didn't!"

Danielle chuckled. "No, I didn't. But I did tell him that if he was worried about his paintings, perhaps he should keep them in his room when he's not working on them, because my guests are welcome to go into the library. I'm not locking the door."

"Good for you!"

"I'll give him his privacy while he's painting, but considering their attitudes, I'm not feeling so accommodating."

CHILI SIMMERING in the slow cooker filled the kitchen and beyond with an enticing aroma. Even Clint and Stephanie appreciated the tempting fragrance. Yet not enough to cancel their Friday dinner plans.

Clint had just stepped out of the living room, where he had been watching television, and was on his way to find Stephanie when the first dinner guests arrived. It was Chris Johnson and Heather Donovan. The neighbors hadn't intentionally arrived together, but since they both lived on Danielle's street, they happened to arrive at the same time.

Neither Chris nor Heather bothered knocking; they simply entered the house, yet came to an abrupt stop when faced with Walt's cousin.

Standing just five feet from Clint, Heather blurted, "Walt, what did you do with your hair, your clothes?"

Expressionless, Clint muttered, "Funny." Turning from the pair, he made his way to the kitchen without saying another word.

Heather was about to go after Clint when Chris grabbed her forearm and pulled her back. "That's not Walt. That's the cousin."

Turning to Chris, Heather frowned. "No! Walt's just messing with us. I know his cousin resembles him, but there's no way he looks exactly like him. That's impossible. They aren't even that closely related."

"What's impossible?" Walt asked when he appeared the next

moment.

"Hey, Walt, we just met your cousin—sort of. But Heather scared him off." Chris chuckled.

"Don't be lame," Heather snapped. She looked at Walt and said, "You look better with your hair like that."

The next moment Heather discovered Walt wasn't playing tricks when Clint and Stephanie returned from the kitchen and walked by them, heading for the front door. They made no attempt to greet Chris or Heather.

"My cousin isn't particularly friendly," Walt noted, watching the pair leave out the front door.

"Oh my gosh, it really wasn't you!" Heather gasped. "How can he look so much like you?"

"I have no idea, but it's exceedingly annoying," Walt grumbled.

HAD JOE BEEN DATING someone else, Danielle would probably not have invited him to her gathering. But his girlfriend, Kelly, was Ian's sister and a new resident of Frederickport; plus, Kelly was curious to get another glimpse at Walt's cousin. Unfortunately for her, Clint and Stephanie had already left before they arrived.

Melony was also curious to see the cousin, but like the other guests, aside from Chris and Heather, he was already gone when she and Adam showed up. Most of the group gathered in the living room for cocktails before dinner, and Adam was telling them of the rude encounter he'd had with Clint and what he had heard him say to Lily. Lily kept muttering how embarrassing it had all been, while Adam told the story.

Chief MacDonald was the only one who had arrived with a child—his youngest, Evan. Eddie Jr. was at a sleepover with friends for the night. Evan spent his time in the hallway with Sadie, rolling the ball for her down the long entry.

Later, when the group gathered in the dining room for chili, Melony said, "I wonder if they'll be back before we leave. I'm curious to see if he really looks that much like the portrait."

"Oh, he does," Heather told her as she took a place at the long dining room table with her bowl of chili.

"I thought maybe the artist would be here," Joe said. He and Kelly sat down.

"Jim Macbeth went to Astoria. Or so he says," Lily piped.

"I thought his name was Jim Hill?" Kelly asked.

All eyes turned to Lily.

"Really, Lily? You're going to accidentally call him that." Danielle placed baskets of warm cornbread on the table.

"So? I don't have anything to hide; he does," Lily said.

"Who is hiding what?" Joe asked.

"Apparently the artist Clint Marlow hired is using an alias," the chief explained.

"Does that mean he's not a real artist?" Melony asked.

"No. By all accounts he's an excellent artist, but he has a shady past," Danielle said. "And I would appreciate it if this conversation stays here. He doesn't know I know who he really is, and I would prefer it if you all would say nothing for now."

"This is why it's not a good idea for you to welcome strangers in your home," Joe said.

"Please, Joe, don't start," Danielle groaned.

"Yes, Joe," Kelly snapped. "It's really none of your business what Danielle does."

CHRIS HAD FOLLOWED Danielle into the kitchen when she went to get more cornbread. He wanted to know what she wasn't telling the others—those who had no idea Walt haunted Marlow House.

"Why is it important to learn more about the artist who painted Walt's portraits?" Chris asked after Danielle filled him in. The two stood alone in the kitchen. "I imagine he's been dead for years."

"We're just wondering why Macbeth is using an alias," Danielle explained.

Chris shrugged. "I can understand why. I use an alias, and it doesn't mean I have nefarious intentions."

"How can we be sure of that?" Walt asked when he appeared a moment later.

Chris looked at Walt and grinned. "You can't."

"For one thing, this guy has a sketchy past," Danielle suggested, ignoring Chris and Walt's exchange.

"Which is more reason for him to use an alias. I imagine he doesn't want people to start asking him embarrassing questions," Chris pointed out.

"Ian suggested the same thing. Yet he doesn't think that's the reason. He's having one of his gut feelings that there is more to the story," Danielle explained.

"Plus, this Macbeth guy did spend an exorbitant amount of time examining the backs and frames of my portraits," Walt told him. "He was looking for something."

"You don't think he's just here to copy the portraits?" Chris asked.

"No," Danielle said. "Because of Macbeth's history and the fact he was so curious about the canvases, my first guess was that maybe there was something under one of the paintings. Like a stolen masterpiece."

"Except that can't be it because those were painted on new canvases. I saw them," Walt said.

"So what now?" Chris asked.

"I still want to find out what I can about the original artist," Danielle said.

"Why?" Chris frowned.

Danielle shrugged. "I don't know. I just want to. I kind of agree with Ian, something feels funny about all this. Especially after meeting Walt's cousin. I know he was kind of a jerk in the emails, but I didn't expect him to be...well..."

"As jerky?" Chris suggested.

Danielle nodded. "Exactly. And Lily is right. For someone willing to pay a fortune to have two paintings reproduced—and I can't believe it isn't costing Clint a fortune—he doesn't seem that interested in the originals."

"Lily mentioned that to me," Chris noted.

"Joanne noticed it too. Before she went home tonight, she said it was odd that someone who didn't seem to have any appreciation for Marlow history would want a copy of the portraits."

"So what are you going to do about it?" Chris asked.

"I'm going to talk to the only person I know who might remember the artist's name. That way, I can look him up. See if there is anything about him that might explain why Macbeth is so interested in those paintings. Who knows, maybe it's the frame he's interested in. Maybe Walt's artist was a notorious jewel thief and hid a fortune in the frames." Danielle grinned at the idea.

"Who are you going to talk to, Eva?" Chris asked.

"No. I already talked to Eva. Tomorrow, I'm going to talk to

Angela."

———

CLINT AND STEPHANIE sat side by side in a Pearl Cove booth, overlooking the ocean view. If not for the outside lighting, they wouldn't have much to look at. Clint's right hand covered Stephanie's left hand while his thumb gently rubbed her wrist.

"I adore you," Clint whispered.

"Not as much as I adore you," Stephanie purred, resting her head against his shoulder.

"I can't wait until we're away from here and all these annoying idiots," Clint grumbled.

"Aren't you the one always telling me to be patient?"

With a sigh, he kissed the tip of her nose. "I know. But sometimes it's hard."

"You know, Clint, I understand there is nothing that annoys you more than having to waste your time on people you don't care about—"

"Which is one reason I'm so happy to be giving up real estate. You've no idea how painful it was to pretend I actually cared what my clients wanted. It was excruciating. Never again."

"I understand that. But we need to get through these two weeks here or else none of that will matter. We won't be able to leave."

With a frown, Clint pulled away from Stephanie and looked at her. "What are you talking about?"

"You know I'm nervous about all this."

"I know. But we'll pull it off," he insisted.

"Not if Danielle starts asking questions. Everything could blow up in our faces."

"Why would she start asking questions?" he asked.

"I overheard Joanne and Danielle talking in the kitchen tonight. Joanne finds your lack of interest in the portraits odd. She said you don't care about family history—"

"I don't. I've made no secret of that. Anyway, Joanne was just saying that crap because I busted her tonight. The woman has absolutely no customer-service skills."

"It doesn't matter. Joanne has Danielle wondering why you're so interested in the portraits."

"Obviously because I look just like Walt Marlow." He laughed.

Stephanie shook her head. "But that doesn't explain why you would bother reproducing his wife's portrait."

Clint studied Stephanie, his expression somber. "You really think we could have a problem?"

"When you first emailed Danielle about buying the originals and you threw in that bit about painting my face on the other portrait, I asked why you told her that since you obviously would never do it. You explained that Danielle probably wouldn't up the price if she felt you were willing to paint over one, because she wouldn't start wondering if there was some other reason you wanted them. I thought that was pretty clever of you. It was also smart of you to say you wouldn't paint over it if it bothered her. It doesn't matter if those portraits were worth nothing, someone like Danielle would probably balk over painting over anything old like that."

"So?"

"So it would make more sense to them if you were having the artist paint my face on the wife's reproduction."

"But we can't do that."

"Obviously, Clint. But you see the problem? Maybe you need to take a little interest in family history so they stop wondering why you want those portraits, especially the wife's."

Clint considered her suggestion for a moment. Finally, he said, "I guess you're right. I didn't really consider that. At this point, I don't want to do anything to screw this up. But what do I do now?"

"Well…one of my aunts was into family history. If she were you, she would be totally goofy over those portraits. If she were here, the first thing she would do is take a trip to the cemetery."

"Cemetery? Why would I want to go there?"

"Because that's where people go when they're into family history. From what I read online, your look-alike cousin and his family are buried there. We go in the morning, take a bunch of photos, and then go back to Marlow House and act all excited and show them to Danielle. I'd say bore her to death, but chances are she might really find it interesting."

"Chances are Danielle Boatman has already taken her own photographs of my dear cousin's grave. She seems a little too engrossed in my family history."

"Whatever, but we need to do this. It's the only thing I can think of to get the thought out of her head that there might be another reason you're interested in the portraits."

ELEVEN

The night before, Macbeth Bandoni hadn't removed his paintings from the library to his bedroom. However, he had covered them each with a sheet and had secured a sticky note on each one, asking that they not be touched. After taking a closer look at each covered canvas, Danielle was relieved to discover they weren't her sheets. Bandoni must have brought them with him.

The fact he had left the paintings in the library while she had dinner guests made Danielle wonder if he wasn't as concerned about his paintings as he let on. *Was there another reason he didn't want anyone in the library?* she wondered.

It was Saturday morning, and no one—aside from Danielle and Joanne—was enjoying the breakfast offered at Marlow House B and B. Bandoni was still sleeping in his room. He had gotten in very late the night before, several hours after the last of her dinner guests had said their goodbyes. As for Clint and Stephanie, they were gone when she got up that morning. According to Joanne, they told her they were going out for breakfast and then sightseeing.

"Are you sure you want to do this?" Walt asked Danielle as she went up to her bedroom to retrieve her purse after breakfast.

"I'm not thrilled to see your wife." Standing in her bedroom, Danielle opened her purse to make sure her wallet was inside. "But I need to do this."

"Please don't call her my wife. As I recall, we said *until death do us part*; therefore, I no longer consider her my spouse."

Shutting her purse, Danielle smiled up at Walt. "Fair enough. But you got that from Marie, didn't you?"

Walt grinned. "Yes. And she's right. So what do you really hope to find?"

Danielle shrugged. "I seriously doubt anything. But I don't know what else to do. I guess it's probably up to you."

"Up to me?"

"Yep. Just keep a close eye on our houseguests, and if they do anything suspicious, let me know. Hopefully this is nothing more than Ian's overactive imagination, and when your cousin leaves at the end of two weeks, it will all be very uneventful."

DANIELLE HAD JUST STEPPED onto the cemetery lawn when Angela appeared before her. Dressed in the same outfit as she had worn when sitting for the portrait—including the hat—Danielle wondered why she had chosen that particular ensemble.

"You're here to tell me I can go now?" Angela asked excitedly.

Danielle came to an abrupt halt, startled by Angela's sudden appearance. "What are you talking about?"

With a disappointed sigh, Angela slumped dejectedly, her hat disappearing from her head, revealing her shortly cropped blonde curls. "I just assumed that's why you were here. To tell me I could go."

Puzzled, Danielle cocked her head slightly and studied the apparition. "I have no idea what you're talking about, Angela. Why would I have any say in if you can come or go?"

Angela shrugged. "Of course you don't have any say. I just assumed you were here to tell me it all worked out."

"What worked out?"

"I knew it was too good to be true," Angela grumbled. She turned from Danielle and began walking toward her grave.

"Aren't you even going to ask me about Walt?" Danielle followed Angela. "You normally do. It's typically the first thing you ask about."

"If it worked out for Walt, I wouldn't be here, would I?" The

65

clothes Angela wore morphed into a different dress, one more casual yet typical of her era, with a fringed hem. She sat atop her headstone.

"You aren't making any sense."

Angela shrugged. "Why are you here?"

"I wanted to ask you about the artist who painted your portraits."

"Why?"

"I...I'd just like to find out more about him. Walt doesn't remember anything about him, and Eva only remembers his name was Jacque, but went by Johnny."

"That's because of his middle name, Jehan, spelled J-E-H-A-N. He told me that was French for John."

"Do you remember his full name?"

Angela shrugged. "Jacque Jehan Bonnet, spelled like a hair bonnet." Angela laughed. "That's how I remember, I used to call him Johnny Hair Bonnet."

"I can't imagine he liked that."

Angela giggled. "Are you serious? He was quite a flirt. If I wasn't marrying Walt, I might have been tempted, but I wasn't about to get involved with a starving artist, no matter how handsome he was."

"What do you know about him?"

"I didn't know him well, but I rather envied him, his freedom and spirit of adventure. He had been traveling through the States, working mostly with theater groups, painting an occasional portrait to make a little extra money. One of my girlfriends introduced him to me when we were at the theater. He had just come back to town and wanted to look at Eva's portrait. He had heard she'd died." Angela shrugged again.

"How did you happen to hire him?"

"He mentioned he was only in town for a short time. Said he planned to go back to France. He hadn't been back in a number of years, said he wanted to see his family, but first he needed to raise a little extra money. Wanted to know if we knew anyone interested in having a portrait done. And I thought, why not? I needed to get Walt a wedding gift, and there was some irony in having Eva's artist paint them. I couldn't resist."

"Did you ever hear what happened to him?"

"No. I assume he went back to France. But I didn't see him

again after he finished the portraits, and as you know, I died not long after Walt and I married."

"Is there anything else you know about the artist?"

Angela considered the question a moment and then shook her head. "No. Why?"

"It's kind of a long story."

"You don't have to tell me. To be honest, I don't really care." Angela let out a sigh and uncrossed and re-crossed her legs, shifting her position slightly on the headstone. "I'm feeling a little depressed. When I saw you, I thought…well, it doesn't matter."

"What did you think?" Danielle asked. "What did you expect me to tell you?"

"That I was free to go. That I could finally move on. That Walt's destiny had been set back on course. I should have known it was foolish to listen to rumors. Especially here."

"Was it something another spirit told you?" Danielle asked.

Angela looked down at Danielle, silently studying her for a moment. "I really shouldn't be discussing this with you. It will just get me in more trouble. If I ever want to leave this place, I have to follow their rules."

"Whose rules?" Danielle asked.

"The Universe, of course." Angela vanished.

Danielle glanced around. There was no sign of Angela. She walked to a nearby bench, sat down, and then pulled her cellphone from her purse and dialed Ian.

When Ian answered her call, she said, "Hi. I have the artist's name for you."

"Angela remembered?" Ian asked.

"Yes. It's Jacque Jehan Bonnet." Danielle then spelt out the middle and last names. "According to Angela, he was planning to go back to France after he finished her portraits. Of course, she died not long after that and never really knew for sure if he left or not."

"I'll see if I can find out anything about him. Thanks, Danielle. You're a regular Nancy Drew—if Nancy Drew were a medium."

Just as Danielle ended her phone call and was about to slip the cellphone back in her purse, she heard Angela call out excitedly.

"Walt! You came! You really came! Does this mean I can leave now? That I'm free?" Angela asked.

Danielle looked up to find Clint and Stephanie walking in her direction.

67

The moment Clint recognized Danielle, he came to an abrupt stop. "Danielle, what are you doing here?"

"I was about to ask you the same thing." Danielle stood up yet found it difficult to focus on what he was saying, considering the shouting coming from Angela.

TWELVE

"Walt, is that why you're here?" Angela squealed, unable to contain her excitement. "Are you here to tell me I can go now?"

Clint stared at Danielle. "Do you always hang out at the cemetery on Saturday mornings?"

"Walt, please don't ignore me!" Angela said impatiently. "I know you were angry with me, but now…" Angela frowned and looked from Walt to the woman by his side. They held hands.

"A dear friend recently died. I like to visit her grave." It wasn't a complete lie. Danielle's dear friend Marie had recently died, and she was buried at this cemetery. Yet, the fact was, Danielle hadn't visited her grave since the funeral. Why should she? Marie's spirit was a frequent visitor to Marlow House.

"I'm sorry to hear that," Clint said politely.

"Walt, why are you holding that woman's hand? What is she to you?" Angela demanded. "This is not how it's supposed to work out. I don't understand. Stop ignoring me!"

"Clint Marlow, are you here to visit your cousin's grave? Walt Marlow, who looks exactly like you?" Danielle said loud and clear for Angela's benefit.

Stephanie and Clint exchanged glances, and Danielle could only imagine what they were thinking: *That Danielle Boatman is an odd one.*

"Yes. We. Are. Here. To. See. Walt. Marlow's. Grave." Clint chuckled.

"Walt's cousin?" Angela gasped. "He looks just like him!"

Stephanie tugged gently on Clint's hand, a silent reprimand. "Yes, Danielle, that's why we're here. Clint wants to visit his family's graves—and take pictures. He's putting together a family history scrapbook."

"He is?" Danielle frowned.

"Oh yes!" Stephanie said excitedly while Clint stood mutely by her side, letting her speak. "I know Clint likes to play the tough guy, that family doesn't mean anything to him. But you don't know how excited he was when he received that link to your business website and saw his cousin's portrait!"

"Well, they do look exactly alike. I can understand why that would pique his interest." Danielle looked to Clint, who smiled sheepishly.

"It's not just the portraits," Stephanie insisted. "You see, Clint really doesn't have any family. His father died a few years ago, and he lost his mother when he was just a child. He doesn't have any cousins or family. No one who can really tell him more about his family's history."

"I...I can relate," Danielle told her.

Stephanie frowned. "You can?"

Danielle nodded. "Yes. My cousin died over a year ago. And she was really the only family I had left. I don't have anyone now."

"Then you can understand how excited Clint was to discover this branch of his family. It gives him the opportunity to learn more about his family history, since there's no one left who can tell him anything."

"In the email, he said he wasn't interested in family history."

Squeezing Clint's hand, Stephanie looked to him and smiled lovingly. "That's just Clint trying to hide his feelings. He's really a marshmallow."

"Yeah...I'm a marshmallow," Clint grumbled, smiling weakly at Danielle.

"If you want, I can show you where the family crypt is," Danielle offered.

"They have a crypt?" Stephanie asked excitedly.

"Yes. Walt's not buried in it, but his parents are and his grandparents," Danielle explained.

"I can't believe how much he looks like Walt," Angela stammered. "I wonder if this has something to do with that other thing."

Danielle glanced at Angela, wondering what that other thing was, yet unable to ask.

"Please take us there!" Stephanie said.

"Okay, but we'll be going right by Angela's and Walt's graves. We can stop there first," Danielle offered.

"Angela?" Stephanie frowned.

"I'm Angela!"

"Angela was Walt's wife. The one in the portrait," Danielle told her.

"Oh, the gold digger who killed my cousin," Clint said.

Angela gasped. "I did not kill him! I tried to stop his murder!"

"It's believed Angela's brother killed Walt. We don't really know for sure if Angela was involved or not," Danielle lied. "She was killed the day before him by a hit-and-run driver in Portland."

"I bet her brother killed her too," Clint said.

"My brother would never hurt me!" Angela insisted. "I know he was wrong, and he has paid for his sins, we all have. But he would never hurt me; he loved me!"

"Then she really could not have been responsible for Walt's murder," Stephanie said. "I might feel a little uncomfortable hanging her portrait in my house if I thought she had killed her poor husband."

"What is she talking about?" Angela asked.

Danielle showed the couple first to Walt's and Angela's graves. Stephanie handed her phone to Clint.

"No, babe, you take the pictures. You take better pictures than I do." Clint smiled at Stephanie.

After Stephanie took a number of photographs of each grave site, Danielle showed them to the family crypt.

"That's kind of cool looking," Stephanie murmured while taking photographs of the crypt's perimeter.

"An interesting story about the crypt. Last year, a local woman died and her uncle hid her body in it," Danielle told them.

Stephanie stopped taking pictures and turned to Danielle. "He murdered his niece?"

Danielle shook her head. "No. She died from natural causes."

"Then why would he hide the body?" Stephanie asked.

"It had to do with the estate. As long as she was believed to be alive, he controlled their family business. But once she died, he believed her share was going to a nonprofit organization and out of his control."

"Who found the body?" Stephanie asked.

Danielle didn't answer immediately. Finally, she said, "I did."

"Seriously?" Stephanie asked.

Danielle nodded. "Long story. Basically, I was dog sitting for my neighbor, the dog got out, I found her here, and while here I noticed the crypt seemed to be open." It wasn't exactly what had happened, but close enough, Danielle thought.

"That's just creepy." Stephanie shivered.

"Yes, it was," Danielle agreed.

"I'm bored," Angela said before disappearing.

Stephanie snapped a few more photographs while Danielle and Clint watched silently. Finally, Stephanie turned to Danielle and said, "I still find it odd how much Clint looks like his distant cousin. Do you have any idea how closely related they are?"

"If Clint is interested in his family history, he might want to get an account at Ancestry.com. I found some information there on the Marlow family," Danielle suggested.

"Oh yes! I'm sure he'll want to do that. Won't you, Clint?"

Clint smiled at Stephanie. "Yes, love. I will do that as soon as we get back to California."

Stephanie grinned at Clint.

"One thing that may explain why Walt and Clint look so much alike, Walt's great-grandparents—the ones who were the first in his line to come to the US were twins—and their twins married each other. Double cousins of identical twins. Clint is a direct descendant of the brother of Walt's great-grandfather and of the sister of Walt's great-grandmother. I always heard that double cousins of twins were genetically siblings. Not sure that's really true." Danielle shrugged.

"So that's why they look so much alike?" Stephanie asked.

"I'm sure that's a contributing factor," Danielle said.

"This is very interesting," Clint said. "But I'm sure we're keeping Danielle."

Danielle glanced at her watch. "I probably should get going. Plus, I imagine you'd like some privacy here."

"I DIDN'T THINK she was ever going to leave," Clint said after Danielle was out of earshot.

"You have to admit it was a little interesting. Especially about the body hidden in your family crypt." Stephanie held Clint's hand as they walked slowly down the path away from the crypt and toward Walt's and Angela's grave sites. Beyond the grave sites was the parking lot.

"First of all, I already knew about all that. I read about it online when I was looking up information on Marlow House after that guy sent me the link."

"Why didn't you tell me?" Stephanie asked.

Clint shrugged. "It didn't seem important. Hell, if I told you about all the insane things I read on the internet, we wouldn't have time to talk about anything else."

"I know, but this was about your family crypt."

"Not my family crypt. The crypt of some people who I happen to share a little DNA with. They are nothing to me. Walt Marlow is nothing to me."

"But you have to admit, Walt Marlow was good looking." Stephanie giggled and leaned up to kiss Clint's cheek.

Clint stopped abruptly, turned to Stephanie, and pulled her into his arms. The two kissed and then Clint pulled away slightly, still holding Stephanie in his arms; he gazed into her eyes. "In a few weeks you'll be my family. There is only one thing in this world that truly matters to me, and that's you, Stephanie. You have no idea how much I love you."

Smiling up at Clint, she stood on her tiptoes and kissed his lips. When she pulled away, she whispered, "The feeling is mutual."

"There is one good thing about running into Danielle today." Clint grinned at Stephanie.

"What's that?"

"When we go back to Marlow House, we don't have to show her all the pictures we took and have to pretend I give a crap about Marlow family history."

Stephanie grinned. "True. So why don't we do something fun today?"

"Fun like what?"

"I don't know. Take a drive along the ocean. Play tourists. After all, this will probably be the last time we're ever on the Oregon coast."

"Thank God for that!" Clint kissed her again.

"SO WHAT DID YOU FIND OUT?" Walt asked when Danielle returned to Marlow House on Saturday.

Danielle walked into the parlor with him and shut the door. She didn't need Joanne or Macbeth hearing her supposedly talking to herself.

"I found out who the artist was, but I don't think it's important now."

"Why do you say that?"

Danielle tossed her purse on the small desk and sat down on the sofa. She kicked her shoes off and propped her feet on the coffee table. "It turns out your cousin is a closet genealogist."

"A what?" Walt sat down in a chair facing Danielle, a lit cigar in his hand.

"It turns out Clint really is interested in family history. I ran into him and Stephanie down at the cemetery. They were there to take pictures of family headstones."

Walt cringed. "That's rather gruesome."

Danielle chuckled. "Not really. People into family history typically visit cemeteries and take pictures of headstones. If you think about it, there can be a lot of useful information found on a headstone—unless the deceased family was cheap."

"Cheap? What do you mean?"

"I had a friend who was into genealogy. She took a trip back East to visit a cemetery where some of her ancestors had been buried. She was rather excited because she was having a hard time finding some birth and death dates. But when she got there, the headstones just had names. No dates."

Walt nodded. "Ahh, the extra cost for a stone cutter."

"Exactly. She was pretty annoyed at her ancestors." Danielle chuckled.

"Back to Clint—why are you no longer interested in the artist?"

"It's not that I'm no longer interested. I'm just not interested for the same reason. I don't think there is anything nefarious going on in spite of the fact Macbeth is using an alias. Clint obviously cares more about his family history than I thought, and I now understand why he would want a copy of those portraits. If he didn't care about his family history, I couldn't understand why he would bother having Angela's portrait reproduced. I could understand why he wanted yours, because of the resemblance."

"Out of curiosity, what did Angela tell you about the artist who painted our portraits?"

Danielle recounted her conversation with Angela. "I already called Ian and gave him the artist's name. I was going to do a Google search on him myself, but I don't see the point now. But I'll let Ian look; he might find something interesting to give the museum. According to him, the museum wanted to have a bio on the artist, but never knew his name."

"Did Angela see my cousin?"

"Ahh yes! At first she thought he was you." Danielle paused a moment and frowned. "Angela also said some strange things when I was there. She acted like I knew something that was going to let her move on."

"Knew something like what?"

Danielle considered the question a moment and then shrugged. "I have no idea. It was really odd."

THIRTEEN

C lint and Stephanie's afternoon drive took them down the coast and back again. Before returning to Frederickport, they stopped for a late lunch at a little restaurant overlooking the ocean. Large picture windows dominated the west-facing side of the quaint rustic building, its exterior wooden panels aged by salt air and persistent sea breezes. Famous for its clam chowder, the restaurant's special for the day was fish and chips. Clint ordered fish and chips while Stephanie ordered a sourdough bread bowl filled with piping hot clam chowder.

"I should feel guilty eating this," Stephanie said while blowing gently on a spoonful of soup. She had tried to taste it, but it was too hot.

"Why?" Clint picked up the ketchup bottle and squirted some ketchup on his plate.

"The carbs are going to kill me." She tasted the now cooled spoonful of soup.

"You don't need to worry about carbs." Clint picked up a French fry and dipped it in the ketchup.

"Oh, it is good. To heck with the calories. I'm going to enjoy this." She took another bite.

Clint chuckled. "Babe, you look perfect how you are. I don't think a bowl of clam chowder is going to hurt."

"You're sweet, Clint." She ripped off a bit of the bread bowl and took a nibble.

"Just being truthful." He popped the fry in his mouth.

"I wonder if they have clam chowder in France?" she asked.

"I remember once in college one of my roommates claimed it was the French who introduced clam chowder to the colonies. We were at the beach at the time, at some little restaurant." Clint paused a moment and glanced around. "It kind of reminds me of this one. Down by Newport."

"It's a French dish?" Stephanie asked.

Clint shrugged and picked up a piece of fried fish. "One of the other guys there insisted the British introduced it, not the French. Never did find out who was right—I didn't really care." Clint chuckled. "But I bet we can get clam chowder in France."

"I just can't wait. There is so much to see! I'm so excited!" With a grin, Stephanie scooped up more soup with her spoon.

"Less than two weeks now, babe. I think you were right about me showing more interest in my family history. Sometimes I get so focused on what I want I forget to tie up the annoying strings."

"Those annoying strings are what can get us in trouble."

"I know." Clint reached across the table and patted Stephanie's hand. "That's why I need you, babe. I'd never be able to pull this off without you."

OFFICER BRIAN HENDERSON couldn't recall the last time he'd had a date. His track record in the romance department wasn't terrific. He had been married and divorced twice. His last serious relationship was with a married woman, and if it wasn't for Danielle Boatman, he might now be serving time for murdering that ex-lover.

Over the last few months he kept running into Beverly Klein, the widow of Steve Klein, who had been the general manager of Frederickport's bank until his fateful fall off the Frederickport Pier after going into anaphylactic shock.

Younger than Brian, in her mid-forties, Beverly was an attractive woman with startling green eyes, a trim body, and just the right amount of curves. Rumor had it she was an ex-beauty queen, and Brian never understood why Steve had been a habitual womanizer. He couldn't fathom why Steve had taken up with Carla, a waitress from Pier Café. As far as Brian was concerned, Carla, with her ever-changing pastel-colored hair, wasn't in the same league as Beverly Klein.

Another thing Brian couldn't quite fathom—Beverly was interested in him. Joe had noticed it first and encouraged his partner to ask the attractive widow out. Brian finally took a chance—and she said yes.

It was their first date, and he was taking her to a little seafood restaurant on the outside of town, along the coast. The drive there would give them the opportunity to get to know each other a little better.

"I saw Marie Nichols's house is on the market," Beverly remarked. She sat in the passenger side of Brian's car, watching the coastal scenery roll by.

"I was a little surprised he didn't keep it and put it in his rental department."

Leaning back comfortably in the seat and gazing out the side window, Beverly said, "Maybe Adam didn't want to see renters in his grandmother's house. I know they were very close. Plus, I imagine he can get a good price for it. I didn't see what it's listed for, but I heard she sold the Beach Drive house for over a million."

"I guess Ian must do pretty well to afford a house like that." Brian then muttered, "I think I'm in the wrong business."

"He is a successful journalist. I've seen a few of his documentaries. Plus, I'm sure Lily got a good settlement from Stoddard's estate."

"True."

"I heard Sunny took a plea deal," Beverly said.

"Yes. But I think it was a mistake not to charge her for Marie's death. Considering all the evidence; I think they could have made it stick."

"She's already going to prison. Does it really matter now?" Beverly asked.

"Yes. I think if someone does a crime, they should be held accountable."

Turning to Brian, Beverly smiled. "And how do you define crime?"

Brian chuckled. "Isn't that fairly obvious?"

Beverly shrugged. "Sometimes there are extenuating circumstances, or the person didn't intend for the inevitable outcome."

"In Sunny's case, there were no extenuating circumstances, and I'm sure when she put that pillow on Marie's face, she knew exactly what the outcome was going to be," Brian said.

WHEN BRIAN and Beverly walked into the seaside restaurant twenty minutes later, they spied one empty booth by the front window. As the pair made their way to it, a man sitting at the next booth caught Brian's attention. The man looked exactly like Walt Marlow—or at least the man depicted in the life-sized portrait sitting in Danielle Boatman's home library.

The Walt look-alike was engrossed in a conversation with the woman sitting across the booth from him. The pair held hands across the table, and Brian caught a glimpse of the large solitary diamond glittering on her left hand. He wondered if this was the couple he had heard about, Walt Marlow's cousin and his fiancée. According to Joe, the cousin looked just like the portrait, and if this was the man, he would have to agree.

Beverly failed to notice Brian's fascination with the couple and instead continued to prattle on about some local gossip as they made their way to the empty booth. Just as Brian sat down—his back to the man who looked like Walt Marlow—Beverly excused herself to visit the restroom.

Waiting for Beverly, Brian picked up his menu and leaned back in the booth seat. Yet instead of focusing his attention on the menu items, he couldn't help but listen to the conversation in the next booth.

"Danielle Boatman must be a little simple to hold onto that house and run it as a B and B," the man told his companion.

"I think she's a little simple not to just sell those portraits to you. Who would want those monstrosities in their house? Especially if they're paintings of strangers. That's just weird," the woman said.

"Not my thing. Neither is Marlow House. That entire Second Empire mansard design does absolutely nothing for me," the man said.

"By the way, I forgot to tell you I overheard Joanne talking to Danielle this morning. You know last night, when she told us she was going to have some friends over and said we were welcome to stay if we wanted?"

"I don't know why she imagined we'd be remotely interested," he said.

"Well, according to what I overheard, she originally planned that get-together so her friends could meet you," the woman said.

"Why would we want to meet her friends? It's our vacation. That's rather presumptuous of her."

"I guess she changed her mind. I think because you hurt her friend Lily's feelings."

"When did I do that?" the man asked.

"When Lily came up to us when we were at that little restaurant on the pier, and you pretty much told her you didn't want to talk to her."

The man laughed. "See. I told you it's always best to be direct with people. Saved us time. You know I think it's a waste to go through all that politically correct crap of pretending you care about getting to know someone when you really couldn't care less."

"I understand, Clint, but even you know sometimes you have to play nice."

The man laughed again. "I love you, Stephanie. And I am playing nice with Danielle Boatman. I smile and everything."

The woman giggled. "And it's killing you."

"Hey, I can be nice to Danielle Boatman if it gets us what we want. After that, I won't waste my time on her."

"Gosh, Clint, I hope you never get bored of me," the woman said with a pout.

"Babe, that will never happen."

AFTER BEVERLY RETURNED to the booth, the waitress arrived to take their order. After she did, the waitress brought the table next to them their bill, and less than ten minutes later, the couple Brian had been listening to left the restaurant.

"What is it?" Beverly asked when she noticed Brian watching the front door of the restaurant.

"That couple that just left, I think they're staying at Marlow House."

"Really?" Beverly craned her neck to get a better view, but the couple was no longer in sight. "Why didn't you introduce yourself to them?"

Brian chuckled. "I don't think so."

Beverly frowned. "Why not?"

"They weren't speaking very flatteringly of their host."

"Really? I've always heard good things about Marlow House. I understand Danielle is an excellent cook."

"Did you hear about Walt Marlow's cousin coming to town? I'm pretty sure that was him sitting in the next booth."

"Walt Marlow? You mean the man murdered in the attic of Marlow House?"

Brian nodded. "Don't you remember seeing those life-sized portraits of Walt and his wife in the library at Marlow House?"

"Sure, why?"

"Because the one of Walt Marlow looks just like the man who was just in here. And according to Joe, who's seen the guy, the cousin looks just like the portrait."

"Wow. It must be a close cousin."

Brian shrugged. "No idea. But considering the resemblance, he has to be a close relative."

"Gee, then why didn't you introduce yourself? I would love to have met this guy."

Brian shook his head. "I don't think you would. From what I overheard when you went to the restroom, he sounded like a major jerk."

Beverly reached out and touched Brian's hand. "Why, Brian Henderson, were you eavesdropping?"

Brian chuckled. "Guilty as charged."

FOURTEEN

Lily entered the side yard of Marlow House through the unlocked gate and made her way down the walk to the kitchen door. Pausing at the back porch, she peeked in the side window and spied Joanne at the counter, prepping food for tomorrow's breakfast. Lily knocked on the door, but didn't wait for Joanne to answer; she walked right in.

Looking up from her work, Joanne flashed Lily a smile. "Afternoon, Lily. What are you up to today?"

Shutting the door behind her, Lily said, "Not much. Ian's been in his office all morning working."

"I thought he didn't work on Saturdays when you're off?"

Lily shrugged. "Something came up. So I thought I'd come over and see Dani. I noticed Clint's van was gone. I'm assuming he's not here?"

Joanne set the paring knife she had been using on the cutting board and then picked up a dish towel and wiped off her hands. She turned to Lily. "He and his fiancée took off early this morning. They didn't even stay for breakfast. I'm not sure why I'm even prepping for tomorrow's breakfast. I imagine it will be just Danielle and me again."

"I'd be happy to come over and help you eat it if I knew he wasn't going to be here."

"I don't know why, but for some reason I expected Walt's cousin

THE GHOST AND THE DOPPELGANGER

to be like him—or how I imagine Walt Marlow might be if I ever met him, considering the two look so much alike." Joanne tossed the dish towel on the counter.

"I'm pretty sure the only resemblance between Walt and Clint are their looks. Beyond that, nothing alike."

"I have to agree with you. One thing I know about Walt Marlow, he hired Brianna Boatman's mother as a housekeeper when many people probably would not have, considering she was an unwed mother. That was rather taboo back then. And then he left her his estate because he understood how evil his brother-in-law was. Whereas Clint Marlow tried to get me fired just because I didn't appreciate him making disparaging remarks about Marlow House."

"Yeah, Dani told me. What a jerk. Where is she, by the way?"

"I think she's still in the parlor. Mr. Hill is in the library, working on his paintings."

"Have you seen them?" Lily asked.

"Not since he first arrived. I was surprised he'd already started working on them." Joanne turned back to the counter and picked up her knife. She grabbed a bell pepper from a small stainless steel bowl and cut it in half.

"I guess he used the photographs Dani sent Clint to start them. I can understand. No way could he paint both of them in two weeks."

"I haven't seen them since then. He won't let anyone in the library when he's working, and when the library is open, his paintings are covered." Joanne removed the seeds from the bell pepper.

"I'll leave you to your dicing and go find Dani."

"IS WALT HERE?" Lily whispered when she entered the parlor. She found Danielle lounging on the small sofa, reading a book.

Danielle glanced up over the open book. "He's in with Macbeth."

Lily closed the parlor door and walked to the chairs across from Danielle. She sat down.

"Although, when he comes out, I think I'm going to tell him he really doesn't need to keep watching him," Danielle said.

"What do you mean? I thought you were worried that they're up to something?"

Closing the book, Danielle tossed it onto the coffee table. "I ran into Clint and Stephanie this morning. I understand why he wants the portraits." Danielle then told Lily about their encounter at the cemetery.

"I still think he's a jerk," Lily grumbled after Danielle told her about the morning.

"What's Ian doing?"

"Ever since you called this morning, he's been locked up in his office."

"I'm assuming he hasn't found anything on the artist. He probably won't."

"I don't know." Lily shrugged. "I asked him why he didn't search on his laptop in the living room with me. But he said it was easier for him in his office, so he could jot down notes. I checked in on him a few times, but he just waved me away. Rather annoying, really." Lily frowned.

"Waved you away?"

"I have to assume he found something on Walt's artist. Ian gets like that when he's researching. He doesn't like to share what he's found until he's put most of the pieces together." Her cellphone began to ring. She pulled it from the pocket of her sweater and looked at it. "It's Ian." She answered the phone call.

"Come in my office," Ian demanded.

"Umm…I'm not there. I'm across the street at Dani's."

"Good. Bring Danielle with you. Hurry. This is important. I found something."

"Okay…be right there." With a frown, Lily looked up at Danielle and tucked her phone back in her pocket. She stood up.

"You going back home?"

"Ian wants us both over there. He's found something. It sounds important."

WHEN DANIELLE AND LILY ARRIVED, Ian was no longer in his office. They found him pacing the living room, his right hand holding several printouts from his computer's printer.

Sadie didn't jump up to greet them. She lay in the corner of the living room, her chin resting on her front paws as she watched Ian pace—back and forth. The moment Ian noticed Lily and Danielle standing at the entrance to the living room, he stopped pacing and faced them. Sadie lifted her head and looked to the new arrivals, her tail now wagging. Yet she made no attempt to jump up and greet them.

"You need to sit down," Ian said impatiently, using his hand holding the printouts to point to the sofa.

Lily and Danielle exchanged questioning glances and then did as Ian instructed. Once they sat down, Sadie stood up and came to greet them, her tail still wagging.

"I found Walt's artist," Ian said excitedly.

"I sort of figured that." Danielle reached down to pet Sadie, her eyes on Ian.

"This is big! Bigger than the Missing Thorndike!" He started pacing again.

"Ian," Lily snapped, "sit down. You're making us dizzy. What did you find out that has you so worked up?"

"How is it bigger than the Missing Thorndike?" Danielle asked. The Missing Thorndike was the necklace found hidden in Marlow House. Originally owned by Eva Thorndike, it had been stolen by Walt at Eva's request, when she believed her ex-husband had switched the original gems for fakes. After Eva's death a short time later, her parents had left the necklace to Walt in their will—should it ever be found. This meant that when it was found, it legally belonged to Danielle. The Missing Thorndike was valued at over a million dollars and currently resided in a safe deposit box at the local bank.

"As it turns out, your Jacque Jehan Bonnet is a very famous French artist." Ian sat down on the recliner facing the sofa. Sadie wandered over to him and lay down by his feet, once again resting her chin on her front paws.

"According to both Eva and Angela, he was nothing more than a struggling artist. I don't understand." Danielle frowned.

"He didn't become famous until the late thirties. According to what I found on him, he came from a very wealthy family in France. He was starting to get recognition in the art world when World War II broke out. His stepmother was Jewish, and when France surrendered to Germany, the family went into hiding and lost everything."

"Did they survive?" Lily asked.

"Yes. But most of Bonnet's early paintings were seized by the Nazis. After the war, he continued to paint and became one of France's renowned artists of that era."

"How is it we didn't know this? After all, one of his paintings is at the museum. If he's so famous, wouldn't they know?" Lily asked.

"For one thing, take a look at his signature." Ian stood up and handed Lily a printout to share with Danielle. Lily accepted it and showed it to Danielle. It was a close-up of the squiggling signature, similar to the one on Walt's and Eva's portraits.

Lily looked up with a frown. "I don't get it. That's the same signature on Walt's portraits."

"Yes. That's Jacque Jehan Bonnet's trademark signature—the one he used on all his paintings. For someone unfamiliar with his work, they wouldn't be able to figure out the name of the artist. Just like we couldn't."

Danielle slumped back in the sofa and looked at Ian. "And no one knew our artist was famous?"

"I suspect Clint knows. And Macbeth. That's probably why they're here. To steal the original paintings. It'll be pretty easy for them. All they have to do is swap the originals for the reproductions before they leave."

"You think that's what they're up to?" Lily asked.

"That would be my guess. Look how Macbeth insists on keeping the library door locked when he's in there alone," Ian said. "Rumor has it, private collectors have spent a fortune obtaining the paintings the Nazis stole. The last Bonnet painting went at auction for over five million."

"Five million!" Lily and Danielle chorused. Startled, Sadie lifted her head and looked at the women.

"How is that even possible that the paintings have been here all these years, and no one knew about them until now?" Danielle asked.

"If you look up Bonnet's bio, there is virtually nothing about his time in the States. You have to remember, during the war, his family lost everything—letters, diaries. Everything. But there were rumors he had spent his youth in the States, and some speculate that he may have done some portraits here to earn a living."

"Why would he have to do that if he was from a wealthy family?" Lily asked.

"According to his bio, his father wanted him to go into the

family business, and when he refused because his passion was art, they disowned him. He left for about ten years, but was back in France—and the family fold—by 1930. There are no details on his time here, only speculation."

"Have any of the portraits he supposedly painted in the US ever surfaced?" Danielle asked.

"Not unless someone found one and sold it to a private collector. That segment in his bio suggesting he may have painted portraits to earn a living in America was purely speculation."

"We know he painted sets for a theater group," Danielle said.

"There was nothing in his bio about that. I imagine if any of those were uncovered, they would be worth a fortune—if you could prove he painted them," Ian said. "And considering how he signs his paintings, it would be easy for one of his portraits to get over-looked unless an art expert familiar with his work happened on one."

"But how did Clint figure out what they were?" Danielle asked.

Ian tossed the papers he had been holding onto the side table. "I have a theory on that."

"Let's hear it," Lily urged.

"There was an art show in San Diego this past fall—featuring some of Bonnet's work," Ian began.

"Clint lives in the San Diego area," Danielle noted.

"Yes. My theory, he went to the art show, noticed the unusual signature, and then recognized it when he looked at the pictures of the portraits posted on your website."

"He would've had to enlarge that image to see the signature," Danielle suggested.

"Bonnet has a very distinct style," Ian pointed out. "Clint may have recognized that when he saw the pictures of Walt's portraits and then took a closer look."

"That wouldn't surprise me. When I saw Eva's portrait for the first time, it reminded me of Walt's," Danielle said.

"Oh my gosh!" Lily gasped. "The museum has a Bonnet too!"

"Does Clint know about Eva's portrait?" Ian asked.

Danielle shook her head. "I don't think so. He's never mentioned it, and since he's not one for engaging in small talk, I don't think anyone has said anything to him about it."

"Unless he's seen it online," Lily suggested.

"So what do we do now?" Danielle asked.

"I think we need to let the chief know what's going on," Ian suggested.

"We don't know for sure Clint knows the originals are so valuable," Danielle said.

"I'm sure he knows. And so does Macbeth. I'd bet anything that's why they're here, to steal your paintings."

"You're probably right. But even if we go to them now, with everything we know, there's nothing we can do. They haven't broken any laws yet. I can't really say using an alias is illegal, considering Chris uses one," Danielle said.

"Then what do you want to do?" Ian asked.

"I think we need to go ahead and let the chief know what we know. But let's not say anything to anyone else right now. Let's see what Clint does. Walt can keep an eye on them. Until they actually break the law, there's nothing we can do."

"Shouldn't you let the museum know?" Lily asked.

"As long as none of Danielle's current houseguests learn about Eva's painting, I don't think we have to worry about it right now," Ian said.

"I can let Eva know about it. Maybe she'll want to keep an eye on her painting, and if someone makes a move on the portrait, she can let us know. But I would really like to wait until after Clint leaves to tell the museum. By then I can figure out what I want to do with our portraits. I'll have to talk to Walt. If they really are that valuable, I certainly can't leave them in my library."

"There is another option," Lily suggested.

Both Danielle and Ian looked to Lily.

"You could say you just found out about the artist and put the portraits under lock and key now. That would be a reasonable thing for someone to do if they found out two priceless portraits were sitting in their house. Of course, it gets Clint and Macbeth off the hook, because you'll pretty much foil their little heist before they can carry it off."

"That might not be a bad idea," Ian said.

The three sat in silence for a few minutes. Finally, Danielle said, "Let me talk to Walt. See what he wants to do. They are his paintings—and Clint is his cousin."

FIFTEEN

W hen Danielle arrived back at Marlow House, she found Macbeth sitting in the kitchen eating a sandwich Joanne had prepared for him. While lunch and dinner were not included in the normal bed-and-breakfast package, Danielle assumed Joanne had offered to make him something to eat since he had slept through breakfast—again. Under other circumstances, Danielle might be tempted to remind Joanne that a guest who makes it a habit to miss the one meal offered with the room was not really entitled to have a meal at his convenience. If they got into that habit, they would be preparing meals all day long. However, Danielle was happy to see Macbeth was out of the library, which gave her an opportunity to talk with Walt. Therefore, she said nothing to Joanne.

She found Walt in the parlor, and he was not alone. Marie and Eva were with him.

"I still haven't seen this cousin yet. I keep missing him," Eva told Danielle.

"He's not here right now. But I'm glad you are," Danielle told Eva. She shut the parlor door behind her. "I need to talk to you and Walt." Danielle turned to Marie. "And I have a huge favor to ask you."

"What is it, dear?" Marie asked.

"Can you go into the library and keep an eye on the artist when he returns? Right now he's in the kitchen eating a sandwich. And if he starts messing with the original portraits, let me know right away. I'll explain everything later."

Marie frowned a moment, looking toward the closed door and back to Eva and Walt. Curious to find out what Danielle needed to tell Eva, she reluctantly gave a nod and then vanished.

"What's this about?" Walt asked. He sat on the arm of the sofa, smoking a cigar, while Eva sat in one of the chairs across from him. The two spirits looked at Danielle, waiting for her response.

"It seems your artist did very well for himself," Danielle began. She then went on to tell them what Ian had learned.

"I knew Johnny was talented," Eva mused. "I'm rather proud of him!"

Danielle looked to Walt. "What do we do? Should we do as Lily suggested, and lock up the paintings now? Or wait until Clint makes a move? Assuming that's his intention."

Standing up, Walt absently puffed the cigar and began pacing the parlor. After a few moments he stopped and turned to Danielle. "I'd like to wait. I want to know if my cousin is a thief."

"I agree." Eva spoke up. "You need to let this play out—it's a test of Clint's character. I think that's what the Universe would want."

Danielle arched her brow. "The Universe?"

"It's a feeling I have," Eva explained. "Something else is going on here. I've felt it for some time now. Ever since I heard Walt's cousin was coming. This is a test."

"A test?" Danielle asked.

Eva smiled. "Despite what some people think, they're not all tests. Sometimes it's simply about free will."

Danielle frowned. "I don't understand; what are you talking about?"

"The Universe, dear. Sometimes it has its own plan."

"Are we talking God? What do you mean when you say universe?" Danielle asked. "Is there a god?"

"Danielle, that's for each of us to figure out—in our own time." Eva stood up. "As for me, I'll keep an eye on my portrait until you and Walt figure this thing out." In the next moment, Eva vanished.

DANIELLE DIDN'T FIND Chief Edward MacDonald at the office

THE GHOST AND THE DOPPELGANGER

Saturday afternoon. She found him down at the beach with his sons, flying kites.

"This looks like fun," Danielle said when she reached Edward. He was watching his two sons, who stood about fifty feet away from him, each maneuvering a string holding a kite. "Don't you have one?"

He chuckled. "It's enough helping those two with theirs. What are you doing down here?"

"Looking for you." Danielle watched the boys, impressed with their kite skills.

"Me? How did you know I was down here?"

"I tried calling you. But you obviously don't answer your cellphone when you're flying kites. So I stopped at the station; they said you were off today. I drove by your house. One of your neighbors said they saw you loading up your kites. Said you normally fly them down here."

"Putting your Nancy Drew skills to work again." He grinned. "For the record, I didn't ignore your call. The battery's dead. In fact, I told the boys they only had ten more minutes. I don't like being without a phone."

"Likely story." Danielle grinned.

"So what did you need to talk to me about?"

"I just found out those portraits of mine could be worth millions. And I think Walt's cousin might be planning to steal them."

DANIELLE SAT with the chief in his living room while his sons were in the family room watching television and eating pizza.

"I have to agree with Walt," the chief said. "Only because if those paintings really are worth what you think they might be, strategically securing them while having your current guests under your roof might have some unforeseen consequences. It would be nice if we could just arrest them now, but they haven't broken any laws. Of course, if Walt wasn't there, I wouldn't suggest letting this play out."

"Walt wants to find out if his cousin is a thief. Plus, this could all be a coincidence. After all, I did run into Clint and Stephanie at the cemetery, so he obviously is more interested in his family history than he first let on. I know he is a major jerk, but I just feel funny suddenly locking up the portraits, telling him they can't finish the reproductions. I would rather they finish, leave—and if they are thieves, Walt will help deal with it. If not, then after they leave, we figure out what to do with the original portraits."

"I am a little concerned about the Eva Thorndike portrait. We need to let the Historical Society know what it's worth. But once we tell them, it's sure to be all over the news," the chief said.

"If it makes you feel any better, Eva's keeping an eye on her portrait. If anyone makes a move on it, she'll let us know."

IT WAS DECIDED that when they went to the Historical Society about Bonnet, they would tell them the chief had also just been informed. They didn't want the Historical Society to question the police chief's judgment in keeping that news to himself for over a week. This also meant Joe and Brian had no idea of the potential art heist.

Marie and Eva took turns watching over Eva's portrait at the museum. As the days went by, Clint, Stephanie, and Macbeth seemed oblivious to the existence of a local museum, much less a priceless painting on display there.

During the beginning of their second week at Marlow House, Stephanie happened to try one of the Old Salts cinnamon rolls sometimes served with breakfast. Joanne had left a few sitting on a plate in the kitchen. After that, Stephanie talked Clint into eating breakfast at Marlow House. They discovered the breakfasts Danielle served far surpassed any served at the Frederickport restaurants they had thus far tried.

Clint's personality didn't improve as time went on. The only person he seemed to care about was Stephanie. While they waited for Macbeth to finish the paintings, Clint and Stephanie spent their time taking walks on the beach, sightseeing, going to an occasional movie, and eating lunch and dinner out.

Easter Sunday fell on their second Sunday in Frederickport. Danielle hosted an Easter dinner for her friends—something she liked to do at Marlow House so Walt could attend—and while she invited Clint, Stephanie, and Macbeth, they all declined her invitation, which didn't bother her at all.

While out and about, Clint and Stephanie occasionally ran into one of Danielle's friends, and like Clint's initial encounter with Adam and Lily, his personality didn't improve. In a small town like Frederickport it didn't take long before people started talking about the guests currently staying at Marlow House.

Many in the small community had seen the portraits of Walt and Angela Marlow, and others, those who had not been to Marlow House, had seen his likeness online. They knew what Walt had looked like, and many recognized Clint as the cousin who had come to visit. Some Frederickport residents tried to introduce themselves to Clint. They received a welcome no warmer than what Adam and Lily had received.

"So what do you want for your birthday?" Lily asked Danielle on Tuesday, the day before Clint and his group were scheduled to leave.

"I just want my birthday to get here. That will mean Clint and the others will be gone, and all of this will be over!"

"So Macbeth finished the paintings?" Lily asked.

"It looks that way." Danielle then added, "I can't believe we didn't slip and call him Macbeth."

"I know." Lily chuckled.

"A couple of times I caught myself. And it would have been all your fault!"

Lily grinned at Danielle. "Sorry about that. So what about the art heist? Have they made any move to switch the portraits?"

Danielle shook her head. "Not yet. But Walt's keeping a close eye on the paintings. In fact, Marie's in with him. That way, she can come tell me if they start to do something."

SIXTEEN

L ate Tuesday afternoon, Danielle sat in the living room reading
a book. Although, truth be told, she wasn't doing much reading. She kept glancing up at the open doorway leading to the entry
hall. Walt and Marie were in the library keeping an eye on the original portraits, and as far as she knew, Macbeth was in his room, and
Clint and Stephanie were upstairs in their room, packing. They
were all leaving in the morning.

Danielle didn't realize how on edge she was as Clint's departure
neared, until the doorbell rang, and she about jumped off the sofa.
Taking a deep breath, she closed the book she wasn't reading, tossed
it on the coffee table, and went to answer the door. It was Chief
MacDonald. She assumed he was on his way home from work, as
he was still in uniform.

"I wanted to stop and see if you were okay," he said in a
whisper.

Danielle glanced to the closed door leading to the bedroom
where she had put Macbeth. "They're all in their rooms." Nodding
toward the living room, she let the chief into the house.

"Anything going on?" he asked when they walked into the living
room.

"No. Walt and Marie are in the library, watching the portraits."
Danielle took a seat on the sofa, while the chief sat across from her
on one of the chairs.

He started to say something but heard someone out in the hallway, so he stopped talking. Both he and Danielle glanced to the open doorway. A moment later, Clint Marlow stepped into the room.

"Danielle, I was looking for you, I wondered—" Clint stopped talking when he noticed MacDonald sitting in the room. He stared at him a moment and then asked, "Is there a problem?"

Danielle smiled at Clint and stood up. She motioned to the chief. "This is my friend Edward MacDonald. He's the local police chief. I believe you met him briefly once, but he wasn't in uniform then." She smiled sweetly and watched as the chief stood up and shook Clint's hand.

"I didn't realize he was the police chief," Clint murmured.

"What did you need to talk to me about?" Danielle asked after the two men finished their perfunctory handshake and then each took a step back away from each other.

"I was wondering if you might be able to ask your friend across the street if he could help us carry the crate in, so we can load the portraits."

"The crate?" Danielle frowned.

"Yes. We can't very well just toss the portraits in the back of the van." Clint grinned. "They traveled here in the crate."

"Oh. And you have to bring the crate inside to load them?" Danielle asked. "You obviously didn't have to do that when you unloaded them."

"True. But we didn't have to be quite as careful as we do now. If one got a little dinged up taking it out of the van before they were finished, Jim could have easily fixed it. But now, well, now, we don't want to risk damaging them; plus, I'm a little concerned the paint might not be completely dry. The crate will protect them."

"I'm afraid Ian's not home. He and Lily went out to dinner with his sister and her boyfriend. I don't expect them back for a couple of hours."

"I can help," MacDonald offered.

Clint looked at MacDonald. "You can?"

"Sure. No problem." The chief grinned.

DANIELLE AND STEPHANIE FOLLOWED MACDONALD, Clint,

and Macbeth outside to where Clint had parked his van. The two women stood on the sidewalk and watched as the men maneuvered the large wooden crate out of the back of the vehicle.

"Stephanie, can you grab a corner?" Clint called out. She quickly scurried over and grabbed hold of one corner.

And I call myself a feminist, Danielle told herself when she didn't offer to lend a hand. But then she realized they would need someone to open the front door, so she quickly jogged up the front walkway while they carried the crate up to the house.

"It would be much easier if I simply brought it in," Walt said when he appeared next to Danielle. The two stood by the open doorway, watching them slowly approach the house with the cumbersome crate.

In response to Danielle's questioning frown, Walt said, "Marie's in the library. I wanted to see what you were up to."

Once they moved the crate inside the entry hall, Danielle closed the door. She and Walt watched as the four people slowly moved the crate down the hallway. Once in the library, they set it in the middle of the room.

When Stephanie let go of her corner of the wooden crate, she let out a curse and grabbed her hand. "Darn it, Clint, I got a splinter from that stupid crate!"

Clint grabbed her hand and looked at it. "You're going to need tweezers to get it out."

"I've got a pair," she grumbled, snatching her hand from him and starting toward the door. Before leaving the library, she shouted, "You'll have to get someone else to help load those portraits!"

Danielle wondered briefly if Stephanie had faked the splinter, thus giving Clint and Macbeth an excuse to load the portraits and make the switch when she and the chief were no longer around. But then Clint asked the chief something that made her wonder if it all really had just been a coincidence.

"Any chance you could stick around for a minute and help us load the portraits? It takes three people, and they're kind of heavy."

Surprised by Clint's request, MacDonald stood there a moment and then said, "Why, sure."

Danielle stood with Marie and Walt by the bookshelves, silently watching as the three men carefully loaded the two reproductions into the crate. It was a process that required at least three strong people. Considering Stephanie's petite frame, Danielle didn't see how she could have helped, even if she hadn't gotten a splinter in her hand.

"Does this mean your cousin isn't an art thief?" Marie asked.

Walt shrugged. "Unless he swapped those paintings when I wasn't looking."

Momentarily panicked, Danielle looked to Walt.

He chuckled. "Don't worry, Danielle, those are the reproductions they're loading into the crate. No one has been in the library without either Marie or myself in here."

With a sigh of relief, Danielle looked back to the crate. When the men were finished loading the artwork, Clint shut the crate's lid. He then locked it.

"You're locking it?" Danielle hadn't noticed the lock before.

"Not that I'm worried about someone stealing them on the way home," Clint said with a chuckle. "It's more for a precaution if we have an accident. I don't want the crate to fly open."

"We're not going to have an accident. I'm driving," Stephanie said when she walked into the room the next minute.

Clint glanced to her right hand. "Did you get it out?"

"Yes. And don't lose that key," Stephanie told him. "It's the only one."

Clint shoved the key in his pocket. "Have more faith in me. I'm not going to lose the key."

"I can help you load the crate into the van," MacDonald offered.

Clint looked at the crate a moment, as if considering. Finally, he shook his head. "No. I appreciate the offer. But I don't want to leave it in the car all night. With my luck, someone might steal my van while we're sleeping, and then the last two weeks would be for nothing."

"And if they are stolen, at least I got paid already," Macbeth said with a laugh.

"How are you going to get the crate in the car with just the two of you?" MacDonald asked.

"We'll figure out something. Maybe I can get Danielle's friend to help me in the morning. But what I would like to do is to take you all out to dinner."

"Dinner?" Danielle asked.

"Yes. I'd like to thank you for letting me do this. And I would like to thank your friend here for helping us load the portraits in the crate. To be honest, loading them in the crate just the right way so they don't get damaged is really the difficult part. Getting the crate back into the car shouldn't be a problem for us. Please accept my offer; let me take you both out to dinner. I'd like to take you both to Pearl Cove," Clint told them.

UNDER OTHER CIRCUMSTANCES, the chief might have politely declined the offer. He needed to get home to his sons. But he also wanted to keep an eye on Clint Marlow and make sure he left town without taking the original portraits with him. After accepting the dinner offer, he agreed to meet them at Pearl Cove in an hour, after he went home, changed his clothes, and took his boys to his sister's house.

"You think they're going to try to make the switch after you leave, and I'm up getting ready for dinner?" Danielle asked the chief as she walked him to the car.

"I honestly don't see how that would be possible. Those canvases are heavy—and cumbersome. I don't see how they could remove the originals from their frames and make the switch. You could walk in on them at any time, and that would be dangerous for you."

"Don't worry, Walt and Marie are keeping an eye on the paintings while I'm upstairs. If they start to make the switch, Marie will let me know, and I'll call you. You can get your officers over here and catch them in the act."

"My guess, if they are planning a switch, they intend to do it tonight when you're sleeping. It'll give them more time. They'll need all three of them, and even that will not be easy considering the weight of the canvases. Walt or Marie hasn't heard them say anything, what their plans are?"

Danielle shrugged. "Clint and Stephanie haven't really had much to do with Macbeth this week. He just does his thing, and they do theirs. Most of the time, Clint and Stephanie have been off somewhere. Marie tried eavesdropping on them a few times, but she said all they really talked about was some trip they were planning, I assume for a honeymoon. Nothing about the portraits."

"Be careful, Danielle."

She smiled. "Don't worry. I have Walt."

IN HER BEDROOM, Danielle glanced at her watch. It was time for her to go downstairs and leave for Pearl Cove. Just as she was about to open her bedroom door, Marie appeared in her room.

"Are you leaving now?" Marie asked.

"I assume they haven't messed with Walt's portraits?" Danielle asked in a whisper.

"No. No one has been back in the library. Walt wanted me to check on you. See when you were leaving."

"Now, I guess." Danielle glanced at her watch again. "I think the chief might have been right. If they plan to switch the paintings, they're doing it tonight when I'm sleeping."

AS IT WAS ARRANGED, the chief picked up Danielle for dinner, while Clint, Stephanie, and Macbeth would be driving to the restaurant in the van.

Danielle and the chief arrived at the restaurant first. They were already seated at a table when Clint and Stephanie arrived.

"Where's Jim?" Danielle asked as the couple joined her and the chief at the table.

"He told us he wasn't hungry. Said he wanted to go to bed since he plans to get up early in the morning and take off," Clint explained.

"Yeah, right." Stephanie laughed. "Is he really going to get up early? I don't think I ever saw him in the mornings while we were here. I'm just glad he actually finished the paintings."

"He did." Clint smiled. He stood up briefly and then pulled the key to the crate from his pocket. He handed it to Stephanie. "Here. Put this in your purse so I don't lose it."

"Now you listen to me." Stephanie laughed.

Danielle and the chief exchanged glances.

After the server arrived at the table and took their drink orders, Stephanie and Clint excused themselves to go to the restroom.

"If Macbeth doesn't have the key, then he can't switch the portraits while we're at dinner—even if he could manage it by himself," Danielle said.

"I imagine he could get the lock open someway. That would be easy. Making the switch himself would be the difficult part."

"Maybe we're looking at this all wrong. Perhaps Clint doesn't intend to steal the portraits—but maybe Macbeth intends to grab the originals and take them while we're all at dinner."

The chief considered the possibility a moment and then shook his head. "No. Why would he spend the last two weeks painting when he could have just grabbed the paintings any time during the last couple of weeks? Plus, everyone would know he took them. No. They're either planning to make the switch tonight while you're sleeping, or they really don't know about Bonnet."

SEVENTEEN

"I would like to wallop my grandson for emailing that annoying cousin of yours," Marie told Walt. They sat together in the library playing a game of checkers. Since Marie was unable to move the game pieces, Walt had to do it for her.

"They leave tomorrow. Maybe my cousin isn't a thief after all."

Walt started to move one of the pieces when Marie gasped, "Don't move it!"

Walt frowned. "It's my checker, why can't I move it?"

"We have company," Marie whispered.

Walt turned to the open doorway. Macbeth was just walking into the room.

"You don't have to whisper, Marie. He can't hear us," Walt reminded her.

"I thought he was going to the restaurant with them."

Walt shrugged. "That's what I thought too. When Danielle left with the chief, I heard Clint say the three of them were driving together."

"You don't think he stayed so he could switch the paintings?"

"There's no way he could do that alone."

They watched as Macbeth approached the framed portraits. He reached out and reverently caressed the frame of Angela's painting.

"You're probably right. He isn't a very large man. I can't see him lifting one of those canvases by himself," Marie noted.

"The way he's staring at that painting, he reminds me of a man looking at his lover."

"Are you jealous? It's your wife's painting he seems to be lost in." Marie chuckled.

"Not particularly." Walt sighed.

"Do you think he knows what they're really worth?" Marie asked.

"If he does, I don't think he'll leave here without trying to take them, considering his history."

Macbeth pulled a cellphone out of his pocket, and just as he started to make a call, he glanced over to the small table holding the checkerboard. He frowned. "I could swear those checkers were stacked up," he muttered. With a shake of his head, he turned from the table and finished dialing his number.

"Oh dear, I do believe he noticed the checkers had been moved," Marie said.

"He doesn't seem overly concerned." Walt took a puff off his cigar and continued to watch Macbeth.

Whomever the man was calling had obviously just answered his phone, considering Macbeth's next words. "Okay, I'm ready for you. But you're going to have to park down the street and walk here. I don't want the neighbors to notice a car parked in front of the house. I'll unlock the front door. Just come in, but be careful the people across the street don't see you. They're friends of the owner. They aren't home right now, but they could be back at any time, and I don't want them to see you when they get back."

Macbeth ended the phone call, shoved the cellphone in his pocket, and then walked to the door.

"Does this mean they're coming after the paintings?" Marie gasped.

"It appears so."

Both Walt and Marie followed Macbeth. He walked down the hallway to the front door. After he unlocked it, he headed back to the library.

"What are you going to do?" Marie asked.

"For the moment, I'm just going to watch. I'd like to know if my cousin is part of this, or if Macbeth is working on his own."

They watched as he removed a key from his pocket and unlocked the crate.

"It seems my cousin was wrong, and he didn't have the only key —or else he gave Macbeth the key before he left."

"I don't see how that's possible. Right after they packed the crate, Macbeth went to his bedroom, and the next time Clint said anything to him was when he told him they were leaving for dinner. In fact, Macbeth didn't even answer his door for Clint. Clint just knocked, said they were leaving, and Macbeth shouted something back to him. There was never an opportunity for Clint to give him the key. I would have seen."

Walt shrugged. "I wonder who ordered the crate? Was it custom made for this job? I would assume that would be something Macbeth would do; he's the expert. He would know what was needed to store paintings that size without damaging them. If he's the one that handled that, then I would assume he could have had an extra key made without my cousin's knowledge."

After opening the crate, Macbeth walked back to his bedroom. Walt and Marie followed him. In the bedroom Macbeth retrieved a small suitcase.

"What's in the suitcase?" Marie asked.

"I suppose we'll find out in a minute."

Suitcase in hand, Macbeth returned to the library, two spirits trailing behind him. He opened the suitcase, revealing a number of tools.

Looking into the open suitcase, Marie frowned. "What's he going to do with those?"

"My guess, he needs them to remove my paintings from their frames." Walt puffed his cigar.

"Aren't you going to do something?"

"Not right now. We have plenty of time."

Aside from unlocking the crate and retrieving a suitcase of tools, Macbeth made no move to tamper with the portraits. He sat on the sofa and glanced at his watch, obviously waiting for whoever he had called to arrive.

"Maybe you should send Edward or Danielle one of those text messages," Marie suggested. "Let them know what's going on."

Walt glanced over to the computer. "I don't think that will be possible at the moment. He might overlook the checker game, yet I suspect if I turn on the computer right now, he might run out of the house."

"But wouldn't that be a good thing?"

Walt shook his head. "No. I'd rather this play out so we'll know what they're up to—and who's involved. I'm rather curious to see who he's waiting for."

Fifteen minutes later, Walt and Marie heard voices calling out from the entry hall. "Hey, Mac, you here?"

Macbeth stood up from the sofa and walked to the open doorway. "Down here!"

"Mac?" Walt arched his brows. "He doesn't go by Macbeth?"

"I imagine he was teased mercilessly as a child for that name."

"Which led him to his life of crime?" Walt snickered.

"Oh my!" Marie gasped when three large men walked into the library. They all wore black—black turtlenecks, black slacks, and black ski hats.

Now sitting on the sofa's arm, absently fiddling with his cigar, Walt studied the men. "I suppose they're wearing black to blend in with the night, but if any car was to drive up the street and their headlights landed on these palookas, someone is going to call the cops." Walt chuckled.

"This doesn't look good. We need to do something!" Marie urged.

Walt arched his brow at Marie, flashing her a lopsided grin. "We? You can't even move your own checker."

"You know what I mean," she huffed.

"Let's get this done," Macbeth said.

"Settle down, Marie, and enjoy the show. Don't worry. I won't let them get out of here. Even if that means I have to levitate them to the ceiling until the chief and Danielle get home."

"You can do that?"

He shrugged. "Just ask Max."

With a sigh born of resignation, Marie took a seat on the sofa and watched with Walt.

Under Macbeth's detailed instructions and guidance, the men used the tools to remove Walt's portraits from the frames, careful not to destroy the material concealing the back of the canvases. They removed the reproductions from the crate and then replaced them with the originals.

"Walt, I—" Marie began.

"Not now," Walt cut her off. "I need to see exactly how they're doing this." He tossed his cigar into the air and it vanished. "I need to concentrate."

Walt was fascinated at how Macbeth fit the reproductions into the frames and adeptly replaced the backing. He had to admit, it was virtually impossible to tell the originals from the reproductions.

The men carefully loaded Bonnet's paintings into the crate, and when they were done, Macbeth relocked the container and slipped the key back in his pocket. Gathering up the tools, they quickly tidied the room.

"We'll see you tomorrow," one of the men told Macbeth. "At the same time?"

"Yes. I'm leaving first so I can get there and make sure everything is ready," Macbeth told them.

"You sure that's a good idea? Letting Marlow take off with the paintings?" one of the men asked.

Macbeth laughed. "He's not going to double-cross us now. He doesn't have the buyer, I do. Without me, he'll be stuck with a couple of hot pieces of art that he can't unload. If he tried to do this on his own and cut me out, he'd get a fraction of what I'll be getting him, and he knows that."

"Oh dear," Marie muttered. "It seems your cousin is a thief."

Walt let out a sigh. "It appears that way."

"What are you going to do now?" Marie asked.

"It looks like they aren't intending to take the crate out of the house now, so I'll wait until Danielle gets back and discuss it with her."

Walt and Marie followed the thieves out into the hallway. After the three men left out the front door, Macbeth relocked it and took the suitcase of tools back to his room. Walt followed him.

"What are you going to do?"

"Horsefeathers, Marie, you keep asking me that!"

"Are you going to clobber him with something?" She followed Walt through the wall into the downstairs bedroom. There they found Macbeth, now sitting on the side of his bed.

"No. I'm not going to clobber him. But I would like to see where he's putting that key."

They watched as Macbeth removed the crate's key and tossed it on the end table. He then pulled his cellphone from his pocket and sent a text message.

AT PEARL COVE, Danielle was just finishing up her dessert when Clint's telephone buzzed. She glanced up and watched as he picked up the phone and looked at it.

"It's from Jim," Clint said after reading the message. He looked up to Danielle. "He wants to know if you have any aspirin; he has a headache."

"Yes. Tell him there's some in the medicine cabinet in the upstairs bathroom."

EIGHTEEN

M acbeth was in his room, the lights out, when Danielle returned to the house with Stephanie and Clint on Tuesday evening. She had driven back to Marlow House with them instead of going with the chief. The van had just a bench seat in the front, no seats in the back, which made for a crowded drive. Once home she thanked them again for the dinner, locked up the house, and then headed for her bedroom. When she got there, she found Walt waiting.

"My cousin is a thief," Walt announced when Danielle entered the room. Instead of responding to his proclamation, Danielle shut and locked her bedroom door, tossed her purse on the dresser, and arched her brows at Walt. Silently asking, *What happened?*

Walt moved from where he had been standing by the fireplace to the right side of the bed, his shoes disappearing from his feet as he got onto the mattress, leaning against the pillows—still covered with the bedspread. He patted the empty spot to his left, waiting for Danielle to join him.

Kicking off her shoes, she took the empty place next to Walt. They lay side by side on the bed, both fully clothed and shoeless, staring at the ceiling.

"So tell me what happened," Danielle whispered.

After Walt told her about the evening's unexpected guests and the switching of the paintings, Danielle silently contemplated all that she had just been told. Finally, she said, "Interesting, first Clint makes sure we all know it was the only key, and at the restaurant he makes a point of giving the key to Stephanie. Why?"

"They made a show of loading the paintings this afternoon. I suspect he wanted to erase any future doubt you might have that anyone could have tampered with the crate. It's probably why he wanted MacDonald to help load them, so he'd know firsthand it wasn't something Macbeth could do on his own."

"Technically, he didn't ask the chief. The chief volunteered. Clint wanted me to ask Ian," Danielle reminded him.

"Not so sure he did."

Danielle turned to Walt and frowned. "Why do you say that?"

"Max told me this evening Clint was outside when Lily and Ian left for dinner. Clint knew Ian wasn't home when he asked you to call him."

"Hmmm...maybe...but he didn't know the chief was going to stop over."

"No. But he saw an opportunity. I suspect he intended all along to ask you to help him load the paintings, that way he would have a reason to ask you to dinner and get you out of the way while Macbeth made the switch.

"He also wanted you to believe he held the only key to the crate, and while you were at the restaurant, he wanted you to know he had it on him. That way, when you got home, there would be no reason to believe it had been opened again. Of course, he also wanted you to help load the paintings so you would understand firsthand it wouldn't be something Macbeth could do alone, even if he had managed to open the crate without the key. The chief arriving just sweetened his plan.

"You have to remember, he probably figured you might someday discover the identity of the original artist, and when that time came, he wanted to shore up an alibi so you wouldn't be able to accuse him of switching the paintings."

Danielle let out a sigh. "Considering the years this house sat empty, and the attorney my aunt had overseeing this property for years was a known thief and murderer, it would make it easy for Clint to avoid scrutiny, especially since we witnessed the reproductions being locked up in the crate before being removed from the house."

Walt nodded. "Exactly."

"Did you see Macbeth send a text message after those men left?"

"Yes. Why?"

"Did Macbeth come upstairs and go to the bathroom after he sent that message?"

"No. Why?"

"It must have been a signal to let Clint know it was safe to come home." Danielle then explained the message Clint had received during dessert from Macbeth.

"I'm sure it was," Walt told her.

"So, what do we do now? Call the chief and tell him what happened?" Danielle groaned. She leaned back on the bed and closed her eyes.

"It's going to be alright, Danielle."

"Is it? I really don't look forward to another drawn-out court case. I'll have to press charges. There will be all that negative press, *again*. I'll have to go to the trial. Not to mention I'm going to have to concoct some story about how I know the paintings were switched, and that will probably involve running tests on the paintings to prove he has the originals. I was really hoping they would all just leave in the morning, and then I could figure out what to do with your paintings. I sure can't keep them here. Even if your cousin hadn't learned the truth about them, eventually someone else would."

"So, what do you want to do, Danielle?"

Opening her eyes, she looked at Walt. "I just wish they could leave in the morning with the reproductions."

"Okay. That's what they'll do." Walt smiled.

Danielle frowned. "What do you mean?"

"I'll go switch them back."

"But should we do that? Won't that mess up the chief's case against them?"

"I thought you said you don't want a long drawn-out court case?"

"I don't."

"Then I can just switch them back tonight while everyone is sleeping."

"You can do that?"

"Certainly. In the morning they'll leave believing they have the originals. By the time they discover they don't, you'll have moved my paintings to somewhere more appropriate for art of that value—

plus notified the museum about Eva's portrait. While they won't pay for their crimes in the typical fashion, I imagine whomever they try to sell those paintings to will not be forgiving when they realize they're fakes. They'll have some explaining to do."

"Just trying to figure out what happened will drive them insane." Danielle chuckled. She then looked seriously at Walt and said, "I better not tell the chief about this tonight. He'll want to arrest them."

"You're probably right." Walt studied Danielle. "Are you sure you want to do it this way? If you're hesitant to have Clint arrested because he is my cousin, I—"

"No, Walt," Danielle interrupted. "That's not why. I just…the thought of dealing with another court trial is exhausting."

"Okay. If you're sure."

Danielle started to grin.

Walt looked at her inquisitively. "What is it?"

"I was just thinking how I handled Adam and Bill after they broke into Marlow House. I didn't involve the police that time, and now look. Adam and I are friends."

"So, you think you might become friends with my cousin?"

Danielle considered Walt's suggestion a moment and then wrinkled her nose. "Nahh, that's not happening."

BEFORE WALT WENT DOWNSTAIRS, he checked on Clint and Stephanie. They were both sleeping, Clint's arms wrapped around his bride-to-be while her head nestled against his bare chest. Walt's next stop was Macbeth's bedroom. Once there, he stood at the foot of the man's bed. He wanted to make sure he was sound asleep. It looked as if Macbeth had been wrestling in his dreams, the way half of the blanket fell to the floor, the only thing preventing it from slipping all the way off the mattress was his left leg draped over it. Wearing just boxers and sleeping on his back, Macbeth's belly rose slightly and fell with each snore.

Walt spied the extra crate key sitting on the nightstand. He couldn't very well take it through the wall with him, and he didn't want to open the door and chance waking Macbeth. His only option was to slip the key under the door and retrieve it from the other side.

"WHERE HAVE YOU BEEN?" Marie asked when Walt entered the library. "I've been waiting forever, and I kept worrying someone would come for the crate, and then what could I do if I couldn't find you?"

"I had to tell Danielle what happened tonight, so we could decide what to do next."

"And what did you decide?"

Walt tossed the key he had been holding into the air. It floated over to the crate. "I'm going to switch the paintings back." The key slipped into the lock and turned.

"Didn't Danielle call Edward? Isn't he coming over? Arresting those men?"

Walt shook his head. "No, Marie. Danielle doesn't want to involve the police."

"So, she's not going to tell Edward what happened?"

"Yes. But after I switch the paintings back—and after Clint and the rest leave tomorrow."

The crate opened.

"But—" Marie began, only to be cut off by Walt.

"Quiet, please, Marie. I need to focus on what I'm doing. I don't want to drop anything."

Marie let out a sigh and then sat back on the sofa and watched as Walt performed his spiritual magic. First, the originals lifted from the crate, one by one, and gently settled on the floor, leaning against the bookcase, waiting for their frames.

Unlike Macbeth, Walt needed no tools to free the canvases from the frames. Once free, they floated across the room, each settling in the crate, Angela's first, followed by Walt's, the same order as the originals had been loaded.

Marie watched in fascination as Angela's portrait floated from where it had just been set to the antique frame and seemingly rein- serted itself. Once it was in place, the material covering the back of the frame and canvas resumed its original position.

Walt then turned his attention to his portrait. It levitated up from the floor and began floating across the room when suddenly Marie called out, "Walt!"

His concentration momentarily broken, the portrait began fall- ing. But the thud was not from the priceless art crashing to the hardwood floor—Walt managed to freeze it in midair—the thud was from Macbeth, now passed out at the doorway into the library.

"He saw the painting flying through the air," Marie explained.

The two spirits looked down at Macbeth.

"He's fainted," Walt muttered. "And I wouldn't say it was flying."

"Odd, he didn't look like the fainting type." Marie looked up to Walt. "Now what?"

Not wasting time, Walt looked over to his portrait still hovering in midair. It practically flew into its frame. Walt looked to the crate, its lid still open. He surmised Macbeth had probably seen not just the flying portrait but the open crate. The next moment its lid closed; the key secured the lock and then floated back to Walt.

"What are you going to do?" Marie asked.

"I'm going to put him back in his bed before he wakes up."

Like the paintings had done minutes earlier, Macbeth lifted off the floor, his unconscious body floating down the hallway. Just as they reached the door leading to the downstairs bedroom, it flew open.

Walt was about to move Macbeth in the room when a dark shadow standing in the hallway caught his attention. He glanced over to it. It was Max, watching, his tail twitching back and forth.

Walt looked to the cat. Their eyes met. Walt chuckled. "So, you think it's funny as long as it's not you?"

Max meowed.

"Hush, Max. He might not be able to hear Marie and me, he can hear you."

Max blinked but resisted his temptation to meow again.

Macbeth's body floated into his room. Just as he landed on the bed, he began to move. Walt quickly returned the key to the side table and closed the bedroom door.

MACBETH JOLTED up in his bed. He looked around the room. It was dark. He glanced at the clock on the end table, noting the time.

"That was one crazy dream."

NINETEEN

"Wake up...time to get up...it's morning..." Walt whispered.

Danielle's eyes flew open. She found herself curled up on her right side under a pile of blankets, looking into Walt's smiling face.

"I was having such a good dream," Danielle said with a pout.

"Was I in it?" Walt grinned.

"No." Disgruntled, she sat up in the bed, clutching the tops of her blankets. "Why did you wake me?"

"Because your guests are up, and I thought you might want them to get that crate loaded, and keep them out of the library before they leave this morning."

"What are they doing?" Danielle glanced at the clock on her nightstand. It was 7:32 a.m.

"Macbeth was getting into the shower when I checked on him a few minutes ago. Not a pretty sight." Walt sat down on the side of the mattress.

"Is Joanne here?"

Walt shook his head. "Not yet."

"And Clint and Stephanie?"

"I know they're awake; I could hear the giggles through the door. But I thought it best not to go in their room. Although, I expect they'll be downstairs as soon as they finish...*giggling*."

Danielle cringed. "You know, Clint is such a jerk to everyone, but he does seem to sincerely care for Stephanie."

"Of course. Men are always nicer to women they can giggle with."

Danielle chuckled. "Why am I never going to think of giggling in the same way?"

His blue eyes twinkling, Walt stood. "Get up, get going. We have a big day today, and tomorrow is your birthday."

"Oh…my birthday." Danielle tossed the blankets aside. "All I want for my birthday is for it to get here."

"Yes, yes, I know. Because then your current guests will be gone."

"And the sooner we get that crate loaded in Clint's van, the sooner we can get them out of here. I imagine they are just as impatient to leave as we are to see them go." Danielle picked her cellphone up off the nightstand.

"Who are you calling?" Walt asked.

"Ian. I know we could probably get the crate loaded without him—with me, Stephanie, Clint, and Macbeth, but considering Stephanie's splinter yesterday—"

"Despite what she said last night, I seriously doubt Stephanie will let the prospect of another splinter keep her from helping her load that crate, considering what she believes it's holding."

"True. But that is assuming she knows. From what you heard last night, do you think she does?" Danielle asked.

Walt considered the question a moment. Finally, he shook his head. "I don't really know. I would think so, but perhaps not."

"Plus, if Ian is here and I tell Clint he only has a few minutes to spare, it might get them to hurry up and move the crate, and I'm pretty sure once they get it in the van, they aren't sticking around long."

Walt nodded. "You're probably right."

Danielle focused her attention back on the cellphone.

"But do you think it might be a little early to call Ian?" Walt asked.

In the next moment, Ian voiced the same sentiment. "Danielle, do you know what time it is? You know, Lily has spring break this week. That means we get to sleep in. Unless, of course, someone calls us on the phone."

114

"Good morning, Ian. Aren't you going to ask if there's something wrong? Like, why am I calling you so early?"

After a moment of silence, Ian hesitantly asked, "Is something wrong, Danielle?"

"Yes. My houseguests are annoying, and I can't wait for them to leave. Can you please, please come over right now and help them load the crate in the van so they can get out of here? Please."

"Crate?" Ian asked.

"Yes. The crate with the paintings in it. It weighs a freaking ton and will take four of us to move it."

"I assume the crate contains the reproductions, not the Bonnets?" Ian asked.

"Yes. I wouldn't ask you to help carry the Bonnets out of my house."

"I guess we were worried about nothing. Clint isn't a thief?"

"He's not stealing anything today," Danielle told him.

"Have Walt move it."

"Ha-ha, funny. I would if I could."

"Okay, I'll be over there in fifteen minutes. You better have cinnamon rolls."

DANIELLE WASN'T the only one looking forward to Clint's departure. Marie couldn't wait for the group to check out so she could be relieved of guard duty. Glancing up to the ceiling, she wondered what was taking Walt so long. The next moment, he entered the library.

"Danielle's up. She's getting dressed and will be downstairs in a minute," Walt explained.

"I was thinking about that, Walt."

He summoned a lit cigar. Just as it appeared in his hand, he looked at Marie and frowned. "Thinking about what?"

"About the propriety of you going into Danielle's bedroom. I really should have been the one to wake her up. It's not proper, you going into her room like that."

"Need I remind you, I'm dead." Walt took a puff off his cigar.

"But you're still a man," she said primly.

Walt exhaled and smiled. "Thank you for that, Marie."

Before they could continue to discuss the appropriateness of

Walt going into Danielle's bedroom, Clint and Macbeth walked into the library.

"I'm just going to be glad when this is finished," Macbeth told Clint in a low voice.

Marie and Walt sat quietly, watching and listening, and prepared to move should one of the men head for their places on the sofa.

"No kidding." Clint walked over to the crate and pushed his hand against it, as if testing its weight. "I wish we had someone else to help load it back in the van. It's going to be heavier than hell with those canvases."

"We'll manage."

"Just remember to call me, and let me know it's all a go," Clint reminded him.

"I got it. I leave first, make sure everything is set, and then give you a call and tell you to come on in."

"I hope we don't have to wait long. Stephanie and I have a flight to catch this evening."

"I want this done just as much as you do. By the way, I had the craziest dream last night." The two men stood by the crate. "I dreamt I heard something and got up. When I walked in here, the crate was open and the painting of Walt Marlow was floating across the room."

Clint chuckled. "Where was it going?"

"Back in its frame, I think. Damn. It felt so real."

"A painting floating across the room felt so real?" Clint laughed.

"No. The dream. It didn't feel like a regular dream."

"Some people say this house is haunted," Clint told him. "I read about it online."

Macbeth glanced around the library. There was no artwork floating about, and he and Clint appeared to be alone in the room. "Who do they say haunts the house?"

"Walt Marlow. The guy you saw floating around the room." Clint laughed again.

"It was a dream, not a ghost."

"So what happened? Did the portrait start talking to you or anything?"

"No. I woke up. It was the middle of the night."

Clint shrugged. "I guess I can understand. We'll both relax when this is over. Although I can't say I've had any nightmares over it."

Macbeth wandered over to the framed portraits and began studying them. After a moment he said, "Damn, I'm good."

Moving to Macbeth's side, Clint whispered, "Not so loud. Someone might hear you."

"Oh, stop being so jumpy. No one is going to hear me."

"Hey, you're the one having the dreams, not me."

"I'm just rather impressed with myself. There's no way anyone will ever suspect those aren't the originals."

Clint looked at the paintings and then nodded. "Yeah, they really are good."

"Oh dear," Marie muttered.

"I was thinking the same thing." Walt stood up.

"How do you know what I'm thinking?" Marie asked.

"You're worried they might realize someone switched the portraits back."

"Yes." Marie nodded. Walt disappeared.

DANIELLE WAS JUST WALKING down the stairs when Walt appeared by her side.

"You need to get in the library and distract Clint and Macbeth. And get them to move the crate, now!"

Holding onto the handrail with one hand, Danielle continued down the stairs. "What's wrong?"

"They're in the library looking at your paintings, and Macbeth is starting to notice how brilliantly close his paintings are to the originals—too close."

"Oh dear." Danielle picked up her step.

"Where's Ian?" Walt asked.

"He's on his way over. I saw him crossing the street from my bedroom window."

WHEN DANIELLE ENTERED THE LIBRARY, she found Clint and Macbeth studying the paintings while Marie stood by nervously, wringing her hands.

"I called Ian, and he said he would be right over to help you move the crate," Danielle announced. She joined the men at the portrait. "So you're saying goodbye to my paintings?"

"Umm...yes..." Macbeth frowned, looking from the painting to Danielle.

Just as he looked to Danielle, she stepped closer to Walt's portrait and cocked her head slightly. "Well...that's odd..."

Both men exchanged quick glances while Danielle continued to stare at the painting, tilting her head from side to side. "It looks... well, different..."

"Different?" Macbeth stammered.

"Yes. Something about the eyes. I love Walt's eyes. It's the twinkle...the twinkle seems different..."

The doorbell rang. While still focusing on the painting, Danielle murmured, "That's probably Ian now."

Clint grabbed Danielle by her arm and turned her from the painting. "We really don't want to take all your friend's time. I think we should move the crate now."

MARIE STOOD with Walt by the door leading to the parlor, watching Ian, Macbeth, Danielle, and Clint carry the crate down the hallway while Stephanie stood by the open front door.

"Clever of Danielle, how she got those men out of the library," Marie said with a chuckle.

"One of the things I love about her, she thinks quick on her feet."

Marie turned to Walt and smiled. "You love her?"

Still watching Danielle and the others, Walt shrugged. "You do too."

"I imagine not the same way as you do."

"I imagine not," he whispered.

Marie looked back to the crate. "Danielle and Ian don't seem to be having trouble carrying their end like those other two. You don't suppose the weight shifted in the crate somehow?"

Walt took a leisurely drag off his cigar and shook his head. After he exhaled, he said, "No. I'm helping Ian and Danielle carry their end of the crate."

Marie turned back to Walt and arched her brows. "From here?"

Walt shrugged. "Why does that surprise you? You saw me switch the paintings last night."

Marie let out a sigh. "Yes, you're right. Oh, how I would love to be able to do that!"

DANIELLE FOUND it amusing how Stephanie had closed the library door after they had carried the crate into the hallway. It was fairly obvious none of them wanted her to go back into the library and start checking out Walt's twinkling eyes—at least not until they were long gone.

After the crate was loaded in the van, Macbeth went back into the house for his two suitcases. Ten minutes later he was gone. Fifteen minutes later, Stephanie and Clint were saying their good-byes while Stephanie got into the driver's seat of the van, and Clint got into the passenger seat.

Danielle waved as the van pulled out into the street. Together Ian and Danielle stood on the sidewalk in front of Marlow House.

"So they really didn't know your portraits are worth a fortune?" Ian asked as the van drove away.

"Oh yes, they did." Danielle glanced towards Ian's house and spied Lily jogging toward them.

"So they weren't thieves after all?"

"Yes. They were. They think they have the Bonnet paintings."

TWENTY

"Why did we have to leave before breakfast?" Stephanie steered the van down the road. "One nice thing I can say about our stay at Marlow House, Danielle serves a delicious breakfast. Would it have hurt to have eaten before we left?"

"I'm sorry, babe, but yeah. It might have. Danielle was looking a little too closely at my cousin's portrait, and I was afraid she was going to ask me to open the crate so she could compare the paintings. If it had been loaded on the bottom of the crate, I could have used that as an excuse not to open it. Letting her compare those paintings is the last thing I wanted to do."

"You know, she's going to eventually find out they're worth a fortune, and what will she do when she realizes hers are fakes?"

"Now you ask that?" Clint laughed.

Hands clutching the steering wheel, Stephanie shrugged. "I've always been worried about that. And now that we've gotten this far, well, it all seems a little more real to me."

"Don't worry. Danielle and the police chief saw us load the reproductions and lock the crate."

"Can't she say we switched them when she was sleeping?"

"I suppose it would be possible. But those paintings have been in that house for almost a century, and anyone could have gotten to them, including that attorney who worked for her aunt. The one who murdered Danielle's cousin and embezzled from the estate," Clint reminded her.

"Yeah, but that means he would've had to have hired an artist to reproduce them. When did he do that? Joanne told me she used to work for the aunt and cleaned Marlow House every week. Wouldn't she have seen something?"

"Damnit, Stephanie, stop! By the time Danielle ever figures out the truth about the paintings—which she may never do—we will be long gone with new identities in Europe."

Stephanie let out a sigh, her eyes still on the road. "I'm sorry. I'm just hungry. I always get anxious when I'm hungry."

"Then let's stop somewhere and grab a bite to eat. We have plenty of time."

"But you said you don't want to leave the paintings in the van."

"We don't have to. I noticed a drive-through not far from here. Take the next left."

Stephanie let out another sigh and smiled. "Thanks. I love you, Clint."

"I love you too, babe. It will be okay, I promise you. We've gotten this far, haven't we?"

DARLENE GUSAROV PERCHED on the cliff at Pilgrim's Point, contemplating her life and subsequent death. On days like this, when she felt particularly melancholy, she preferred her white chiffon, ankle-length dress. Even when the air was still, she could create the illusion of a breeze gently rustling her skirt and tossing her blond curls.

Resting her chin on a balled fist, her elbow perched on one bent knee, she gazed out to the ocean and watched as the breakers crashed onto the shore below   one after another. There was no one on that stretch of the beach, there rarely was.

After what seemed like an eternity, she gazed upward. Rain clouds filled the blue sky, gradually turning it gray.

"What is it you want from me?" Darlene asked aloud.

There was no answer.

"How long am I to serve this penance here? Yes, I was wrong. I am prepared to move forward—prepared to take the rest of my punishment. But please, I beg you. Let me leave this place!"

There still was no answer.

"I know none of the lives I've saved while here will replace the one I took." She paused a moment and then said, "Okay, technically I took more than one life. But please, I can't bear this. Unable to venture more than a few hundred yards in any direction. No one to talk to. Unless, of course, I count one of the spirits who occasionally pass by. But then, they just remind me of my limitations."

It wasn't an answer, more a question she heard.

"Danielle Boatman? Yes, she can see and hear me, but it's not like she stops by to chat—"

Dropping both hands to her lap, Darlene sat up straight and frowned, still looking upward. "Oh yes. Of course. She's hardly someone who would want to be my friend. I—I wasn't talking about making friends, I—"

Still frowning, Darlene cocked her head to one side. "I'm not sure what you mean? That doesn't make sense…are you sure?"

"Talking to yourself again?" Eva asked when she suddenly appeared by Darlene's side.

Startled, Darlene jumped down from where she perched, now facing Eva.

"What are you doing here, Eva? Come to taunt me?"

In response, Eva waved her right hand, sending a flurry of glitter bursting out and over the cliff, disappearing before it reached the beach below. "No. I've come to help you."

"Help me? Why would you want to help me?" Darlene frowned.

"I loved my career on the stage, but it was cut short, no fault of my own. You, on the other hand, had immense talent, yet gave it all up for a man—a man you hardly loved. For what? Financial security? And what did it get you?" Eva glanced around, taking in the prison that was Darlene's.

"You think I had immense talent?" Darlene whispered in awe.

Eva smiled. "In life taking a turn down the wrong road can change everything. Just one little turn. And everything changes."

Darlene stared at Eva for several moments. Finally, she asked, "You know I wasn't talking to myself just a minute ago, don't you?"

Eva nodded. "Yes. I'm here to help you understand. It is not about you changing the future; it's about someone else choosing where to turn. There is no predestined future, but gentle nudges along the way to get you on the right path. And sometimes, under extreme circumstances, the Universe tries to right wrongs. Yet even in that, there is no guarantee."

"Free will?" Darlene whispered.

Eva nodded.

"Then what will happen to me if I do this?"

"Have faith, Darlene." Eva vanished.

"THAT WASN'T as good as the breakfast at Marlow House," Stephanie grumbled as she turned back onto the highway.

After ordering breakfast sandwiches and coffee from a drive-through restaurant, they had eaten the meal in the van while sitting in the restaurant's parking lot. Clint had tossed all the trash in the garbage can before they started back on their way.

"I'm sorry, babe. But just think, tomorrow we'll be in Paris, and I bet the food there will make Boatman's look like that drive-through's."

Stephanie grinned. "You're right. Sorry I'm such a whiner today. I don't know what my problem is."

"I imagine this whole thing has been stressful for you. But we're almost there, babe."

Clutching the steering wheel and peering down the highway, Stephanie nodded. "I know."

"You sure you want to drive?" he asked.

"You know how windy roads make me car sick if I don't drive."

"I know." Clint sighed and leaned back in the passenger seat, resting his head on the headrest. He gazed out the windshield, reading the highway signs as they passed by. They hadn't traveled up this stretch of the highway when coming to Frederickport. But they weren't returning to California, and they needed to meet with the buyers before heading to the airport in Portland.

"Pilgrim's Point, one mile," he muttered.

"What?" Stephanie glanced briefly to Clint.

"I was just reading the signs."

"What's Pilgrim's Point?" Stephanie asked.

"It's up ahead."

"Funny name. I wonder why it's called that."

Clint shrugged. "No idea. But it sounds familiar. I think I read about it online."

"This is really a beautiful stretch of the highway," Stephanie noted, glancing over to catch a glimpse of the ocean.

"Just keep your eyes on the road," he reminded her.

"I am," Stephanie said impatiently.

Several moments later, just as they turned the bend at Pilgrim's Point, a blond woman appeared in the middle of the highway, her white chiffon dress fluttering around her bare ankles.

"Watch out!" Clint shouted.

Stephanie screamed, her eyes locking with the blonde's, who made no attempt to dodge the fast-approaching van. Panicked, Stephanie jerked the steering wheel toward the ocean side of the highway, sending the vehicle careening toward the cliff.

With Clint now screaming while attempting to take the steering wheel from Stephanie, the van continued on its lethal course despite Stephanie's attempts to apply the brake. A moment later they were literally flying, airborne over the edge of Pilgrim's Point while the pair continued to scream in unison.

After catapulting off the cliff, the van sailed for just a few moments before it made a nosedive and then clipped a protruding boulder along the mountainside, sending the van in a flip, turning it upside down, which was how it landed when it finally reached the beach below.

The screaming stopped. All was quiet in the van, as if it and the passengers were holding a collective breath.

"Stephanie?" Clint finally whispered.

"Oh crap," Stephanie groaned.

"Are you okay?" he asked.

"For a minute there, I thought I broke something. But I think I'm okay." Stephanie looked out the windshield. "We're upside down."

"Let's get out of here. But be careful. There's glass all over."

When they climbed out of the vehicle, they found themselves standing on a desolate beach, their van's tires facing the sky, one rear wheel spinning.

"I about killed us," Stephanie groaned.

"It wasn't your fault. It was that crazy woman."

They both looked up the mountain and to the cliff.

"Where do you think she went?" Stephanie asked.

"I don't know. But at the moment, I'm more concerned about the paintings."

Stephanie and Clint ran to the back of the van and looked inside. One of its rear doors had flown open during impact, but the crate was still inside.

"It doesn't look like it's damaged," Clint said.

"What now?" Stephanie glanced around. She could hear the waves crashing on the beach.

"The only thing we can do. We need to call Mac. He's going to have to rent a vehicle and get his guys down here. This will delay us, but it's not the end of the world."

Stephanie stepped away from the van and looked back up the mountainside. "But where is that woman? I didn't hit her, did I?"

"Even if you had, it wouldn't have been your fault. I don't know what she was doing, standing in the middle of the road like that, trying to get herself killed."

Still looking up the mountain, Stephanie shook her head. "She must have been trying to get us to help her."

"What, by getting us to run her down?" he asked angrily.

"Clint, did you see her face? She looked just like Marilyn Monroe."

"Come on, Stephanie, pull yourself together; we need to get going."

Stephanie glared at Clint. "You aren't the one who about killed someone!"

"No one died! But she about killed us. So come on, we need to get going."

"Are you sure I didn't hit her?"

"Yes. I'm positive. Now come on, we need to get the cellphone and call Mac."

Stephanie let out a sigh and then reluctantly made her way back up to the front of the vehicle. When she reached the driver's door, she leaned down and peered inside. To her horror, she came face-to-face—with herself.

Just as she screeched, "Clint!" Clint leaned down and looked into the passenger window. He found himself looking into his own face, blood running down from a gash in his forehead. He appeared to be sleeping. And beyond the sleeping Clint in the vehicle was another Stephanie, this one battered and bloody, her head turned in an unnatural position and her vacant eyes open, staring blankly in his direction.

"Oh crap," Clint muttered. "This doesn't look good."

125

TWENTY-ONE

J oanne had gone home after stripping the linens off the beds in the guest rooms and gathering up all the towels. She had started one load of laundry and then went to clean the guest rooms and baths. When she was done, there was another load of laundry to put in, but Danielle had told her to go ahead and go home and take the rest of the day off. Danielle said she would finish up the laundry. Joanne was happy to oblige, as it was spring break, and she had some family visiting her for a few days.

Marie had taken off too. Eva had stopped by just after Clint and Stephanie had driven away. She told Marie there was something she needed to do and wondered if she would keep an eye on her portrait. While Marie wasn't thrilled to still be on guard duty, she didn't mind going to the museum and eavesdropping on some of the docents, like Millie and Ben—assuming either of them were on duty.

Chris had arrived at Marlow House not long after Joanne went home and found Ian and Lily with Danielle and Walt in the library. After they brought Chris up to speed on what had gone on since the previous evening, they all sat in silence for a few moments while Chris processed all that he had just been told.

"I can't believe you didn't call me last night," Chris finally said, looking at Danielle. "And I can't believe you didn't tell the chief."

"She didn't tell us either," Lily grumbled. She sat with Ian on the sofa, while Danielle and Chris sat in the chairs across from them. Walt stood by the bookshelves, smoking a cigar.

"Hey, guys, there was nothing you could do. And we had it under control," Danielle insisted.

Chris nodded over to the life-sized Marlow portraits. "What are you going to do about those?"

"We were just discussing that," Ian said.

"And it's not just the portraits here, we have to deal with the one at the museum. They need to be told what it's worth," Lily said.

"When are you going to do that?" Chris asked.

"That's one of the things we were talking about," Ian said.

"I think the first priority is getting Eva's portrait secure. Walt can keep an eye on his until we work it all out, but I'm worried that someone connected to Clint's art heist—and we know there are more than seven people involved, considering the men who showed up while we were at the restaurant and the fact there has to be at least one buyer. It wouldn't take long for someone curious to start doing a little online sleuthing and stumble across Eva's portrait, considering so many of the online articles mention both Walt and Eva," Danielle explained.

"And if the buyer realizes those portraits are fake this afternoon, one of them might turn to the internet for answers. That seems to be what you people do these days," Walt interjected. While Lily and Ian couldn't hear what Walt had said, Danielle and Chris could.

"What do you think we should do?" Chris asked Danielle.

"I think Ian should go to the Historical Society today and tell them he's been doing some research on the portraits. Reasonable, considering everyone in town knows Clint paid an artist to reproduce our paintings. Plus, Ian has already talked to Millie over there about the possibility of him doing another article on Eva. He can say he just came across the information on the artist. Let them know the painting might be worth a small fortune. It's all basically true except for telling them he just stumbled on the information. Don't let them know he's known for almost two weeks."

"But how do we explain how Ian found the artist? We can't very well say Angela gave us the artist's name," Lily said.

"No. But Ian could have happened across the information the same way we believe Clint did. Maybe not that he attended the art show, but he can say he happened across the information on the art show when searching for artists of that era. And then he can say he noticed the similarity in style, looked at the signature, and realized it was the same one on the portraits here," Danielle explained.

Walt grinned and muttered, "That's my girl. Always thinking."

"You still have to do something about the Marlow portraits. Even with Walt here, it's not safe to keep something like that in your house," Chris told them. "Remember, Ian told us a Bonnet went for over five million at auction. That means your paintings could conceivably be worth ten million. Maybe more, considering their size."

"I hate to say this, but I agree with Chris," Walt begrudgingly admitted.

"Why does this always happen to me?" Danielle groaned.

Lily broke out into laughter. Everyone looked to her.

When Lily regained her composure, she said, while wiping tears of laughter from the corners of her eyes, "What, you mean always falling into buckets of money? Your aunt's inheritance, the Missing Thorndike, an unexpected inheritance from Cheryl, the gold coins, and now priceless art?" Lily began laughing again. Ian and Chris could not suppress their grins.

Danielle scowled at Lily for just a moment and then broke into a smile. She chuckled and then said, "Dang, Adam is really going to hate me."

POLICE CHIEF MACDONALD stood on the sidelines, hands on hips, surveying the carnage. The first responders had already removed the bodies, and now they were waiting for the tow truck to arrive.

Brian Henderson and Joe Morelli, both in uniform and wearing their baseball-style hats embellished with the department insignia, approached the chief. In one of Brian's hands was a small pad of paper, in the other a pen.

Still looking at the upside-down van, MacDonald asked, "So what do we know?"

Brian glanced at his open notepad. "The van doesn't belong to Marlow. It's a rental from a company in Portland. I've already called them. They didn't have any information on Marlow aside from his credit card and driver's license, which we have."

"Apparently they weren't going back to California," Joe told the chief. "There were one-way tickets to France in his fiancée's purse. They were leaving from the Portland airport late this afternoon."

MacDonald frowned and glanced to Joe. "They were headed in the wrong direction if they were going to the airport."

Joe shrugged. "Maybe they took a wrong turn."

"That's an understatement," Brian grumbled.

"There's a huge crate in the back of the van. I assume it has the paintings in it," Joe noted.

MacDonald nodded and then asked, "You said one-way tickets?"

"Yes," Joe told him.

"Interesting. They didn't mention anything about a trip to France after leaving here," the chief muttered.

"You think Danielle knows who we might contact for the next of kin?" Joe asked.

"Walt Marlow," Brian said with a snort.

MacDonald ignored Brian's crack and said, "From what Danielle told me, he doesn't have any family. No siblings, his parents are gone. I don't know about his fiancée. But I'm going to stop by Marlow House before I go back to the station. I want to let Danielle know what happened and see if she might have any contact information for Clint and Stephanie."

———

POLICE CHIEF MACDONALD stood on the front porch of Marlow House, waiting for someone to answer the door. Hat in hand, he turned his back to the house for a moment and looked out toward the street. Chris's car was parked in front of his patrol car, but Joanne's vehicle wasn't anywhere in sight. He glanced up to the sky. The gray clouds that had been gathering earlier had disappeared, leaving behind a blue sky.

"Chief!" Danielle greeted him when she opened the door.

He turned around to face her, his hands fidgeting with his hat. Before he had time to respond, she reached out and grabbed him by the forearm, pulling him into the house. "Come, everyone is in the library."

"Everyone?" He watched as she closed the front door.

"Walt's in there, but Marie's not. Come on!" Danielle said,

turning her back to him and heading down the entry hall toward the library.

"I need to talk to you," he called out.

"Come. We can talk in the library." She continued on her way.

With a sigh, MacDonald followed Danielle. He tossed his hat on the entry table as he passed it and continued on to the library.

"LOOK WHO'S HERE!" Danielle said cheerfully. All eyes turned to the doorway leading to the entry hall. "It's like he had ESP and knew we needed to talk to him." Danielle went to a chair and sat down.

Not smiling, the chief paused at the doorway and surveyed the room.

"Clint and Stephanie left," Lily said brightly.

"Yes, that's why I'm here." MacDonald walked all the way into the room.

Noting the police chief's peculiar expression, Ian asked, "What's wrong?"

"There was a car accident," he said solemnly. "Clint's van went off the cliff at Pilgrim's Point."

Collective gasps went around the room. Danielle stood up. "Was anyone hurt?"

The chief nodded. "Stephanie didn't make it. It looks like she died on impact."

"And Clint?" Danielle asked.

"He's in the hospital. I don't know the extent of his injuries yet. He was unconscious when they took him out of the van and put him in the ambulance. I haven't heard if he's regained consciousness yet."

"Oh my," Danielle muttered, sitting back down in the chair.

"What happened?" Ian asked.

"Stephanie was driving. By the tire marks on the highway, it looks as if she swerved to miss something on the road, an animal perhaps, and then lost control of the vehicle," the chief explained.

"That's where Darlene haunts," Danielle blurted. All eyes turned to her.

"You think Darlene had something to do with this?" Lily asked.

Danielle shrugged. "The only time her spirit's ever done something malicious was when she went after her killer. Yet other times, well, I know she's saved a few lives."

"I was hoping you'd have some information on who we might contact for either Clint or Stephanie," the chief said.

Danielle motioned to the desk chair for the chief to sit down and then said, "She never talked about her life. In fact, I didn't talk to either of them much. But I think you should know something." Danielle then went on to tell the chief about how the paintings had been switched.

After Danielle finished her telling, MacDonald let out a sigh and said, "I guess that explains the tickets to France."

"France?" Lily and Danielle chorused.

MacDonald nodded. "There were plane tickets in Stephanie's purse, for her and Clint. One-way tickets leaving late this afternoon for Paris."

"So they weren't planning to return to California?" Danielle asked.

"They must have been on their way to meet with the buyers before going to the airport," Ian suggested. "Because if they were headed to Portland, they were going the wrong way if they ended up at Pilgrim's Point."

The chief nodded. "That's what I was thinking too."

"That means Macbeth and the buyers are somewhere waiting for Clint to deliver the paintings," Lily said.

The chief groaned. "It also means that they believe the contents of the crate are worth a fortune, and once they find out what happened, they're probably going to be coming for it."

Walt flicked his cigar into the air. Before it vanished, he said, "My cousin better have a speedy recovery. I don't need him coming back here."

TWENTY-TWO

D anielle stood with the police chief at the front desk of the intensive care unit. Since she was not a relative of Clint's, she would never have made it past the door into the ICU without the chief's help.

"This is Danielle Boatman," the chief introduced her to the nurse. He knew most of the ICU and ER staff at the local hospital.

"Yes, I know who she is." The nurse smiled.

"Clint Marlow and his fiancée were staying with Danielle before the accident happened," he explained.

"I'm so sorry about the fiancée. So tragic, such a young woman."

"How is Clint doing?" Danielle asked.

"Technically, since you're not a family member, you really shouldn't be back here." The nurse smiled sheepishly.

"Clint doesn't have any family," Danielle explained. "His father died a few years ago, and his mother died when he was a child. He doesn't have any siblings. I guess I'm as close to family as he has."

The nurse arched her brow. "How is that?"

"You did mention you know who I am. I inherited the Marlow estate, through my aunt. And Clint and I have been in communication for some time. That's why he was here, to visit me. We consider ourselves family, since neither of us have any living relatives," Danielle embellished.

"Oh…I can see how that would draw you close…" the nurse conceded.

"Can you tell me how he's doing?" MacDonald interrupted.

The nurse focused her attention back on the chief and smiled. She gave him a nod and said, "Of course, Chief. He still hasn't woken up, yet his vitals are good, and there doesn't seem to be any internal damage. He did break a leg and got a nasty cut on his forehead. But aside from that, physically he seems to be okay."

"But he hasn't woken up?" he asked.

The nurse shook her head. "No."

"Do they know why?"

"No. But the doctor has ordered some more tests."

"Do you think I could see him?" Danielle asked.

The nurse shook her head. "I'm sorry. Even if you were his sister, I couldn't let you in there right now. Like I said, the doctor ordered some more tests for him, and I know they're coming to get him in a few minutes. Anyway, it's not like he'll even know you're there, since he's still unconscious."

"Do you know when someone can see him?" Danielle asked. "I understand he won't know I'm there, but I'd still like to."

The nurse stared at Danielle for a moment before answering. Finally, she said, "It will be about an hour, but then, I'm afraid I wouldn't be able to let you see him." She smiled apologetically.

"But I told you I'm as close to family as he has," Danielle insisted.

"I really am sorry. But those are the rules." The nurse then paused a moment and glanced around. She leaned toward Danielle and whispered, "My shift ends in two hours. You can tell Mr. Marlow's sister that he will probably be back from his tests by then. When she comes in, she needs to just tell the nurse on duty that she's his sister." The nurse smiled. "You can tell his sister that for me."

"DID she just tell me to lie to the next nurse on duty?" Danielle asked the chief after they left the ICU and started down the hall toward the elevator.

"Which should be easy for you to do, considering all that BS you gave her in there about how you and Clint are practically family." The chief chuckled.

Danielle shrugged. "It was just a little embellishment."

"Embellishment?" he said with a snort. "I'm getting concerned when you can't objectively tell your lies from the truth."

"Okay, okay. It was a freaking lie." She stepped into the empty elevator with the chief. The door closed.

"I know you wanted to come with me to see how he was doing, but why are you so determined to see him?" He pushed the button for the first floor. "The man is unconscious."

The elevator started moving downward.

"Because he's been unconscious for a few hours, and according to the nurse, there doesn't seem to be a physical reason for it."

The elevator door opened. Just as Danielle and the chief stepped out onto the first floor, a nurse stepped into the elevator. The door closed. Danielle and the chief headed toward the exit leading to the hospital's front parking lot.

"Remember Lily and Chris?" Danielle asked.

The chief glanced briefly to Danielle. "You telling me Clint's spirit is wandering around somewhere?"

"I'm hoping it's not wandering around. I'm hoping it's in his hospital room."

"I'm curious, why do you want to know?" he asked.

"Because I've learned from Lily and Chris that when a traumatic accident happens, the spirit—or soul—whatever you want to call it—doesn't necessarily understand what's happening, which accounts for people who are in comas for a long time. Clint may not be my favorite person, but I don't want to think of him being detached from his body while it lingers in some rest home somewhere."

"You think he's in the hospital room with his body?"

"To be honest—not really. That was the issue with Lily and Chris; they got separated from their bodies, which was part of the problem. But before I go looking for him, I figured since we're at the hospital anyway, I should at least see if he's still with his body. I'd feel pretty foolish if I run around town looking for him and then discover he's simply lingering in the hospital room, trying to figure out what's going on."

"Since you can't get in to see him for another two hours, you want to stop by the scene of the accident?"

Pushing through the exit doors, Danielle let out a sigh and said, "I suppose that would be the most logical place to start."

———

THE MAN in the hospital bed appeared to be sleeping. The bruise along the right side of his face added color to the unnatural paleness of his current complexion. Running down the right side of his forehead was a deep cut, now with ten stitches, giving the otherwise handsome face a Frankenstein's monster look. His left leg, encased in a cast, was elevated, while various cords hooked him to the monitors.

Standing by his bedside was his fiancée and—himself.

"I don't understand. Why are you there—" Stephanie nodded down to the unconscious body and then looked back to the Clint by her side "—and here?"

Afraid, Stephanie had refused to leave Clint's side after climbing out of the van. When they had loaded her lifeless body into a vehicle and the paramedics had freely discussed the fact she was dead, Stephanie didn't for a moment consider staying with her body and leaving Clint.

Unlike herself, Clint was alive. At least, that was what the paramedics on the beach had said when they had put him in the ambulance. *And what was that old cliché?* she asked...*where there is life, there is hope.* Yet, as hours unfolded, she began to realize life no longer applied to her.

"I wish I didn't have to leave you!"

Clint looked from his body to the woman he loved. "Leave me? No. You can't. I need you!"

"Clint, it's obvious. You lived; I didn't. I can feel it. I have to go. It's pulling me." She glanced to her right, seeing a light not visible to Clint.

"No." He shook his head. "If you can't stay here, I'm coming with you!"

Stephanie's eyes widened excitedly. "You would do that?"

Turning to her, he smiled softly. "There's nothing here for me. You're the only one that ever mattered."

Stephanie glanced to the light and then back to Clint. "I'm afraid," she whispered.

"Don't be afraid. I'll be by your side," he promised.

"But we did something we shouldn't have. We stole Danielle's paintings. Are we going to hell now?" Nervously she glanced back to the light.

"It wasn't your fault. You just went along with me. And it's not like we killed anyone," Clint insisted.

"I know…but…" Stephanie's brow furrowed as she continued to glance from Clint to the light and back to Clint.

"I'll be by your side. We'll face this together. I promise."

"I love you, Clint."

"I love you, Stephanie."

"Are you afraid?" she whispered.

"It doesn't matter. As long as I'm with you, nothing matters. I won't leave you to do this alone."

Stephanie nodded toward the light—the light Clint did not see —and started walking. Just as she reached it, she put out her hand to Clint. He walked toward her, but in the next moment, she vanished.

"Stephanie!" he screamed. There was no answer.

FROM THE HOSPITAL Danielle and the chief stopped by Pilgrim's Point. But Danielle saw no sign of Clint—nor of Stephanie or Darlene. Standing along the cliff, Danielle and the chief looked down to the beach. The van had already been towed away. The only sign of the accident were the fresh tire marks along the highway. After they left Pilgrim's Point, the chief dropped Danielle at Marlow House; he needed to get back to the office.

At Marlow House, Danielle filled Walt in on his cousin's condition. She was home for about an hour, contemplating going back to the hospital to see if she could get in to see Clint, when Lily called her. She and Ian were down at Lucy's Diner, and they wanted her to join them for a late lunch—or early dinner. They also wanted to fill her in on Ian's meeting with the Historical Society's board of directors.

"So what did they say when they found out the painting is worth a fortune?" Danielle asked after she joined her friends at the diner.

"To say they were in shock would be an understatement. Ben didn't quite believe it could be possible until I showed him the Bonnet paintings online," Ian told her.

"I wonder if Marie and Eva were at the museum when you were talking to them," Danielle mused.

"They've all agreed to keep this quiet until they can provide the proper security for the painting while finding a buyer. And they understand you'd probably appreciate they keep it quiet until you figure out how you want to handle your paintings," Lily explained.

"So they're going to sell Eva's portrait?" Danielle asked, sounding somewhat disappointed.

"I don't see how they have any other choice," Ian said. "And neither do they. The money from the sale of that painting will help fund a small museum like theirs for years. Not only would keeping it increase their insurance premium, they would probably end up spending a fortune on improving security around the museum."

Danielle picked up a menu from the end of the table. As she opened it, she said, "I wonder what Eva is going to think of that."

Lily shrugged and opened the menu she was already holding.

"What did the chief do with Clint's paintings?" Lily asked as she skimmed the menu.

"I guess the police department has a couple of storage units that they use to store items—like unclaimed property," Danielle told them.

"They know who it belongs to," Lily said.

"True, but Clint's in the hospital unconscious, and if there weren't people out there who thought the paintings were worth a fortune, then I'd offer to hold them for Clint. But I don't need those people showing up at my place."

"Isn't the chief concerned about someone breaking into the storage rooms?" Lily asked.

"According to him, the storage units' location isn't common knowledge, and it's always been protocol with his officers not to discuss where property is being held. Apparently, it's not just price-less artwork that becomes a target after property is held for some reason," Danielle explained.

"I suppose it's a good thing the police department has them. Keeps the attention off Marlow House while you get your portraits settled," Lily said.

Danielle set the menu down on the table and glanced around. "Where is our waitress? I need to order, eat and then get back down to the hospital."

TWENTY-THREE

Danielle was in her car, on her way from Lucy's Diner to the hospital, when her cellphone rang. It was Chris. She put the call on speakerphone.

"I stopped by your house. Walt said you were at Lucy's with Lily and Ian," Chris said.

Hands firmly on the steering wheel, Danielle's eyes looked down the road as she talked to Chris. "I just left them. I'm on the way to the hospital now."

"Walt said you weren't able to see Clint when you stopped there earlier. Is he still unconscious?"

"As far as I know. But maybe I'll get lucky, and when I get there, he'll have come out of it."

"I hope so. I hate to think of a Walt look-alike wandering aimlessly around Frederickport."

"Chris, you think you can call Heather for me, give her the heads-up about what's going on? I know she had a problem seeing you when you had your experience, but her ability has heightened, and if she does see him, she needs to be prepared to nudge him back to his body."

"What about Evan?" Chris asked.

"When I left the chief earlier, he promised he would talk to Evan about it."

"I'll call Heather as soon as I get off the phone. Do you want me to meet you at the hospital? Render some medium-to-medium support?"

"Thanks, Chris, but I better do this alone. As it is, I'm going to have to pass myself off as Clint's sister in order to get in to see him."

"I thought he didn't have any siblings?" Chris asked.

"Exactly."

"By the way, Eva stopped by my house about an hour ago. She's not thrilled about the museum selling her portrait," Chris told her.

"Ahh, so she was at the museum when Ian talked to the board."

"Apparently both she and Marie were there. She feels her painting belongs in Frederickport. She told me she was unhappy when the theater closed, and she got stuck in a dreary basement for years."

"You mean her painting got stuck there. She didn't," Danielle reminded him.

"You know Eva, a little prone to dramatics." Chris chuckled.

"Ya think?"

———

"YOU'RE MR. MARLOW'S SISTER?" the nurse at the ICU asked after Danielle introduced herself as Clint's sister in order to gain access to that section of the hospital.

"Yes. How is he doing?" Danielle wondered briefly if it was a crime to try passing oneself off as a family member, but then remembered the chief was standing there while the previous nurse had practically told Danielle to do that very thing.

The nurse sighed and shook her head. "I'm afraid there's still no change."

"I know they had some tests done to see why he hasn't come to. Do they know anything more? Why he's still unconscious?"

"I'm afraid you will need to talk to his doctor about that."

Danielle fidgeted nervously with her purse's strap. "Umm...can I see him, please?"

"Certainly. He's in room C." The nurse motioned in the direction of room C.

The patient rooms in the ICU reminded Danielle more of cubicles—cubicles surrounding the ICU nurses' station. Glass windows instead of interior room walls faced the ICU staff, allowing visibility into each room. There were curtains, yet those were only closed to provide privacy when the medical staff or a family member was in with the patient. Instead of solid doors, each room or cubicle had just a doorway for easy and quick access.

As Danielle approached room C, she noted the curtains were drawn. When she reached the doorway, she hesitated to enter. It was one thing to lie about being Clint's sister in trying to track down his detached spirit, it was another to walk in on a nurse inserting a catheter or giving Clint a sponge bath.

She hesitated at the doorway a moment, only the foot of the hospital bed visible from where she stood, when she heard a female voice say, "You can come in."

Reluctantly, she entered the room and was immediately relieved to discover Clint fully clothed, covered with the blankets—save for the left leg imprisoned in a cast and suspended—and the nurse wasn't in the process of inserting anything into any intimate areas of his body.

"Danielle Boatman?" a confused male voice called out.

Danielle's head immediately jerked to the left. She found a man sitting in a chair along the curtained wall. It was Clint Marlow. Their gazes locked.

"You can come in," the nurse told Danielle. "I'm just finishing up. I assume you're a family member?" she asked kindly, flipping through the papers on the clipboard in her hand.

"Umm…yes…his sister. Is there any improvement?"

"My sister?" Clint said with a snort.

At his comment, Danielle's gaze briefly shot back to Clint before returning to the nurse.

Clint stood abruptly. "Oh my gawd, you can see me!"

"I'm afraid not. But on the positive side, his vitals look good. I've seen patients like him just suddenly wake up." She smiled up at Danielle.

"You can see me, can't you?" Clint walked to Danielle and stood directly in front of her, just a few feet away, blocking her view of the nurse.

Danielle stepped to the side slightly so that she could see the nurse. In turn, Clint took several steps, again blocking Danielle's view.

"Yes, I'm hoping that will happen," Danielle said, finding it diffi-cult to focus with Clint bouncing up and down in front of her, now waving his hands and making ridiculous faces. While he was Walt's twin, she couldn't imagine Walt ever making any of the inane expressions Clint was now trying out on her.

"Would you like me to keep the curtains closed while you visit your brother?" the nurse asked, now stepping away from the bed.

"Yes…yes, that would be nice." Danielle forced a smile. She watched as the nurse adjusted one of the monitors, and then the nursed flashed Danielle a parting smile while heading for the door.

"You can see me! Admit it! Why are you pretending you can't? I know you can; I saw it in your eyes! Answer me!" Clint shouted.

"I obviously couldn't talk to you while she was in here," Danielle hissed under her breath after the nurse left the room.

Clint froze. Momentarily speechless, he stared at Danielle. Finally, he muttered, "Oh my gawd, you really can see me."

"I thought we already established that," Danielle whispered. "Now come over here so I can talk to you without drawing attention to us."

Danielle walked to the chair he had been sitting on a minute ago. She pulled it up to his bedside and sat down, leaning close to the unconscious body.

"I don't understand. How is it you can see me, but no one else can?" he asked, now standing by her side.

"I suppose you might say I have a gift. I first realized it when I saw my grandmother's spirit at her funeral," Danielle explained.

"Are you saying I'm dead? I'm a spirit? A ghost?"

She nodded to the man in the bed. "You are obviously not dead. Don't you recognize yourself?"

He glanced from Danielle to his body and then back to Danielle. "Yes…but…I mean…"

"You're more a spirit than a ghost, I suppose. If you were dead, then you'd be a ghost." She looked up to Clint.

"Like my Stephanie?" he asked sadly.

Danielle nodded. "I assume you know about Stephanie?"

"Yes."

"I'm sorry about her. I know you really loved her."

"I want to be with her," he told Danielle.

"Maybe someday. I suppose you will see her again. But you've obviously not finished with life here yet. You need to go back into your body."

He took a step back from the bed, as if the idea repulsed him. "Go back into my body? No. I want to go with Stephanie!"

141

"Have you seen her? Since the accident?" Danielle asked in a whisper.

He nodded. "Yes. We were together after the accident, on the beach. We watched as they took our bodies away, and they said she was dead."

"Did she go with her body?" Danielle wondered if Stephanie had moved on or if she was still in post-death limbo.

"No. She came here with me. She was afraid and didn't want to be alone. But then she felt something pulling her—to some other place. I tried to go with her; she wanted me to. But when she left, I couldn't follow her. I'm stuck here. I don't want to be here. I want to be with Stephanie!"

"I believe there is—*actually, I know there is*—more after this world here. Stephanie has continued on her journey. And someday, when you're finished here, you'll see her again. I'm certain of that."

He shook his head. "No. I'm finished here now. There is nothing more for me here. I want to go with Stephanie. It's where I belong. It's the only place I've ever belonged."

Danielle let out a sigh and looked up sympathetically. "I really am sorry about Stephanie. And I know you're going to miss her—and grieve for her. But the fact is, you aren't ready to move on."

"How do you know?" he snapped.

Danielle pointed to the bed. "Because of that."

Looking at the man on the bed, Clint frowned. "Because of my broken body? I don't understand."

"You can't move on in your journey until your time here is over. As long as you have a viable body, you can't just follow Stephanie. In essence, your physical body tethers you to this world."

"So what are you telling me? That my spirit-self needs to connect with my physical self in order to join Stephanie?"

"That's just part of it. You have to finish your life here. And considering the nurse says your body is relatively healthy, there's no reason to believe that once you reconnect to your body, you couldn't live a long life. Which is something you should want to do. I know it's hard to lose the person you love—I lost my husband—but that's no reason to give up on your life."

"No. I don't want to live a long life. Not without Stephanie. What if I refuse to reconnect with my body?"

Danielle glanced from Clint to the bed and shrugged. "I imagine your body could feasibly linger for years while you're stuck in limbo, with only people like me—and there are not that many of us—who will ever see or hear you. Eventually your body will die, but it could be years from now. Why waste all that time in limbo, when you could be living a full life?"

"You're saying, when my body dies, I should be able to join Stephanie?"

Danielle studied Clint for a moment. "I suppose you'll be able to. But first, you may have some penance to do before you can join her. I imagine Stephanie has her own penance she's dealing with right now."

"What are you talking about?" He frowned.

"During our lives, we all make mistakes. Some mistakes are more severe than others. Crimes we must atone for. I have no idea how you've lived your life up until this point. But I do know about the Bonnet paintings."

Clint stared at Danielle, momentarily speechless.

She smiled at him. "Technically, you didn't actually steal anything. We switched the paintings back after everyone went to bed last night."

Clint smiled and sat on the edge of the mattress.

"You're happy about that?" Danielle asked.

Clint shrugged. "I don't really care about the paintings now. And if we didn't actually steal them—well, I'm thinking of Stephanie. She was afraid. This could be a good thing. It's not like either of us lived a life of crime up until now."

"So what are you going to do? Linger here, or live your life? I'm not pressing charges about what you tried to do, so you won't have to deal with that."

"I don't care about the paintings. I only care about being with Stephanie."

"So what arc you going to do?"

"I suppose the only thing I can do. Reconnect with my body and then commit suicide." He flashed her a broad smile, obviously believing he had stumbled upon a brilliant solution.

Danielle cringed and shook her head. "Ohhhhhh…I really don't think you should do that."

"Why not? It's the only solution," he insisted.

"Umm…not if you want to be with Stephanie when you eventually pass over."

"I don't understand?"

143

"Cheating death—in this case—cheating life—comes with unavoidable consequences. Trust me, going that route is not going to get you to Stephanie any quicker than living out your natural life as the Universe intended. In fact, it will probably take you much longer to be with her again if you kill yourself."

TWENTY-FOUR

D anielle glanced at her watch and then stood up. "I need to go home," she whispered.

"You're just going to leave me here?" Clint asked incredulously.

"It's up to you now. You can linger by your body until it dies, and possibly spend years in some dreary rest home. Or you can make an effort and reconnect with your body and live out your life as it's supposed to be."

He shook his head. "I'm supposed to be with Stephanie."

Danielle shrugged. "I don't know what else to say. I came here and did what I had to do. Now it's time for me to go."

"And what were you supposed to do?" he asked.

"When I heard you were still unconscious, I suspected your spirit-self had disconnected from your body. I've seen that happen a couple of times before. I was worried you might be confused and didn't understand what you needed to do. But now you know what to do, and it's your choice."

Danielle turned from Clint and started for the door.

"And that's it? You're just walking out?"

She paused a moment and turned to Clint. "I'm sorry. There is absolutely nothing I can do to help you. Whatever you choose— even if it's suicide—well, you will have to live with the consequences of your choice—for eternity. Not for the rest of your life, but after your body dies. So think long and hard before you do anything. Goodbye, Clint. I wish you well."

———

WHEN DANIELLE RETURNED to Marlow House that afternoon, she was surprised to find Chris in the library with Walt. Walt sat on the sofa, clad in gray dress slacks and a white dress shirt, its sleeves pushed up to his elbows. Danielle was used to seeing Walt in three-piece suits—often without the jacket, and more often than not, in pinstripes. But she liked this look too.

Chris sat in one of the chairs facing the sofa. Chris's manner of dress was fairly typical for him, faded denims and a *Keep Portland Weird* T-shirt. It was a good disguise for someone who would prefer the world not know he was worth billions. While Chris enjoyed dressing down, his wardrobe was not without trendy clothes befitting a man of his station. Yet it didn't matter if he dressed as a beach bum or a man who had just stepped off the cover of *GQ*, women's heads turned when he walked by.

"What are you two up to?" Danielle asked as she walked into the room.

"We were discussing the portraits," Walt explained. "But first, tell us. Did you find my cousin?"

"Oh yes…" Danielle plopped down on the sofa next to Walt and propped her feet on the coffee table after kicking off her shoes. "He was at the hospital with his body. And he's reluctant to—well—get back in it."

"What does he want to do?" Chris asked.

"He wants to move on with Stephanie."

"Isn't that a little drastic, considering she's dead?" Chris asked.

Danielle shrugged. "He even suggested returning to his body and then killing himself so he could be with her."

"If my cousin was a woman, I might wonder if he was Hindu," Walt said dryly.

"Ah, you mean the practice of sati, where a widow throws herself on her husband's funeral pyre," Chris said with a chuckle.

"I don't think he was suggesting anything that dramatic," Danielle said. "But in defense of those women, I believe the practice grew out of a widow's fear of being taken prisoner and raped after battle."

"What does Walt's cousin fear?" Chris asked. "Being arrested for trying to steal your portraits?"

Danielle shook her head. "No. I already told him I knew what he had done, and I have no intention of pressing charges. I really think it's just about Stephanie. He seemed sincere in wanting to be with her. Which I find interesting, because he's not particularly love-able." Danielle glanced at Walt and added, "No offence."

Walt shrugged. "None taken."

"I just find it peculiar that someone who is that—well, cold in many ways actually cares for someone that deeply."

"You know, Danielle, they say there is someone for everyone," Chris reminded her.

"I suppose. And I do feel bad for him." Danielle let out a sigh and leaned back on the sofa.

"So what is he going to do?" Walt asked.

"I assume he will eventually come to his senses after he gets bored hanging around the hospital, talking to an occasional spirit who has recently passed. Maybe he just has to mourn for Stephanie before he can reconnect with his body. But I've done my good deed for the day. Tried to explain to him how it all works."

"Better you than me," Chris said with a chuckle.

"I have an idea why my cousin is reluctant to resume his life, and it's not all about Stephanie."

"What then? I told him I wouldn't press charges."

"Remember, according to the chief, they had one-way tickets to Paris. I have a good idea Clint has already severed ties with his life in California. I imagine he's moved out of his home there and quit his job. He may have burned all his bridges already and has nowhere to go."

Chris nodded in agreement. "Walt's probably right."

"I usually am."

Chris rolled his eyes, and Danielle sat up a little straighter and removed her feet from the coffee table, setting them on the floor. She glanced from Walt to Chris and said, "So tell me, you said you were discussing the portraits. What about them?"

"Chris has offered to buy them," Walt told her. "And I think you should sell them to him."

Now frowning, Danielle glanced from Walt to Chris. "Why would you want to buy them?"

"Eva got me thinking about it," Chris said. "I happen to agree with her. I think her portrait belongs in Frederickport. I also think Walt's belong here too. The museum obviously can't afford them, and it's not safe for you to keep them at Marlow House. Even with Walt here."

"So what do you propose?" Danielle asked.

"I can purchase them—or Chris Glandon can—and then loan them back to the museum. Of course, there will need to be a new section added to the museum to house the paintings and to keep them secure. There is room to do that, and I can pay for it. I can also cover the expense for the extra security. I've already spoken to the board on behalf of my other self." Chris chuckled, because the board of directors of the Historical Society had no idea the affable Chris Johnson, who worked for the Glandon Foundation, was actually its founder, Chris Glandon.

"And they want to do this?"

"I offered them five million for Eva's painting, the same price as the last Bonnet went for auction. They won't be losing the painting, and they'll be gaining two more for their exhibit—yours if you agree—which will put the little museum on the map. I suspect they're relieved I'm handling this. According to Ian, they were a little overwhelmed at the thought of contacting buyers while securing the paintings. We also agreed to bring in an art expert to authenticate them. If they aren't authentic, then I won't be buying them, but it won't cost the museum anything. I'll handle that. And we'll also have the paintings appraised, and if they come in at more than five million, I'll renegotiate the prices. I figure I'll pay you whatever the appraiser says yours are worth."

"Wow. That's a lot of money, Chris," Danielle stammered.

"Yeah, well, I have a lot of money." Chris grinned.

"I think we have company," Walt said dryly.

Both Danielle and Chris turned in the direction Walt was looking. Clint Marlow stood at the doorway into the library, staring at Walt.

"I don't understand," Clint stammered, walking into the room, his attention still on Walt.

"I guess he didn't go back into his body," Chris said under his breath.

"Who are you?" Clint demanded of Walt, now standing just a few feet from the sofa. "And you can see me, like Danielle can."

Clint blinked his eyes in confusion, still staring at Walt. "You look just like me."

"Technically, you look just like me," Walt said.

Shaking his head, Clint backed away from the sofa. "I don't understand. Is this some kind of weird dream? Has this all been a dream?"

"I'd offer to pinch you, but in your state, you can't feel pinches." Walt waved his hand and a lit cigar appeared between two of his fingertips. He took a puff.

Still dazed, Clint took another step backwards and then looked over to Chris, who was staring at him. "You can see me?"

Chris smiled sympathetically at Clint. "Yes. I'm like Danielle; I can see spirits like you. And ghosts." He turned to Walt and added, "Ghosts like Walt here."

Walt glared at Chris and took another puff off the cigar.

"Walt? Walt Marlow...the one in the portrait?" Clint glanced over to Walt's life-sized portrait.

"I think he's starting to get it," Walt said.

"Yes. After your cousin, Walt Marlow, was killed in this house, his spirit never left. He's always been here, yet you couldn't see him before," Danielle explained. "But in the state you are in now, you can see him—just like Chris and I can."

Clint looked back to Danielle. "If my cousin has been haunting Marlow House all these years, and you can see him, why did you tell me I had to go back in my body?"

"Because unlike me, you aren't dead," Walt told his cousin.

"Then why did Stephanie have to leave me?" Clint asked. "Why didn't she stay with me?"

"I don't think she had a choice," Chris told him.

Clint turned to Walt and said, "Danielle told me there's another place after this. A place where Stephanie went."

Walt met Clint's gaze and arched his brow. "And?"

"Why are you here and not there?"

"It's complicated," Danielle said. "Not everyone's path is the same."

"If that's true, then why did you tell me I had to go back in my body and not follow Stephanie?"

"Because that's how it works," she said impatiently.

"No. You just said everyone's path is not the same. If Stephanie had to go, and Walt got to stay, then I don't see why I can't refuse to reconnect with my body and move on."

"You can try that, but I don't think it's going to work out for you," Chris muttered.

TWENTY-FIVE

C lint did not linger at Marlow House arguing about his choices. He vanished, leaving the three wondering what he intended to do. Danielle called Lily to tell her what had been going on, and it was agreed that Lily and Ian would pick up Chinese food later and bring it to Marlow House for dinner. Also invited to the impromptu Wednesday evening meal were Heather Donovan and Chris.

Heather showed up wearing black leggings, black knee-high boots, and a long black, cowl-neck sweater. Instead of the traditional braids or pigtails she frequently wore, tonight her dark hair was down, freshly washed, falling silky and smooth past her shoulders, with her straight-cut bangs covering her eyebrows. Chris showed up wearing what he had been wearing earlier that day.

The five friends sat in the living room of Marlow House, eating Chinese food from paper containers and off paper plates. Walt was there too, but unlike the rest, smoking instead of eating.

Ian and Lily had brought Sadie with them. To leave her at home would have disappointed Walt. Before settling down on Walt's feet, the golden retriever made the rounds, her curious nose sniffing for food while her tail wagged. Yet no one seemed inclined to sneak her a bite. It wasn't Ian's stern, *"Sadie, go lie down!"* that got her to curl up by Walt. It was when in the next moment Walt told her, "I doubt you'll even like Chinese food," that she stopped begging. Of course, Ian assumed she had acquiesced because of his command.

Sitting on a chair, Heather held a small take-out container in one hand and a pair of chopsticks in the other. She wrestled chow mien with the ends of her chopsticks, determined to eat her dinner without the assistance of a fork. While struggling with her food, she asked, "How exactly is Clint supposed to get back in his body?"

Chris and Lily—each of whom had had that experience—exchanged glances and shrugged. "It's kind of hard to explain," Chris said.

"Then how does Danielle expect Clint to just reconnect with his body?" Heather shoveled some chow mien into her mouth and made a slurping sound.

"I think the main thing is just understanding what has happened," Lily said. "After that, it's…well, intuitive."

"Rather like a spirit who understands how to move on after he finally grasps the fact he is dead," Chris added.

After chewing and swallowing her food, Heather said, "I can't imagine just leaving my body unsupervised. Didn't Eva say when you do that, another spirit can jump into it? And heck, his body is in the ICU, and I imagine there are spirits coming and going there, some who would love a fresh body to jump into."

Lily cringed. "That thought kinda gives me the creeps. It makes me think of wearing someone else's unwashed underwear."

About to take a bite of food, Danielle paused. Setting her chopsticks down on her paper plate, she frowned at her best friend. "Seriously, Lily? I'm trying to eat here."

Lily giggled sheepishly. "Sorry, Dani."

Rolling her eyes, Danielle shook her head, picked her chopsticks up, and resumed eating.

A new thought suddenly occurred to Heather. She looked at Walt and blurted, "Why don't you take Clint's body? After all, he doesn't want it."

Walt shivered at the thought and shook his head. "What Lily said."

Lily stopped eating and looked to where she believed Walt stood. "Could Walt do that?"

"I think your underwear analogy summed up Walt's feelings on the subject," Chris told Lily.

"Just when I thought my life couldn't get any weirder," Ian muttered, "we start talking about body swapping."

Their conversation was interrupted when the doorbell rang.

Danielle stood up and set her plate on the coffee table. "I'll get that."

Sadie jumped up and started to follow Danielle into the hallway when Ian called her back. Reluctantly, the dog returned to the living room.

WHEN DANIELLE OPENED her front door a few moments later, she found herself looking into the face of Macbeth Bandoni, aka Jim Hill. His appearance startled her, yet not as much as the fact he was not alone. Standing next to him were three large men. She suspected they were the same men who had helped swap the portraits while she was at the restaurant the night before.

"Jim...oh...this is a surprise," Danielle stammered, making no attempt to invite him inside. She glanced nervously into the house, toward the doorway leading to the living room. She could hear the faint voices and laughter of her friends. Danielle briefly wished Ian hadn't called Sadie back into the living room. She looked back to Macbeth and forced a smile.

"I just heard the news. Is it true?" Jim asked.

"I'm afraid so." Danielle continued to stand in the doorway, her right hand clutching the edge of the front door, blocking Jim's entrance into the house. "Their car went off the side of the road and over a cliff. The police think Stephanie might have swerved to avoid an animal on the highway. They said she died on impact. But Clint, well, he's in the local hospital, in the ICU. The last I heard, he was still unconscious."

"And the paintings?" Macbeth asked.

"Returning to the scene of the crime?" Walt said when he appeared—only visible to Danielle.

Danielle relaxed, no longer nervous now that Walt was by her side.

"The paintings?" Danielle asked innocently.

"I know it may seem insensitive of me to ask, but I did put my heart and soul into those paintings. An artist always has an emotional attachment to his work, even if it's just a reproduction of another artist's creation. I have to know; did they survive the crash?"

Instead of answering his question, Danielle smiled sweetly and said, "You haven't introduced me to your friends."

Macbeth glanced briefly to the men at his side and then back to Danielle. "They're my cousins; they live in Oregon. I stopped to see them after I left here this morning." He then rattled off their names so quickly that had Danielle been asked to repeat them ten minutes later, she would have been unable to. The men nodded their hellos, yet made no attempt to shake her hand when Macbeth introduced them.

"From what I understand, the crate wasn't hurt in the crash. It was still locked and in the back of the van when the paramedics arrived. I have no idea if the paintings inside were damaged at all," Danielle said.

"Where is the crate now? I thought they might have brought it back here. If so, I was wondering if I could check on them—just to make sure the paintings are okay. I'm afraid they might have shifted in the crate during the impact. With fresh paint like that, one of them could easily get damaged if the other one managed to get loose." Macbeth flashed Danielle an insincere smile.

"No, they aren't here. Not sure why you imagined they would be. The police have them. Anyway, without the key, you really couldn't get in the crate."

"You're such a brat," Walt said with a chuckle. "You know he has his own key. Although, I don't imagine one of his *cousins* would have a problem breaking that lock."

"WHO WAS AT THE DOOR?" Lily asked when Danielle returned to the living room a few minutes later.

"Jim Macbeth," Danielle told her. "And he had three intimidating men with him. According to Walt, they were the same men who helped switch the paintings."

Ian stood up from his chair and set his paper plate of food on the game table. He walked over to the front window and pulled the curtains to one side. It was dark out, but he could see the lights from a vehicle pulling away from the front of Marlow House.

"What did they want?" Chris asked.

"The paintings, of course," Walt said.

"The paintings?" Lily asked.

"I told them the police have them." Danielle sat back down on the sofa and picked up her plate of food.

"I wonder what they're going to think when it's announced the Bonnet paintings are now at the museum—under heavy guard," Chris said.

IT WAS quiet in Marlow House. Everyone had gone home. Only Walt, Danielle, and Max remained. Max, who had slept through dinner in the attic, was now awake but downstairs sitting on the windowsill in the living room, looking outside, with his head and upper body sandwiched between the curtain and windowpane, and his tail swishing back and forth on the living room side of the curtain.

Danielle had taken a quick shower and shampooed her hair. Now with it shorter, it seemed an easier task. After drying off, she slipped on a pair of fleece pajama bottoms—white with red hearts —and a red T-shirt. Since one of her earliest encounters with Walt, she had made a habit of dressing and undressing in her bathroom. It was because of a bargain she and Walt had struck right after she had moved to Marlow House. Walt had promised never to intrude on her privacy when she was in any of the bathrooms. It was comforting knowing some pervy ghost wasn't going to suddenly appear in her shower when she was bathing.

She didn't have a problem with Walt showing up in her bedroom at night when she was getting ready to turn in. In fact, she had come to expect it. In some ways, she felt like they were an old married couple, who in the evenings, before going to sleep, would lie side by side, hashing over the day's events.

Marie, who had decided to delay continuing on her journey and instead hang around as a spirit, wasn't aware of their nightly ritual. However, she had expressed her disapproval of Walt popping in and out of Danielle's bedroom whenever he felt like it. Fortunately for Walt and Danielle, Marie enjoyed going out in the evenings. And after spending much of the last two weeks helping Walt look after the portraits, she was looking forward to getting away from Marlow House for a while.

Danielle was just climbing into bed when Walt appeared in the room.

"I'm sorry you aren't getting your birthday wish," he told her.

Danielle scooted over to one side of the bed, making room for Walt.

"You mean because your cousin hasn't actually left Frederickport?" Leaning against a pile of pillows, she crossed her arms over her chest and watched as Walt took the place next to her.

"Yes." He settled on the bed, his arms crossed over his chest in the same manner as Danielle's crossed over hers.

"Are you alright with Chris buying your portraits?" he asked.

"You mean *your* portraits. Frankly, I'm a little surprised you're okay with it," Danielle said.

Walt shrugged. "To be honest, I'm not particularly attached to them. I'd like to think I'm not such a narcissist that I need to have a life-sized portrait of myself, and as for Angela's—to be honest, I'll be happy to get that out of the house."

"I had no idea you felt that way." Danielle studied Walt. "And you were so adamant about not selling them to Clint."

"It was the principle of it all. He was cocky to assume you would practically hand them over to him. As if it were his right."

"About Clint…" Danielle uncrossed her arms and scooted down a bit on the pillows. She looked over at Walt.

"About Clint, what?"

"Oh…I was thinking about what Heather suggested. Have you…well…do you ever wish you could be alive again?"

"Just every day," he whispered.

It was quiet for a few moments. Finally, Danielle asked, "Are you ever tempted…I mean…knowing Clint is wandering around… leaving his body vulnerable…look what happened to Kent."

"Tempted?" Walt shook his head. "No. It would be wrong. And I don't need that crime on my soul."

TWENTY-SIX

D anielle opened her eyes and looked down. She was standing in
the basket of a hot-air balloon, travelling down the Oregon
coast. In the distance she could see Ian and Lily's house, and beyond
that was Marlow House. She could see where Heather lived and
Chris's beach house. And there was the pier. Glancing to her right,
she saw she was not alone. Walt stood next to her in the basket as
they glided south.

"Happy birthday," Walt greeted. He wore what he had been
wearing when Danielle went to bed—gray slacks and a white shirt.
Yet now the sleeves were no longer pushed to his elbows, but down
and buttoned at the wrists.

Danielle wore a long floral cotton dress in pastels; it fluttered in
the breeze.

"It's not my birthday," she said with a smile, watching the coast
move by.

"Yes, it is. This dream hop started right after midnight. Technically, it's your birthday."

"This is nice. Thanks, Walt." She flashed him a smile.

"I feel bad I couldn't get you a real birthday gift."

Grinning at Walt, she asked, "What are you talking about?
Because of you I'm probably getting over ten million dollars for my
birthday. Heck, the most birthday money I used to ever get was a
hundred bucks from my parents."

Walt chuckled. "So what are you going to do with all that money?"

Resting her hands on the rim of the balloon basket, she looked out over the ocean. "Eventually give it away, I suppose."

"Chris says if he can work it out, he plans to pick up the paintings in the morning. I think that's a good idea."

Danielle nodded. "I have to agree. Especially since Macbeth resurfaced. I know he thinks the Bonnets are locked up in that crate and not in our library, but it still makes me uncomfortable thinking of them here while he's hanging around with those thug cousins of his. Of course, I doubt they're even his cousins."

They were silent for a moment, each lost in his and her private thoughts. Finally, Walt asked, "What do you really want to do for your birthday?"

Danielle shrugged. "It's just another day."

"No. It's your birthday."

Danielle considered the question a moment and then said, "I really don't want to do it now, but I'd like to go dancing again. Maybe you could take me dancing in another dream hop."

"The Charleston again?" he asked.

"No...I was thinking, what about ballroom dancing?" She looked over to Walt. "Do you know how to ballroom dance?"

"Are you trying to insult me, Miss Boatman? A gentleman of my breeding always knows how to do such things," he said in mock seriousness. He then added, "But the question is, do you know how to? While my firsthand knowledge of your generation is limited, I don't see much ballroom dancing on the television shows I've watched."

Danielle laughed. "When I was younger—back when Cheryl was heavily into the beauty pageants thing—which was practically my entire childhood—my mother was always signing me up for random classes. One year it was ballet, another ballroom dancing. I think she was determined to make me into a little beauty princess like her niece."

"Then ballroom dancing it is."

"I guess if we're to count our blessings—as my grandma used to say—if you were alive, we wouldn't be able to have dream hops where you take me ballroom dancing."

"Who needs a dream hop in real life? Isn't there anywhere where you can go ballroom dancing these days?" he asked.

Danielle shrugged. "I suppose there is."

"We could even go up in a hot-air balloon."

Danielle laughed and shook her head. "No. That is something we most definitely could not do."

"And why is that?"

"Because I'm afraid of heights. No way in the world would you ever get me up in a real hot-air balloon." Danielle shivered at the thought.

"Oh, I suspect I might be able to get you up in one. I think the trick is being able to look down, and you seem to be mastering that without a problem."

"Maybe. But I know if I fall out of this balloon, I'll just wake up in my bed—or, the very worst, on my bedroom floor. If I fall out of a real one, well…then I move over to your side, and since that would mean you are on my side, it would be kinda lonely."

Walt looked at Danielle and chuckled. "I can't believe I actually understood what you just said."

Danielle flashed Walt a wistful smile and then looked back out to the ocean. After a moment of silence, she said in a quiet voice, "I have to admit, ever since Heather asked you about taking Clint's body, I have been fantasizing a bit about what it would be like to have you alive. You wouldn't be confined to the house. We could really walk on the pier together—or down to the beach, not to mention travel. I could show you what the world looks like now—beyond television, in real life."

"Don't think I haven't thought about it. But the fact is, even if Clint said, '*Here, take my body. I don't want it*'—something I don't think he's going to say, and even if he did, I believe it would be taking advantage of him while he was emotionally vulnerable—there are other complications to consider."

Now leaning back against the rim of the basket, her arms crossed over her chest, Danielle looked up to Walt. "Such as?"

"For one thing, I have no desire to be a real estate agent."

Danielle laughed. "Why would you have to be a real estate agent?"

"I have to assume that in your time, as in mine, a person still has to make a living. Clint is a real estate agent."

"Why would you have to do what he did?" Danielle frowned. "Anyway, you have plenty of money. You could do whatever you want."

"The last time I looked, they didn't bury my money with me."

"Don't be silly, Walt. Marlow House would still be your home. And the money from Brianna would really be yours."

Walt looked at her and shook his head. "No, Danielle, that's yours now."

"Don't be ridiculous. After all, there's more than enough money for both of us."

"We really don't need to argue about something that will never happen. Let's just enjoy your balloon ride. Or I'll have to push you out of the basket." Walt smiled at Danielle, his blue eyes twinkling.

CHIEF MACDONALD HADN'T BEEN to the office for more than five minutes on Thursday morning when he was informed there was someone who needed to talk to him: Jim Hill. It took a moment for MacDonald to recognize the name. Then he remembered. It was the artist, the one whose real name was Macbeth Bandoni.

The moment Macbeth entered the chief's office, he extended his hand and said, "Hello, Chief MacDonald, we met at Marlow House on Tuesday night. I'm Jim Hill, the artist Clint Marlow commissioned to copy the Marlow paintings."

Standing up, the chief walked around his desk and shook the man's hand. "Of course." The handshake ended and the chief motioned to one of the chairs facing his desk.

"I've come to talk to you about my paintings," Macbeth said, taking a seat.

"Your paintings?" MacDonald sat down behind his desk. Leaning forward, he rested his elbows on his desktop and studied Macbeth, who seemed nervous. Considering what the chief knew about the man, he understood why.

"Yes. I think of them as mine."

The chief smiled. "Of course. Because you painted them?"

"Yes. That and the fact Clint hasn't paid for them yet. So, technically, they really are mine."

The chief leaned back in his chair, folding his arms across his chest. "I seem to recall, when we were loading the paintings, you mentioned he had already paid you for them."

Macbeth shook his head. "I know I said that, but the truth is, he just paid a small down payment."

"You said you wanted to talk about the paintings. What about?"

"I understand you have them."

"I don't personally have them. I assume you heard about the accident?"

"Yes. I...I heard about it on the news. I stopped by Marlow House yesterday afternoon, and Danielle mentioned the police had removed the crate from the van."

"You stopped by Marlow House in the afternoon? I thought you headed home yesterday morning. How did you return to Marlow House so quickly?" The chief leaned forward again, pulling his chair closer to the desk. Picking up a pencil, he absently tapped its eraser against the desktop while waiting for an answer.

"I...I didn't head home after leaving Marlow House yesterday morning. I stopped to visit some family I have in Astoria. I was there when I heard the news," Macbeth explained.

"As for an answer to your questions, yes. We have the crate. It's in storage along with Clint Marlow's other personal belongings."

"I was hoping I could pick it up—since I'm technically the rightful owner."

"You are aware Clint is still alive, aren't you?"

Macbeth nodded. "Yes. I called the hospital this morning, but they wouldn't tell me how he was doing. According to Danielle, he was still unconscious yesterday. But I am praying that he will come out of this and then be able to go home."

MacDonald arched a brow. "Yet you want to take his paintings?"

"Like I said, they belong to me. I painted them. And aside from a very small deposit, I haven't been paid for my work."

"Unfortunately for you, this is something you will need to work out with Clint after he comes out of this. And if for some reason he doesn't make it, then I suppose you'll need to work this out with his estate."

"You don't understand, Chief MacDonald. I'm doing this for Clint. Because I care about him."

The chief frowned. "And how is that?"

Macbeth let out a sigh and sat back in his chair. He looked to the chief and smiled sadly. "You see, the only reason Clint wanted those paintings was for Stephanie. If you knew Clint, you would know he absolutely adored her. She meant everything to him. He told me numerous times he didn't really want the paintings—he called them *gross monstrosities*."

"Then why did he commission you to copy them?"

"Like I said, it was because of Stephanie. It was something she wanted. From what Clint told me, he showed her Marlow House's website, and when she saw the portraits, she wanted them. She was so disappointed when Danielle refused to sell them to Clint. That's when he came up with the idea to hire me. Stephanie loved the idea."

"I still don't understand why you believe I should turn them over to you."

"Because with Stephanie gone, I know Clint won't want them. It will be a painful reminder of his loss. And then, to add insult to injury, he still owes me for them. I'm doing this for Clint—to make it easier on him. He won't have to deal with any of it when he comes out of the hospital."

"That's very generous of you, Mr. Hill." The chief grinned.

Macbeth perked up. "Then you'll give them to me?"

"No."

"No? But you just said—"

"I'm sorry, Mr. Hill." The chief stood up. "But legally, I can't turn those paintings over to you. Perhaps you could get a court order, prove to the court they belong to you. But as it stands, no. No, I'm sorry." The chief wasn't really sorry.

Macbeth stood. "Can I at least see them? Make sure they weren't damaged? If one came loose in the crate, it could damage the other one."

"Don't worry, Mr. Hill. We already checked on the paintings. There was a key in Stephanie's purse. We used it to unlock the crate. And you have nothing to worry about. The paintings were sitting perfectly in it—just as I helped you put them in there on Tuesday."

TWENTY-SEVEN

T he library looked larger now that one corner was no longer dominated by the two life-sized portraits. Danielle stared at the space and felt a pang of regret.

"I wish Bonnet wasn't a famous artist," she muttered.

"Why do you say that?" Walt asked. They were alone in the room.

Still staring at the space, she shrugged. "I didn't realize how attached I was to the paintings. I'll confess, I'll miss yours more than Angela's." She turned to Walt and gave him a half smile.

"Why would you miss mine? After all, you see me all the time."

Danielle studied Walt a moment. Today he wore his blue three-piece pin-striped suit. He even had the jacket on. She suspected her birthday was the occasion for his more formal appearance. She took note of his incredible blue eyes and found it utterly bizarre that Clint had the very same eyes.

"Danielle, you didn't answer my question."

Jolted from her momentary lapse into daydreaming, Danielle smiled sheepishly and turned from Walt. She took a seat on the sofa, pulling her bare feet up on the cushions and tucking them under her. "You're here now. But you won't always be. And when you're gone, well, I won't even have your portrait."

Walt sat down in a chair across from Danielle. "I'm not going anywhere."

Cocking her head slightly to one side, she studied Walt. "So you're going to stick around until I move to your side?"

"I certainly am not going to stick around if you aren't here. But now that I think about it, when you get married and start a family, I don't imagine your husband will appreciate me hanging around. I know I wouldn't if I was him."

Danielle laughed. "There you are, trying to marry me off again."

"Let's not talk about this. It's your birthday. What do you want to do?"

"You're right. It's my birthday. What do I want to do? I want to talk about this."

Walt let out a sigh and waved his right hand. A lit cigar appeared between two of his fingers. He took a drag and then blew out a series of smoke rings.

"Have you ever seen *The Ghost and Mrs. Muir* on television?" Danielle asked. "The movie, not the old television series."

"I avoid anything with *ghost* in the title. Why?" He took another puff and blew out more smoke rings.

"It's an old classic, really. I rather liked shows like that when I was a kid. *Topper*, *Casper*—anything with a friendly gh—spirit." Danielle grinned. "I found them rather comforting considering my...umm...gift. Of course, not all spirits are as charming or harmless in real life—or death."

"Why did you ask me about *The Ghost and Mrs. Muir* movie?"

"In the movie, Mrs. Muir is a widow—but unlike me, she has children—and moves into an old house. Also on the coast, but I believe it was the east coast. The ghost of a handsome sea captain is in residence. And they..." Danielle paused a moment and then frowned. "Never mind. It was just an old movie. Not sure why I mentioned it."

"Could it be because Mrs. Muir and the sea captain fell in love?" Clint Marlow asked from the doorway.

Danielle turned abruptly toward the newcomer. "How long have you been standing there? And why aren't you at the hospital?"

Clint walked into the room, his hands tucked into the pockets of his slacks. He wandered over to the empty chair next to Walt and sat down. Walt watched his cousin, yet said nothing.

"It seems you two are in the same situation as Stephanie and me." His hands no longer in his pockets, Clint leaned back in the chair, crossed one leg over the opposing knee, and folded his hand over one trousered thigh.

"What are you talking about?" Danielle asked.

"It's pretty obvious." Clint glanced from Walt to Danielle and smiled. "You two are in love. But one of you is alive—the other is a ghost."

"I find the term *ghost* rather grating," Walt noted.

"Grating or not, it's what you are, cousin." Clint chuckled and added, "I noticed neither of you disagreed with my assertion about you two being in love."

"Why are you here?" Walt asked.

"Being that I'm in limbo and not prepared to rejoin the living, I thought I'd come back and ask Danielle a few questions."

"Questions about what?" Danielle asked.

"I was curious; when did you realize the portraits were valuable? Was it when Walt caught Mac changing them? Mac is Jim's real name."

"Actually, Mac's real name is Macbeth," Danielle corrected.

Clint chuckled. "So you know about that too?"

"It was Ian, actually. He recognized him the first night you were here," Danielle explained. "That got us to look a little closer at the paintings, and after Angela told us the artist's real name, we were able to find out who he was."

Clint frowned. "Angela? Walt's wife? The one in the portrait." He sat there a moment, processing the information. When it finally clicked what Danielle was talking about, he shook his head and let out a bitter laugh. "Good lord, I never had a chance of stealing those paintings, did I?"

"Not really. So tell me, is this something you do a lot?" Danielle asked.

"What? Art theft?" Clint asked.

Danielle nodded.

"Hardly. My father used to say, if you're going to be a thief, it better be worth it. For the record, I don't imagine my father stole a thing in his life. His point, I believe, was that if you're ready to risk everything, then the payoff better be more than a few thousand bucks."

"Does this mean there is a monetary minimum on your heists?" Walt asked.

"I've never stolen anything before."

"So why this time?" Danielle asked.

With a sigh, Clint slumped back in the chair. He uncrossed and re-crossed his legs. "I'd come to hate my job. There is a reason they say buyers are liars. And sellers aren't much better. Don't even get me started on other real estate agents, incompetent imbeciles!"

"So you hated your job. Why not just find another career?" Danielle asked.

"Like what? I never went to college. I've been doing this since I was eighteen."

"What made you decide to become an art thief?" Walt asked.

Clint looked at Walt a moment and then smiled. "Don't act so superior. Maybe this is in my genes. I've read about how you stole that necklace from your friend. At least I don't steal from friends."

"Should I be insulted?" Danielle grumbled under her breath and then added, "Walt didn't steal the Missing Thorndike for himself."

Clint shrugged. "Frankly I don't care why he stole it. I just find it amusing he's so judgmental over all this, considering what he did."

"It doesn't really matter what Walt may have done. We were talking about you. Why did you decide to become an art thief?" Danielle asked.

Clint studied Danielle a moment before answering. Finally, he shrugged and said, "The only thing going right in my life was Stephanie. But I hated my job, and my broker was a jerk. I caught him stealing a couple of my clients. Take my advice, never work for a competing broker."

"Why the Bonnets?" Danielle asked.

Clint drew in a breath and then let it out before continuing. "When that other real estate agent sent me a link to your page, I didn't pay much attention at first. Like I said in one of my emails, I really didn't care about family history. Stephanie and I had decided not to have kids. Neither of us wanted them. So what would I care about a bunch of dead people I just happened to share DNA with?"

"Indeed," Walt muttered, taking another puff off his cigar.

"I told Stephanie about the website, and she asked to see it. She's the one who opened the webpage showing pictures of your portraits. I hadn't opened that page when I first went to your site. She was immediately fascinated by Walt's portrait and the likeness to me. Out of curiosity, she enlarged the image, trying to find the name of the artist. Stephanie was an art major in college, so she was always interested in that sort of stuff."

"Did she recognize the artist immediately?" Danielle asked.

Clint shook his head. "No. Neither of us could figure out the artist's name by the signature on the painting. We just figured that whoever it was, was basically a talented nobody, considering you didn't mention anything about him on your site."

"And then you went to the Bonnet art show?" Danielle asked.

Clint frowned. "How did you know?"

"During Ian's research, he discovered there had been a Bonnet art show in your area right before you sent me that first email. We assumed that's how you figured out the paintings' worth."

"Steph and I went to that show, and she almost flipped out. She recognized his style immediately, but the signature—that clinched it. That's when we decided to email you and offer to buy them."

"You mean steal them," Walt said.

"No. Maybe take advantage of the fact you had no clue what you had. But all perfectly legal. After Stephanie read my emails to you, she was kind of annoyed with me. Said I would get more bees with honey. Claimed I was too abrupt in my emails." He shrugged. "After you refused to sell them, we came up with a plan to steal them."

"How did you find Macbeth?" Danielle asked.

"During college, Steph had worked for a museum and had read about Macbeth Bandoni. It wasn't too hard to find him online. He agreed to do the paintings and find a buyer, and we agreed to take him on as our partner."

"He was here yesterday, trying to find the paintings," Danielle told him.

Clint chuckled. "I'm not surprised. Did you tell him you switched the paintings back?"

"No. For one thing, the Bonnets were sitting in this room at the time, and Macbeth had three burly men by his side."

"Ahh, you mean his cousins?" Clint asked.

Danielle frowned. "They really are his cousins?"

Clint nodded. "Yes. That's how Stephanie tracked Bandoni down. She found an article about his cousins. They live in Astoria. We thought that was a sign. I mean, imagine that? Bandoni's cousins live just a stone's throw from Marlow House."

CLINT HAD BEEN MILDLY curious as to what Danielle had known about his plot to steal her portraits. Now that he had the answers, he had no reason to hang around Marlow House. He didn't find her any more interesting than when they had first met. As for his distant cousin Walt, he found it rather creepy being in the same room with him. It wasn't just because he was a ghost, it was that Walt had his face. Clint didn't understand how identical twins dealt with that. He cringed at the thought.

Just as he stepped onto the sidewalk in front of Marlow House, a bright light appeared before him. He froze, wondering for a moment if perhaps his body had died back at the hospital and this was the portal to take him to his Stephanie.

Yet, instead of a doorway into forever, the light swirled about, sending glitter like rain bursting in all directions. Just as the light faded, a beautiful woman appeared before him, her pale blue chiffon dress fluttering in the breeze.

"Are you an angel?" he gasped in surprise.

She looked him up and down and said, "I'm no more an angel than you are Walt Marlow."

TWENTY-EIGHT

"Who are you?" Clint asked. They continued to stand on the sidewalk in front of Marlow House.

She smiled and waved her right hand to one side, sending more glitter into the air before it vanished. "My name is Eva Thorndike."

"What are you?" he asked.

"I suppose I am a ghost." She twirled around merrily, her hands waving gently in the air, while releasing more glitter. She reminded him of a fairy godmother from a Disney movie. Not the plump one from Cinderella, a more glamourous one. When he shared that observation with her, she stopped twirling and then laughed.

"In some ways I am a fairy godmother. You might say I'm yours, in a manner of speaking."

He frowned. "I don't understand."

"I've come to help you, Clint Marlow."

"How do you know who I am?" he asked. "And a moment ago you mentioned my cousin, Walt Marlow."

"I'm a close friend of your cousin. Walt and I grew up together."

"Eva Thorndike!" he gasped when recognition dawned. "You're that actress, the one Walt stole the necklace from."

Eva gave a little curtsy and then said, "At your service. And, in fairness to dear Walt, he only took my necklace because I asked him to. Unlike you, who were prepared to take something without the

169

owner's permission." She gave a little tsk-tsk sound and shook her head.

"You know about that?" he asked.

"Of course. Everyone knows. At least, everyone who matters."

He frowned. "I don't understand. And why did you say you were my fairy godmother?"

"I said in a manner of speaking. I'm not really your fairy godmother." Eva glanced around and then pointed toward the other side of the street. "Come, we need to talk somewhere else. I really don't need Walt to look out the window and wonder what I'm up to. At least, not yet."

Too curious to refuse, Clint followed Eva across the street and through the opening between Ian's yard and his neighbor's until they were on the beach behind Ian and Lily's house.

"Clint Marlow, I must say you failed the test," Eva announced.

"What test?" He frowned.

"It's a matter of character," she told him. "Yours is seriously lacking."

"Is this about me trying to steal the portraits?" he asked.

Eva shook her head. "That's only part of it. You aren't a bad person, yet you do seem to be utterly incapable of embracing this gift called life. You're not really fighting for yours, are you?"

"What's the point? The only person I ever loved is gone. I just want to go with her."

They were interrupted by a dog barking. Eva looked toward Ian and Lily's house and watched as a golden retriever came racing in her direction. She smiled and leaned down to greet the dog.

"Ah, Sadie, it is so nice to see you," Eva cooed.

Clint looked back to the house and saw Lily, hands on hips, her red hair pulled up casually in a high ponytail, watching the golden retriever, who was excitedly greeting Eva. By Lily's expression and Clint's knowledge on how this all seemed to work, he was certain Lily could not see Eva or himself. He wondered what Lily must be thinking, considering her dog's behavior.

After Sadie greeted Eva, she looked at Clint and cocked her head from side to side. She then started barking—not a friendly bark.

"You're right, Sadie. It isn't Walt," Eva told her.

"Sadie! Come!" Lily called from the house.

"Go, girl," Eva told the dog, pointing toward Lily.

With a final bark, Sadie turned around and raced back to the house. A moment later she went inside with Lily.

"The dog could see us," Clint muttered.

"Yes, most dogs and cats can. Some other animals too, yet I've found not all of them are able to." Eva shrugged.

"Why do you want to talk to me?" Clint asked.

"Come. Let's walk. I love walking along the ocean."

Clint fell in step with Eva as the two strolled leisurely down the beach, the skirt of Eva's long dress fluttering in the breeze. Clint glanced down and noticed she was barefoot. He was certain she had been wearing shoes when she had first appeared in front of Marlow House.

"You need to make a decision, Clint Marlow. Your body is waiting for you."

"I don't want to go on. I want to be with Stephanie. There's nothing here for me anymore."

"I heard you considered going back in your body—and then killing yourself."

"Did Danielle tell you that?"

She shook her head. "No."

"Then how did you know?"

"It doesn't matter. I just do."

He shrugged. "Well, it seemed like the easiest solution at the time. But Danielle said it wasn't a good idea."

"Danielle's right. The Universe takes unkindly to those who squander precious gifts like life."

"Universe?" he asked with a frown. "Isn't there a god?"

She glanced to him. "Why do you suggest there's no God?"

"You said universe, so I just thought..." He shrugged.

"It's all semantics anyway," Eva said. "You'll eventually understand more about God and the Universe when you're ready."

"Maybe I'm ready now. I want to move on."

"When you say you want to move on in the same sentence as suicide, that is beyond troubling. While the Universe might be more understanding and forgiving of those suffering a debilitating disease, great emotional pain, or mental illness—your motivation seems more self-centered—self-serving."

"So what do I do? Go back and live my life and be miserable?"

Eva shrugged. "If you wish to be miserable, you will be. Or you can wander around half-dead, half-alive until your body finally gives up. Yet, that in itself is almost as bad as suicide, considering it produces the same outcome—a waste of a life."

"So there really is no other choice?" He stopped walking and gazed out to the sea. If tears were possible, he would cry.

Eva stood several feet from Clint, studying him. Finally, she said, "There is one option open to you."

Clint looked to her. "There is?"

"If you found a spirit—someone who was cheated out of life and is as stubborn as you, in that the spirit has refused to continue on in his journey, just as you have refused to return to your life— give your body to him. Once he accepts the gift, you will be free to move on—and free of any penance you might have suffered for your actions prior to death."

"Someone else can take my body? That is actually possible?"

Eva nodded. "Yes, it is. But it is a tricky thing. There have been rare cases of wandering spirits hijacking the comatose body of a confused spirit. While they might believe at that moment they have found a way to cheat death, they eventually learn after the body dies —and all bodies eventually die—that there is a hefty penance to pay. For claiming an unwilling body is tantamount to murder. However, if the original inhabitant of the body—a spirit so opposed to life— turns it over to another spirit—one who was previously cheated out of life—the Universe considers that a matter of setting things right."

"How do I find a spirit willing to take over my body? Hang out at the morgue? The cemetery?"

"Are you seriously asking that question? You really don't know?"

Clint stared at Eva for several moments, allowing her words to sink in. "You're talking about my cousin, Walt Marlow!" he blurted.

"Of course. Isn't it the obvious solution? His adjustment to your body would be minimal. After all, when he looks in the mirror— something he can't do now—he will see himself. Or at least it will look just like the man he remembers from his first life. Even your name is the same. Your real name is Walter Clint, as is his."

"He wouldn't be me."

"No. He would be himself. You would be no more. You would be with Stephanie."

"I don't know," he said with a frown, shaking his head in disbe-lief. "It just seems…wrong."

"Not as wrong as you killing yourself!"

"It's my body. It would feel strange having someone else…use it like that. People would think it was me."

"What people? You have no friends."

He glared at Eva.

"It's true," she said calmly. "You don't."

Shaking his head, he muttered, "I have to go." In the next moment he vanished.

Now standing alone on the beach, Eva let out a deep sigh. She looked up to the sky.

"This isn't how it was supposed to go!"

A moment later, still looking upwards, she said, "I understand, there are no guarantees. Yes, I know…*free will*."

JUST AFTER LUNCH, Danielle opened her door to find Adam Nichols standing on the front porch carrying what appeared to be a cake box. Instead of wearing a smile, his mouth twisted into a half smirk as he pushed his way past Danielle into the entry hall.

"Well, hello to you too," Danielle said wryly as she closed the door. Turning to Adam, she waited for an explanation for his odd behavior.

"I brought you a birthday cake," he announced, quickly opening the box for her to see the contents. While it was impossible to tell what kind of cake it was, the frosting appeared to be chocolate buttercream. Unable to resist, Danielle reached for the cake to swipe a taste of the frosting when Adam jerked the box away from her and shut it, holding it just out of her reach.

Danielle frowned. "Gosh, I thought you said you brought it for me?"

"I did. But for once, I don't think you should have your cake and eat it too. I'm going to make you watch me eat your entire birthday cake!" Adam marched toward the kitchen.

"What in the world?" Danielle shook her head but reluctantly followed Adam. She watched as he jerked open one of her kitchen drawers and snatched a fork. He then slammed the cake box on the kitchen table, sat down and roughly opened the box.

Speechless, Danielle watched while Adam jabbed the fork into the middle of the cake, and then he shoved the bite into his mouth, leaving frosting around the corners of his lips. Glaring at Danielle, Adam stared her in her eyes as he chewed.

Still perplexed, Danielle sat down at the table with Adam, her eyes never leaving his. After a moment of silence, Adam tossed the fork on the table, wiped the frosting off his mouth with the back of his hand, and then pushed the cake box toward Danielle.

He began to laugh. "Are you freaking kidding me? Over ten million dollars?"

Danielle grinned and then pulled the cake box toward her. She picked up Adam's fork and then wiped it off on the edge of the cardboard cakebox before helping herself to a bite.

"You heard about the portraits?" Danielle asked as she took her second bite.

"How do you do it, Danielle? You keep falling into money."

Danielle shrugged. "How did you find out?"

"It's all over town. Everyone is wondering where Chris put the paintings while they have the new section of the museum built—with added security."

"Hey, this is good cake." Danielle stood up and walked to the counter. She grabbed another fork from the silverware drawer and then filled two glasses with cold milk. She returned to the table and handed Adam a glass and a fork.

"I picked it up from Old Salts. That's where I heard the news."

"Ahhh…you were bringing me a birthday cake? How sweet," she cooed.

"It was for…well, later."

"You mean for my surprise party?" Danielle took another bite.

"How did you know?" he asked.

Danielle shrugged. "I figured Lily was up to something when she stopped asking me what I wanted to do for my birthday."

"I guess I'll need to pick up another cake for tonight," Adam grumbled as he took another bite.

TWENTY-NINE

C lint returned to the intensive care unit and stood by his hospital bed. He watched the steady breathing of the body that was his. Aside from the broken leg and stitched-up forehead, Clint begrudgingly admitted he looked relatively healthy. He laughed at the thought, finding it bizarre that he would come to a place where the prospect of a healthy body was a bad thing.

Eva's unorthodox solution stirred his emotions in a most unsettling manner. While he had contemplated suicide in order to be with Stephanie, he was surprised at the wave of possessiveness flooding over him when she mentioned turning his body over to Walt. Her initial suggestion—when she had been using abstracts—*no one specific spirit*—had not inspired any particular emotion. However, the moment she had suggested turning his body over to Walt, something inside him rebelled.

It reminded him a little of the time he was about to break up with his high school sweetheart, Julie Ann, and then discovered the captain of the football team had a crush on her. There was no way he was going to let him have her. Clint had ended up dating Julie Ann for six more months, until the football player started going steady with one of the cheerleaders. That was when Clint dumped Julie Ann.

Turning from the bed, Clint left the hospital again. He ended up back on Beach Drive, in front of Marlow House. To his relief, there was no sign of Eva Thorndike. Not wanting to deal with Walt or Danielle, he decided to stroll down to the pier. After he reached the pier, he headed back down the beach, ending up behind Ian and Lily's house. Bored, he decided to go in and have a look around.

He had forgotten about the dog and was quickly reminded of her when he entered the house from the back and found Sadie sleeping on the bed in what appeared to be the master bedroom. Not wanting to wake the dog and send her into another barking fit, he moved into the living room. The living room was empty. But then he heard voices from the kitchen. Curious, he decided to investigate.

"That darn Adam," Lily said as she emptied what appeared to be dry onion soup mix into a container of sour cream.

"What did Adam do now?" Ian asked. He stood across the kitchen from Lily, at the counter dicing up cheese into bite-size wedges.

"Dani knows about her surprise party." Lily angrily stirred the soup mix into the sour cream.

"He told her?"

"She said he didn't mean to. But I don't think he could resist. He heard about the portraits when he went to pick up the cake at the bakery."

"So?" Ian began organizing the cheese and crackers on a serving tray.

"He thought it would be funny to give her her birthday cake and tell her that for once she could have her cake and not eat it. He then started to eat the cake in front of her."

With a frown, Ian turned from the cutting board and faced Lily. "I don't get it."

Lily shrugged and placed the lid on the sour cream container. It barely fit with the addition of the soup mixture. "He was trying to be funny."

"Ahh...I get it." Ian nodded. "Yeah, I imagine about now Adam —along with most of Frederickport—is wondering if Danielle has some good-fortune fairy godmother following her around."

"Good-fortune fairy godmother?" Lily laughed. "I'm not sure I've ever heard of one of those before."

"If there is one, she's assigned to Danielle. That girl seems to fall into money at every turn. Two inheritances, the necklace, the gold coins, and now Chris is giving her over ten million for those paintings. Considering Danielle's moderate lifestyle, I'm not sure what she's ever going to do with all that money."

"It's true what they say, money can't buy happiness." Lily picked up the container of dip she had just made and set it in the refrigerator.

"You don't think Danielle's happy?" Ian asked.

"Sure, she's happy, I suppose. As happy as she can be considering the man she's in love with has been dead for almost a hundred years. No real future in that."

"You really think she's in love with Walt?"

Folding her arms over her chest and leaning back against the kitchen counter, Lily faced Ian and nodded. "I'm sure of it. I really thought for a while there she would have a future with Chris. Chris is a great guy. They have so much in common. They know each other's secrets; plus she never has to worry about Chris being after her money."

"I like Chris too. And I know he's crazy about her."

Lily let out a sigh. "But that thing with Walt keeps getting in the way of any real relationship."

"Did she tell you how she feels about Walt?" Ian asked.

"She doesn't have to tell me. It's all over her face. I know her too well."

"Maybe it would be best if Walt moved on," Ian suggested. "That way Danielle could get on with her life."

"Or maybe…maybe Heather was right earlier."

"Right about what?" He frowned.

"Clint doesn't want his body. I think Walt should march over to that hospital and just take it!"

Ian chuckled. "I don't think it would be that easy. And what would Walt do in our world? Yeah, he knows how to use a computer now, but how would he survive? What would he do?"

"He could do whatever he wants. Danielle is a rich woman, and most of that money was Walt's. He'd be a very rich man."

"Yes, he would…" Clint muttered.

A moment later Sadie came rushing into the kitchen. She went immediately to Clint and started barking. From Ian and Lily's perspective, the dog appeared to be barking at the wall. Sadie lowered her head and began to growl.

CLINT MADE a hasty departure from Ian and Lily's house. Instead of returning to the hospital, he perched atop Lily and Ian's roof and considered all that he had overheard in their kitchen. Nothing in this world was fair, he thought.

The woman Walt loved and who loved him back was alive. Walt's vast fortune remained intact. However, for Walt to truly be with the woman he loved and to enjoy his money was currently impossible. Unless, of course, Walt stepped into Clint's body.

Clint, on the other hand, had access to a viable body, yet the woman he loved had moved on, and most of his money was now gone. He had taken a hit after selling his condo. Foolishly he had purchased the property at the top of the market before real estate prices had plummeted. While prices had slowly inched upward during the past year, he had still been upside down in his loan, something that did not bother him at the close of escrow, as he had been counting on the money from the portraits and a new life in Paris with the woman he loved.

"If I have to wake up in my body again, I'd rather do it as my cousin," Clint said aloud. He then laughed. "Not so crazy about being stuck with Danielle Boatman, but all that money of hers would make life bearable."

Clint's thoughts wandered for a moment. He imagined what it would be like to wake up in his body and then convince Danielle he was really Walt reincarnated. "All that money," he said with a sigh. Unfortunately, there was one little hitch. It would be impossible to convince Danielle he was Walt while his cousin haunted the house.

The sun had set when cars began arriving in front of Marlow House. Ian and Lily had crossed the street earlier, with Sadie in tow, but Clint had failed to notice, as he was so engrossed in his own thoughts. Weary with contemplation, he began paying attention to what was going on across the street.

They're having a party. The thought made him bitter. It had just been a day since Stephanie's death. His body was lying in a hospital unconscious, and he had been a guest of Marlow House for two weeks. But did they show the slightest remorse? *No, they're having a freaking party,* he thought.

He continued to sit on the rooftop as the hours went by. Finally, people began coming out of Marlow House and getting into their vehicles. One by one the cars drove away. After the street in front of

Marlow House was empty again, Ian and Lily came outside with their dog and made their way across the street.

Lights went out in Marlow House. All except for the attic. Clint noticed a man's silhouette in the attic window.

"That's Walt," he muttered. "I need to talk to him."

———

"HELLO, COUSIN," Clint greeted him when he appeared in the attic.

Startled by Clint's sudden appearance, Walt turned to look at the man who looked like himself.

"Clint." Walt eyed his cousin curiously and took a seat on the sofa.

"We haven't had a chance to talk." Clint sat in the nearby folding chair and faced Walt.

"I'm not sure what we have to talk about." Walt waved a hand for a cigar.

"How do you do that?" Clint asked.

Walt glanced at the cigar. "This?"

Clint nodded.

Walt shrugged. "It's just one of the things I can do."

"Why haven't you moved on?" Clint asked.

"I'm just not ready. I will eventually." Walt took a puff off his cigar.

"You're in love with Danielle, aren't you? I can see it in your face. I imagine I look at Stephanie the way you look at Danielle."

"When are you going back in your body? What are you waiting for?" Walt asked.

"I told you before. I don't want to go back. I want to move on with Stephanie."

"I would like to be alive, but we don't always get what we want, do we? You might as well go back to your body and make the most of it. The longer you wait, the harder time you'll have getting your body back in shape. You're just making it worse for yourself."

"Maybe we can both get what we want." Clint smiled.

"What are you talking about?"

"You take my body. Once you do that, I'll be free to move on."

Walt's cigar vanished. Startled by the offer, Walt studied his cousin. "What makes you think that is even possible?"

"I spoke to your friend Eva. She tells me it's my only option if I want to move on. I need to find a spirit willing to move into my body, and you're the most obvious candidate."

"Eva told you that?" Walt frowned.

"Yes. Do you have any reason to believe she doesn't know what she's talking about?"

Walt considered the question a moment and then shook his head. "No. Not really. Eva tends to be—well, it may sound cliché— but a *free spirit*. As a spirit, she's seen far more of this world than I have and understands more about it than I do, which is understandable considering I'm confined to Marlow House."

Clint frowned. "What do you mean you're confined to Marlow House?"

With a wave of his hand another cigar appeared. "I wouldn't be able to do this, or—" the table next to the sofa lifted in the air and then settled back to the floor "—that, if I enjoyed the same freedom as Eva."

"Are you saying you can't leave Marlow House?" Clint asked.

"I can leave—I just can't come back once I do."

"What would happen to you?"

Walt flicked ashes from his cigar. Clint watched them vanish in midair.

"I suppose I'll move on, like Stephanie did."

"But you have to be able to leave here so you can go into my body!" Clint insisted.

"Go into his body?" said a female voice.

Both Clint and Walt turned to the open doorway and found Danielle standing there. She wore plaid flannel pajama bottoms, a solid blue T-shirt and a stunned expression on her face. By her side was Max, who looked from Clint to Walt, his black tail waving behind him.

"Yes. I'm trying to talk Walt into taking over my body," Clint told her.

"Excuse me. Did you say take over your body?" she stammered.

THIRTY

C lint stood up and looked from Danielle to Walt. "I'll leave you two alone to discuss this. But you need to come to a decision soon. I want to move on and be with Stephanie. Maybe you don't want my body, but I imagine there's someone out there who would jump at this second chance I'm offering. While you consider my proposal, I think I'll go back to the ICU and see if I can find any recently deceased spirits lingering somewhere in the hospital." The next moment he vanished.

"Do you think he's serious?" Danielle walked to Walt and sat next to him. Max jumped up on the sofa with them, settling between Danielle and Walt.

"I think he is," Walt murmured, his forehead drawn into a frown while he considered all that Clint had said.

"How did he even know this is a possibility?" Danielle asked.

"He told me Eva suggested it."

"Eva? He talked to Eva?"

"Apparently."

"Are you…well…considering it?" Danielle asked in a whisper.

"I know Heather spoke of this the other night, and I automatically dismissed it. Frankly, I never thought it was an option. And I would never take advantage of a confused spirit who might regret moving on. However, I do believe Clint is serious in that if it is not me, it will be someone else."

Danielle slumped back on the sofa. "Oh my goodness...this could be real."

They sat in silence for a moment. Finally, Walt let out a bitter laugh and flung his cigar into the air. It vanished. "Who am I kidding? I can't do this."

"Why not?" Danielle studied Walt a moment, tilting her head slightly. "This is about what you said last night, isn't it?"

"What do you mean?"

"You don't want to stay at Marlow House if you cross back over."

"You know I don't want to leave here. Lord, would I still be here if I wanted to leave?" Walt asked.

"Then what's the problem?"

"For starters, I wouldn't be me anymore."

Danielle frowned. "Yes, you would."

"Everyone would think I'm Clint. Wouldn't they find it a little strange if I stayed and then mooched off you?"

Danielle considered Walt's words and then smiled sheepishly. "Yeah, I see what you mean. I really didn't think that one through. But we could work it out. Anyway, most of our friends would know the truth."

"But not everyone," Walt reminded her.

"If it makes you feel any better, we could get you a job with the Glandon Foundation. You wouldn't really have to work, but everyone—those who didn't know the truth—wouldn't think you were unemployed."

Walt let out a snort. "Oh, I'm sure Chris would love that. In fact, I'm not sure Chris would be thrilled with any of this. In fact, I'm certain he won't be."

"Why not?" Danielle asked.

Walt studied Danielle and then asked in a whisper, "If I did this, what would it mean for us?"

"For us..." Danielle choked out.

"Things would change, Danielle. If I did accept my cousin's offer and then accepted yours and stayed here, I don't imagine we'd still have our nightly chats—in your bed."

Danielle's gaze met Walt's. After a prolonged silence she asked, "Why not?"

Walt smiled softly. He reached out to brush a strand of hair from her eyes but stopped when he remembered that would be impossible to do with his fingertips alone. For one thing, he didn't actually have fingertips. "Our entire relationship will change if I do this. I don't think I want to be like Chris."

"Chris?" she whispered.

"Your pal. One you can have platonic sleepovers with."

Danielle blushed. "I've never had a sleepover with Chris— platonic or otherwise. Unless you count the time we were chained up together in Seligman."

"You know what I mean, Danielle," he whispered. "You have to know how I feel about you."

She searched his expression and smile wistfully. "I think you know how I feel about you. But all of this—if it were to really happen—is uncharted territory. You and I have become best friends. That other thing we feel is just out of our reach, something we both understood was impossible. But should you do this, those barriers come down, yet even without the barriers, there are no guarantees. People long for all sorts of things they know they can never have, yet when they are given the opportunity to finally have those things—it doesn't really work out for them. Perhaps the impossibility of the situation made the forbidden more desirable. What we can't have, we tend to want more."

"Is that what you think would happen?" Walt asked. "Those feelings we have been trying to ignore would simply dissolve?"

Their eyes locked and Danielle smiled softly. "I honestly don't know. What I do know, there are no guarantees in life. All we can do is live it and see what happens. If it were up to me, I would want you to live that life and see what happens."

ADAM WAS ALREADY SITTING in Pier Café when Bill walked into the diner the next morning. The handyman glanced around the restaurant, looking for his friend. Once he spied Adam alone at a booth reading a menu, he started in that direction.

"Tell me it's an April Fool's joke," Bill said as he took the seat across the table from Adam.

Adam set the menu down and frowned. "April Fool's joke?"

"I just heard at the barber that those paintings of Danielle Boatman's and the one at the museum of Eva Thorndike are worth millions."

Adam chuckled. "No. It's not an April Fool's joke. It's true. The Thorndike portrait is probably worth five million at least. Danielle's might be worth more, considering the size."

"Damn, I can't believe that woman. I've heard of the Midas touch, but this is ridiculous."

Adam stood up. "I'll be right back."

Adam headed to the bathroom while Bill picked up a menu, still shaking his head. While Adam was in the bathroom, four men walked into the diner and glanced around. They spied the empty booth next to Bill and Adam's.

When Adam returned from the bathroom, he paid little attention to the four men now sitting in the booth behind theirs. Just as Adam sat back down across from Bill, Carla walked up to the table with a pitcher of coffee.

"Did you hear about that painting at the museum of Eva Thorndike?" Carla asked as she filled Adam's and Bill's cups.

"We were just talking about that," Adam told her.

Still holding the pitcher of coffee in one hand, Carla propped her other hand on one hip as she looked down to Adam and Bill. "Some of the board members of the museum were here for breakfast. I can't believe they've had that painting all this time and never knew it was worth a fortune. Oh my gosh, you should have heard them. They were already making plans to spend all that money they're getting."

"I thought the painting was staying at the museum?" Bill asked.

"Oh, it is," Carla said with a nod. "I guess that place Chris works for, Glandon Foundation, is buying the portrait from the museum and then loaning it back to them. The foundation is even paying for an addition to the museum and added security."

"I heard the foundation is also buying Danielle Boatman's paintings—of Walt Marlow and his wife. Are they going to be displayed at the museum too?" Bill asked.

"Yes," Adam told him.

"Can you imagine, those paintings Danielle Boatman inherited are worth over ten million dollars?" Carla gushed. "I hope no one steals them from her before the foundation pays her!"

"I don't think you have to worry about that," Adam said. "The foundation picked up the Marlow portraits yesterday, along with Eva's."

"But I thought Eva's was staying at the museum?" Carla frowned.

"That's where they're eventually going, after the addition to the museum is complete."

"Did they take them to the foundation headquarters?" Bill asked.

Adam shook his head. "I saw Chris last night at Danielle's birthday party. He said the three paintings were shipped to some museum in Portland yesterday. Some expert familiar with the artist —I think the artist's name was Bonnet—is coming in to verify the authenticity of the paintings, and there will be an appraisal before the museum or Danielle are paid."

"Oh my gosh, they're Monet's?" Carla gasped.

Adam chuckled. "No. The artist's name was Bonnet. Another French guy."

ONE OF THE men sitting in the next booth directly behind Adam had been attentively listening to Adam, Bill, and Carla's conversation. After hearing the name Eva Thorndike, he picked up his cellphone and made a quick internet search. After seeing the results, he let out a groan.

"Let's get out of here," he whispered to his companions.

"We haven't ordered," one of the men protested.

"Now," he insisted.

MACBETH BANDONI HURRIED toward the pier parking lot, his three cousins reluctantly following. It wasn't until the four men were back in their car and driving down Beach Drive did Macbeth explain their hasty departure from Pier Café.

"It's over," Macbeth told them.

"What's over?" one of his cousins asked.

"They know about the paintings," Macbeth told them.

"What are you talking about?" one of the men asked.

"Didn't you hear what the guys in the next booth were saying? They were talking about the paintings," Macbeth said. "Everyone knows Bonnet painted them."

"So? They don't know you have the originals. We can still get them and take them to the seller," another one of his cousins suggested.

Macbeth shook his head. "No. One thing about this business is to know when to take your losses and get out. That has kept me out of prison this long. They've taken the fakes to some art expert in Portland, along with another Bonnet painting." He then paused and let out a curse.

"What other Bonnet painting?" a cousin asked.

"It seems there was another original Bonnet in town we weren't aware of. At the museum. They've all been taken to Portland."

"I still don't see what the problem is," one of the cousins whined. "All we need to do is get the originals out of storage."

"That would be fine and dandy if we knew where in the hell the damn cops put them, which we don't. But now it's too late. We need to get out of Frederickport. I need to make myself scarce."

"Why?" two of the cousins coursed.

"Because if that art expert is looking at those portraits right now, he is going to realize the museum one is an original and the Marlow ones are fake. Which is then going to lead them to the two stored by the cops. And once Clint wakes up from his coma, he is going to sing like a canary when they ask him how his reproductions happen to be the real deal. I'll be screwed. They aren't going to care about some two-bit real estate agent who has never had so much as a traffic ticket. But they will love using him to get to me."

THIRTY-ONE

D anielle stood in the kitchen of Marlow House looking at the calendar hanging on the wall. It was April 1—April Fool's Day—which made her cynical-self ask, *Was Clint's suggestion simply a perverse April Fool's joke?* But then she remembered he had made the suggestion prior to midnight—on her birthday. This made her optimistic-self ask, *Was Clint's suggestion a wonderful birthday gift?* The gift of life for Walt? *What would it all mean?* Her head spun at the possibility and absurdity of it all.

"Considering all that we are dealing with right now, I'm rather relieved you didn't book any guests for the next two weeks," Walt said when he appeared in the kitchen, standing by Danielle's side.

"Have you made a decision?" she asked.

"No. Not really." Walt walked to the table and sat down. "I think it may be a good idea to gather some more opinions on Clint's proposal. Others—not as close to the situation as you or me—might see something we're missing."

"I assume you mean talk to those who know about you?"

Walt nodded. "All except for Evan. I don't think he needs to deal with this—at least not yet."

"You want me to call everyone, see if they can come over here today?" Danielle asked.

Walt considered her suggestion and then shook his head. "No. I think you need to do it somewhere else."

"But then you won't be able to be part of the discussion."

"Exactly."

She frowned. "I don't understand."

"Danielle, if I want everyone's honest opinion—an open discussion on this—I think it's best if I'm not there. It will allow everyone to speak freely. Do you honestly think any of them will feel comfortable expressing a reason why I should remain dead? I don't even think Chris would be able to do that."

"I suppose you're right," Danielle said with a sigh.

"Of course, it's always possible my dear cousin has already found someone and it's all a moot point."

Danielle walked to the counter and picked up her cellphone. It was in the process of being charged. She unplugged the cord from the phone and turned to Walt. "I'll call everyone. See if they'll meet me at the foundation office. I know Chris and Heather are working today, so it'll be easier if we all meet there. But before I go, I'll stop by the hospital and have a talk with your cousin."

"Assuming he is still there."

"If he is, we'll know he hasn't found someone willing to take his offer. And if he isn't and his body still hasn't woken up, I'll have to assume the same and figure he is out looking for someone to take him up on it."

"YOU'RE HIS SISTER?" the nurse from the ICU asked Danielle forty minutes later. Danielle had not seen this particular nurse before. The way she narrowed her eyes, Danielle didn't think she believed her.

And here Walt said I was such a good liar. Danielle smiled sheepishly. "Yes. By any chance, has he come to?"

The nurse studied Danielle a moment, yet didn't challenge her claim. "I'm afraid not. You can go in and see him if you want. Try talking to him. Sometimes that helps."

"Oh, I will." Danielle smiled at the nurse and then hurried off to Clint's room. The curtains were not drawn, which meant those at the nurses' station would be able to watch Danielle through the windowed wall as she visited Clint.

To her relief, the moment she walked into the room, she spied

Clint's spirit-self standing in the corner, a few feet from the head of the hospital bed.

"Did you come to tell me Walt is rejecting my offer?" Clint asked.

"No. I came to tell you he's considering it."

Clint brightened. Standing a little straighter, he smiled at Danielle. "He is? But he didn't come with you?"

"He'll only come if he decides to do this."

"You mean because if he leaves Marlow House and decides not to take my offer, he can't return—he'll be forced to move on?"

Tilting her head inquisitively, she studied Clint a moment. "How did you know that?"

He shrugged. "Just something he said."

"So you haven't found another spirit to take your offer?" Danielle asked as she sat down on the chair, pulling it closer to the bed. Leaning forward, it looked as if she were addressing her conversation to Clint's body.

"I thought it best to give my cousin a chance first. After all, he is family."

"I thought family didn't mean anything to you?" she asked.

"Maybe I'm getting sentimental now that it's all over, and I'm getting ready to move on. Although, I can't wait forever."

"Just give us a few days. If Walt decides he can't do this, I'll let you know right away."

After Danielle left the room a few minutes later, Clint stood by the windowed wall and looked out to the nurses' station. He watched as Danielle rushed past the nurses and out of the ICU.

"What would happen if Walt came for my body and I changed my mind at the last minute?" Clint asked aloud. "Would you know I wasn't him, Danielle Boatman? I imagine you would eventually. Of course, I could always pretend to have amnesia. I've heard that's not uncommon after someone's had a traumatic injury. I wonder how long I could pull it off? Would it be worth the money to be with someone you didn't really love? Maybe the real question, what's more important, love or money?"

DANIELLE WAS HEADED for the exit door to the hospital parking lot when Adam Nichols came breezing through the door, briefcase in hand. Wearing dress slacks and shirt, and a tie, he looked like a man ready to do business.

"Hey, what are you doing here?" Danielle asked. She looked him up and down and then said, "Wow, you have a tie on today. What's the occasion?"

Holding up his briefcase for a moment, he said, "I have a client who needs to sign some escrow papers. Unfortunately, his heart condition has him here for the week." He then eyed her and asked, "What are you doing here?"

"I came to visit Clint Marlow."

"He came out of his coma?" Adam asked.

"No. He hasn't come to yet. I was just checking on him." It wasn't completely false, she thought.

"That's nice of you, considering that guy is a tool."

"Adam!" Danielle admonished. "The poor guy lost his fiancée."

Adam's complexion reddened. He shrugged and said, "Yeah, I know. That was horrible and all. I feel sorry for the guy. But he's still a tool. Do they know why he's not waking up?"

Danielle shook her head. "No. But remember, both Chris and Lily went through something similar. It just takes a while."

"Ahh, that's right. I forgot about that. But, Danielle, remember, this guy is not Lily or Chris. It's nice of you to check in on him, but don't make yourself crazy."

"I'm not. I just wanted to see how he's doing. After all, he was our guest for two weeks."

"That or the fact he looks just like Walt Marlow."

"What does that have to do with anything?" she asked.

"Come on, Danielle, ever since you moved into Marlow House, it's like you have some affinity to its previous resident. It was you who proved he didn't kill himself. Why did you care so much? And I remember once you even told Bill and me you didn't want to upset his spirit, or something like that."

"I was just teasing at the time," Danielle lied. "You take everything I say so seriously."

"No. I think you have a crush on Walt Marlow. And frankly, I'm a little surprised you sold his portrait to Chris. I know you don't care about money," he teased.

"Don't be silly. It's just that Clint stayed with us for two weeks, and I feel horrible about Stephanie."

"Yeah, that really does suck. She was pretty hot."

Danielle scowled. "What, and if she were less attractive, her death would not be as tragic?"

"I didn't say that!" Adam grumbled.

"It's how it sounded."

"Maybe it did sound that way." Adam grinned. "But at least I don't have a crush on someone who's dead." He laughed and then looked at his watch. "I gotta go."

THEY SAT in the front office of the Glandon Foundation: Heather, Chris, Ian, Lily, and Chief MacDonald. They were all there, sitting in various chairs in the room, when Danielle arrived.

"So are you going to start with *I have called you all here today...*" Lily greeted Danielle when she walked into the room. Lily laughed at her attempt at humor, yet she was not actually teasing.

"I would have liked Marie and Eva to be here too. But I haven't seen either of them for a few days. I rather thought Marie would show up on my birthday, but she didn't."

"Spirits don't always have a good grasp on time, especially one as new as Marie." Chris reminded her. "So what is this about?"

"Actually, Walt asked me to call you all here. He has a decision to make, and he would like your input."

"Then why did you ask us to meet here?" Lily asked. "Instead of Marlow House?"

"Walt doesn't want any of you to be inhibited by his presence. He wants your total honesty and sincere opinions. If he's here when we have this discussion, he's afraid some of you might be reluctant to say what you really think."

"I don't know about the rest of you, but she has piqued my curiosity," Ian said.

They all looked to Danielle, waiting for her to explain why she had called them together.

Ten minutes later, Chris let out a low, long whistle at Danielle's conclusion. He shook his head and muttered a few words under his breath.

"Damn, I'm not even sure how to comprehend this," Ian said after Danielle was finished. "Much less give advice."

"Exactly when did I cross over to the twilight zone?" the chief asked.

"Walt alive?" Heather murmured. "How interesting."

"I think he should do it!" Lily blurted. "I adore Walt, and I would love to be able to see him more than in a dream hop. Although, I will admit I'll miss those."

Chris studied Danielle and asked in a serious voice, "How do you feel about this, Danielle?"

Nervously chewing her lower lip, Danielle shook her head. "To be honest, since Clint made the proposal, I've been tied up in knots."

"Knots in a good way?" Lily asked.

With a snort, Danielle said, "When are knots ever a good thing? It's not that I don't want Walt to do this. In fact, I'm overwhelmed with the idea he could actually be given a second chance. That he could be part of all of our lives—not just the people in this room and not just at Marlow House. More than anything, I want him to do this, but I worry that there might be some unforeseen consequences we're overlooking. Plus, it has to be his decision, not mine."

"Yeah, and all the people not in this room would think he's Clint," Ian reminded her. "And Clint is not a particularly likeable fellow."

Danielle nodded. "I know. And that bothers Walt, stepping into someone else's life."

"And that is exactly what he would be doing," the chief said. "Frankly, if it were me, I would want to know everything I could about the guy."

"Why do you say that?" Heather asked.

"We know he tried to steal Danielle's portraits. What else has he done? Does Walt really want to have a second chance and then find himself dealing with whatever mess Clint might have left behind?" the chief explained.

"What mess?" Heather asked.

"That's the problem," the chief said. "We have no idea what it might be."

THIRTY-TWO

W hen Danielle returned to her car to drive home, she found Eva Thorndike sitting in her passenger seat. The spirit had changed her chiffon ensemble for a royal blue afternoon tea dress, with long white gloves and a straw hat wrapped in a broad blue bow.

No one else could see the ghost. Heather and Chris had walked them all to the front door of the Glandon Foundation office and had said goodbye, but neither Heather nor Chris had walked outside, much less all the way to the street where Danielle had parked her car. And unlike the chief, Lily, and Ian, they were the only ones there who could have seen Eva, aside from Danielle.

Danielle sat in her car while Lily and Ian walked by and gave her a goodbye wave, totally oblivious to Eva's presence. She watched as they got into their vehicle, and then the chief got into his before their two cars drove away. Danielle slipped her key in the ignition but didn't turn it on. She looked over to Eva. For a brief moment she wondered if Eva was going to start tossing glitter inside her car. Fortunately, Eva's glitter was like Walt's cigar ashes, so it was more a random thought that just popped into her head as opposed to a real concern. What she was more curious about was Eva's role in Clint's offer.

"You told Clint about how he might move on," Danielle said.

"I certainly did." Eva smiled.

"Why?"

"Because it was the truth. And if someone didn't tell him, he might do something foolish and this opportunity would slip by."

"You think Walt should do this?" Danielle turned her back to the driver's door and faced Eva.

"I think it's Walt's opportunity to finish his journey here. Of course, there is no guarantee, but the Universe is willing to give him this chance."

"The Universe?" Danielle muttered under her breath.

"You see, Danielle, when we die, the most natural thing is for us to move on in our journey. But there is always that interim time—between death and that place after life, when a spirit may falter in confusion. It's one reason there are people like you."

"Like me?"

Eva smiled. "Of course. There is a reason you and Chris have this gift. Your purpose is to help those confused spirits you encounter along the way—help them to understand so they can continue their journey. I suppose you could consider yourself guides."

"I never really thought of it quite like that before. But doesn't that mean I didn't do a very good job with Walt? Considering he hasn't moved on?"

Eva pondered the question a moment and then smiled brightly. "I do love movies. If anything, my death has enabled me to watch every movie that has ever been shown in the Frederickport Theater."

Danielle wasn't sure why Eva had suddenly veered off into a new topic. *Perhaps she's changing the subject because she doesn't want me to feel bad for my failure at guiding Walt?*

"Have you ever seen *Heaven Can Wait?*" Eva asked.

Danielle frowned. "Umm…yes. It's one of my favorite movies."

"I just adore Warren Beatty." Eva practically swooned but then straightened up and continued with her train of thought. "In the first part of the movie, after Beatty's character dies and goes to Heaven, he insists he was not supposed to die. Of course, that overzealous angel who *beamed him up*—"

Eva paused a moment and laughed. "I also enjoy watching *Star Trek* when the local theater runs their *Star Trek* marathon."

She then continued. "Anyway…while the overzealous angel is arguing that Beatty is wrong—he is supposed to be dead—the head angel intervenes, saying something to the effect that the degree to which someone persists—if they keep insisting they are right and won't back down—then the probability that the person is indeed right increases exponentially. In Beatty's character's case, he was correct; he wasn't supposed to be dead."

"Are you saying that because Walt has persistently refused to move on for almost a century, it means he wasn't supposed to die?" Danielle asked.

"In a way. Yes. Not in the same way as in the movie. Beatty's character was clearly wrongly jerked out of his body by the angel. There was no overeager angel responsible for Walt's premature demise."

"I'm not really sure I understand what you're getting at."

"We all have a path to follow during our time on earth. A road we are on in our journey here. Because of free will, we can be inter-rupted at any time. It's not just our own free will that can disrupt our journey, but the free will of another person who does something to jerk us from our path."

"Like Walt's brother-in-law murdering him?"

"Exactly. Some people like to think bad things happen for a reason—that they are preordained. But that's not true. What's crit-ical are the lessons learned from those unfortunate circumstances and how we respond...but I digress..."

"Umm...I think I'm following you...I think..."

"Danielle, there are no guarantees we will be able to continue our life's journey. Tomorrow you can walk outside your house and be run over by a careless driver. You might be at the bank and get shot when someone decides to rob it. No guarantees. However, when a spirit persistently refuses to move on—when he stubbornly refuses to go—then perhaps his journey here on earth is not supposed to be over yet. Maybe there is something more he is supposed to do. Because of Walt's persistence, he has been given this second chance."

"But what about Clint and his life?"

"Clint has free will, Danielle. There is no guarantee he will honor his offer to Walt. He is free to change his mind at any time—right up until Walt's spirit moves into his body."

"What about Walt? What if he leaves Marlow House and then Clint reneges?"

"Like I said—no guarantees. And the only way Walt can do this is with Clint's complete agreement. Should Walt do something reprehensible like that Tagg Billings character and steal another man's life, the Universe would not be happy."

"So what you are saying, if Walt does this, he needs to realize that if he gets to the hospital and his cousin has changed his mind, he won't be able to return to Marlow House?"

"Nothing has changed in regards to the conditions of Walt being able to stay at Marlow House. When he leaves there as a spirit —for whatever reason—he will be unable to return there as a spirit. He will have a very short window before he has to move on—just enough time to get to the hospital and accept his cousin's offer."

"If Clint doesn't change his mind," Danielle grumbled.

"Everything we do—in life and after death—has consequences. Walt will need to understand he needs to *live with*—and I use that term loosely—his choice."

Danielle sat there a moment in silence, absorbing everything Eva had just told her. Finally, she asked, "What about you, Eva?"

"Me?"

"You've been dead longer than Walt has, and you're still here."

"I suppose I haven't finished here either." Eva turned in the passenger seat and faced the windshield. "Now I have something I need you to do."

"What's that?"

"I need you to go to the cemetery and talk to Angela."

"Angela?" Danielle gasped. "Why?"

"She wants to talk to you. I promised I'd bring you."

"I didn't even know you ever talked to her."

Eva shrugged. "I tend to avoid the cemetery because of her. I hated how she took advantage of dear Walt and the part she played in his death. But she has paid dearly for her crimes, and...well...I thought in this instance it would be best if I saw her. And after I did, I realized the best thing for everyone would be for you to talk to her."

"I have no idea why I would need to see Angela."

"Of course you don't, Danielle. And if you just keep sitting here, not turning on the engine, then we will never get you to the cemetery where you can find out!"

THE ENTIRE DAY felt like a giant April Fool's joke. Danielle drove to the cemetery and parked her car along the side of the street closest to Angela's grave.

When Danielle opened her car door, Eva leaned back in her seat and looked as if she was about to take a nap. Danielle didn't think ghosts actually did that. At least, she had never seen Walt nap.

"Aren't you going to come with me?" Danielle asked after she stepped from the car, and Eva didn't budge.

"No, Danielle. You don't need me. And I imagine Angela would rather do this without me hovering." Eva vanished.

"Seriously?" Danielle grumbled. She slammed the door shut and walked around to the sidewalk. If Eva hadn't piqued her curiosity as for why Angela wanted to see her, she might be tempted to just go home.

A few moments later, just as Danielle turned onto the path leading to Angela's grave, the spirit appeared.

"You came!" Angela said excitedly. "Eva promised she would get you to come. But I know how much she hates me. I was afraid—"

"What is this about?" Danielle studied Angela and realized she wasn't wearing the dress from the portrait—nor a flapperish outfit—both of which were what Angela had typically worn during Danielle's previous visits. Today, Angela wore a conservative dress suit circa 1925 with a burgundy cloche hat covering most of her blond curls.

"Please, please convince Walt to accept Clint's offer."

Danielle frowned. "You know about that?"

"Of course. Everyone does."

"Everyone?" Danielle glanced around. She didn't see any other spirits lingering nearby.

"This is Walt's second chance at life—and if he takes it, I'll get my second chance."

"At life?"

Angela shook her head solemnly. "No. But I will finally be able to continue my journey—I will be able to leave this place!"

"How do you know that?" Danielle glanced back in the direction of her car, thinking of Eva. "And how did Eva know that?" she muttered under her breath. *She had to have known; this is why she brought me here.*

"It's hard to explain," Angela began. "But I've known for a while now that something was about to happen—I felt it. I sensed it.

I just didn't understand what exactly until I saw Eva and she explained it to me."

"You just said everyone knew…but now you say Eva explained it to you? Did she explain it to them too? And who are they?" Danielle didn't imagine Angela would have a clue as to what she was saying —she barely knew herself.

Angela laughed. "Eva typically knows before the rest of us. She has privileges because of her status."

"Her status?"

Angela shook her head. "I've said too much. It's best that those on the other side not have too clear a picture on what happens next. It will only confuse things for you. But I know you have influence over Walt. I know he wants to do this, or he wouldn't have stayed for so long. And if he can just make a move in some direction—toward life or after-death—then my penance will come to an end. Please, Danielle. Tell Walt I am so sorry for what I did. For my part in his death. I did try to stop it, but it was too late. I was selfish. Please. Please ask him to forgive me."

"Do you want him to forgive you, or move on?" Danielle asked.

Angela considered Danielle's question for a moment. "I can't really move on without his forgiveness—and neither can he." Angela vanished.

Danielle stood alone in the cemetery. She glanced around.

"Angela?"

No answer.

"Umm…is that it?"

Still no answer.

"Angela?"

Perplexed, Danielle walked back to her car. Eva hadn't returned, and Danielle hadn't expected her to. Getting into the driver's side of the vehicle, she rolled down the window and made no attempt to start the car. Leaning back in the seat, she closed her eyes and considered all that Eva and Angela had said. After a few minutes, Danielle lifted her head from the headrest and opened her eyes. Putting her key into the ignition, she turned on the engine and then pulled out into the street.

"Why can't I be a normal person?" Danielle muttered. "Is there even such a thing as normal?"

THIRTY-THREE

W hen Danielle returned to Marlow House on Friday afternoon, she told Walt what had been discussed with their friends. Aside from Lily, no one had given Clint's offer a green light. Nor was it red, more yellow. It was not that they wished to deny Walt life—but they were concerned what that would mean for Walt, stepping into a virtual stranger's life, where he would be forced to suffer the consequences of Clint's past actions—whatever they might be.

Danielle also told Walt about her visits with Eva and Angela. He found it interesting—and somewhat encouraging—that Eva seemed to be promoting this unorthodox move. As for Angela, his feelings on that matter surprised Danielle.

"To be honest, I think I forgave Angela months ago," Walt told Danielle.

"You have?"

"I think getting to know you and Lily has made me understand her more."

Danielle frowned. "Certainly you aren't comparing Lily and me to Angela?"

Walt laughed and waved his hand for a cigar. He and Danielle sat alone in the parlor, Danielle on the sofa and Walt on the chair facing her.

"Just the opposite. You see, you and Lily were raised in a

different time. I never really considered what it was like to be a woman back then—what it was like for Angela. She didn't have the same choices you and Lily do. Even your choice to stay single is not looked at in the same way as it was in my time."

"Yet you are always trying to marry me off," Danielle teased.

Walt smiled. "I suppose I am a product of my generation, as is Angela. Oh, I'm not suggesting she was right to marry me under false pretenses or to plot my murder. But in her own way, I suppose she felt she had no other choice. Women married back then, and their husbands took care of them. And should a wife be divorced and left without financial support—as I believe Angela feared could happen considering my attitude toward her brother—there would be few respectable options left to her."

"But you were newlyweds. Surely she wasn't worried about you leaving her then."

Walt shrugged. "We fought a lot for newlyweds. And she knew the lengths I would take to disinherit her brother. And if I'm honest, I never really loved Angela. I married her because of my pride. She was the prettiest catch of the season and she wanted me, so I reeled her in."

"Comparing her to a fish? Now that might be a bit misogynistic," Danielle smirked.

"True. But the point is, neither Angela nor I married for the right reasons. Back then, I told myself I loved her. But I didn't."

"How do you know you didn't? Maybe you did love her back then," Danielle suggested.

Absently fidgeting with his cigar, Walt studied Danielle for a moment and then smiled. "Because, Danielle, back then I had no idea what true love was. I know now."

Danielle stared at Walt, her complexion reddening. But she made no comment.

He took a puff off his cigar and then said, "So how can I fault Angela when I was no better?"

"At least you didn't plot her murder."

Walt chuckled. "True. But I believe she has suffered for her crimes. I'm no longer angry with her. I do forgive her." He took another puff off his cigar and then added, "Of course, it doesn't mean I have any desire to stop at the cemetery and have a visit with her. Like Marie says about marriage, *until death do us part*. Angela is no longer my wife."

"Does this mean you are considering Clint's offer?" Danielle asked in a whisper.

"You know I am."

They sat in silence for a moment. Danielle watched as Walt smoked and blew smoke rings.

"You know what this means, don't you? If you accept Clint's offer," Danielle said.

"That I will no longer be dead?"

Danielle nodded toward the cigar in Walt's right hand. "You'll have to quit those."

Walt held out his hand holding his cigar and stared at it. "I will?"

Danielle nodded. "When someone has a heart transplant, they're not supposed to smoke. I would think that would also go for something like this."

Still staring at the cigar, Walt let out a sigh. "I suppose you're right. But to be honest, smoking this is something I do because— well, frankly—it's about all I can do now."

They were interrupted when the doorbell rang. Danielle stood up and walked to the parlor window and peeked outside.

"Looks like we're having another party," Danielle muttered.

"Who is it?" Walt asked.

"Everyone."

EVERYONE TURNED out to be all those who had been at the Glandon Foundation meeting earlier that day—including an extra person, the chief's youngest son, Evan MacDonald. Evan was the youngest medium in their small group.

"I thought it best if I told Evan what was going on," the chief said when they all settled in the living room.

"I think that would be neat if you were alive," Evan told Walt. "That way I could take you to the beach with us and teach you how to fly a kite."

Walt smiled down at the second grader. "I might show you a few tricks. I used to fly kites on the beach when I was a boy."

"You did? They had kites back then?" Evan asked.

The adults all laughed. Even those who could not see or hear Walt understood the gist of what he must have said to Evan.

"I believe kites have been around for about two thousand years," Ian told Evan.

Evan's brown eyes widened. "Wow. That's even older than Walt."

"I'm still trying to wrap my head around all this," Heather said. "I've rather gotten used to Marlow House being haunted."

"Considering Marie practically lives here now, and Eva pops in from time to time, it still will be," Lily reminded her.

"But this means Walt will be on our side—not able to see or hear them," Ian noted.

"I forgot about that," Walt muttered. He looked to Danielle. "I suppose that means I won't be able to communicate with Sadie and Max like I do now."

"It's all a trade-off," Chris reminded him. "If you do this, the next time Danielle needs someone to move heavy furniture or boxes up to the attic, she's going to have to hire someone."

Ignoring Chris's flip comment, MacDonald looked to the spot where he believed Walt stood and said, "Walt, after we got together this morning, Ian and I decided to see what we could find out about your cousin. While I would like more time to check him out, I suspect you don't have a lot of time to come to a decision."

Walt didn't bother making a response; he knew the chief would not hear him. But he listened attentively.

"Your cousin does not have so much as a parking ticket. There are no outstanding warrants on him, nothing. I called a few people I know from San Diego, and he didn't come up on any of their radars."

"While the chief was worried about Clint's history with the law, especially considering his bungled attempt at art theft, I searched in another direction. He apparently has paid all his income taxes. No red flags," Ian told them.

"I didn't even consider the IRS," Danielle muttered.

"He closed escrow on his condo and severed ties with his broker the day before he arrived in Oregon," Ian continued. "But all the money from the condo sale went to pay off his mortgage. He only has a couple of thousand dollars in his bank account. Unfortunately, he has about ten thousand dollars in credit card debt, but that's about all. I don't know if he could get his money back for his tickets to France, considering Stephanie's death and his stay in the hospital. Fortunately, he did purchase extra insurance on the van, and Stephanie was covered on the policy, so I don't see how the car rental company could come after him for the van."

"What about his medical bills?" Heather asked. "I imagine he's racking them up."

"I also checked on that," Ian said. "Looks like he has pretty good medical insurance, and he already used up his deductible for this year, so it doesn't look like he's going to have any more out-of-pocket expense. Not if he comes to and this doesn't drag on for months."

Heather frowned at Ian. "How in the world did you find out all that in just a few hours? You can't get all that information online, can you?"

Ian grinned at Heather. "I have my connections."

"Never underestimate Ian's investigational skills," Lily chirped.

"So what are you saying?" Danielle asked Ian.

Ian looked to Danielle. "Unless there's something out there we missed—which is always possible—the worst I see happening is Walt having to pay off eight thousand dollars of Clint's outstanding credit card debt."

"And it's a good thing Stephanie was driving," Chris said.

"Why's that?" Walt asked.

"If Clint had been driving the van, someone from Stephanie's family might try suing for wrongful death," Chris explained.

WALT ASKED Ian if Sadie could stay over at Marlow House for Friday night. Ian didn't ask Walt why, but he thought he knew the reason, so he agreed to let her stay.

Of the human guests, Chris was the last to leave. Walt had told him he needed to discuss something with him—alone.

Danielle left the two in the living room while she went upstairs to take a shower. Sadie had followed Ian and Lily to the front door earlier, when they had left for home, but when they didn't take her with them, she wandered to the parlor, jumped up on the sofa, and fell asleep next to Max.

"What did you want to talk to me about?" Chris asked. The two stood in the living room, Chris looking as if he was preparing to head home.

"You don't have a problem with me doing this—if I do it?" Walt asked.

Chris smiled at Walt. "When did you ever care what I thought?"

Walt smiled back at Chris. "I consider you a friend. But please don't repeat me."

Chris chuckled. "I consider you a friend too. And I would appreciate you not sharing that either. And I hope you take your cousin's offer. However, it has nothing to do with our friendship. It's that other thing."

Walt arched his brows. "Other thing?"

"Danielle."

"You want me to be alive...for Danielle?" Walt asked.

Chris sat back down in a chair and looked up at Walt. "I'm not a total jerk; I want you to have this chance for yourself. You didn't deserve what your brother-in-law did to you. But part of me wants you to have a second chance at life so I'll have a chance with Danielle."

Confused, Walt took a seat across from Chris. "I don't understand?"

"I can't compete with you, Walt. Not like this."

"Are you banking on me accepting my cousin's offer and then him changing his mind at the last moment so I'll have to move on and be out of your life forever?"

"Hardly. That would be the worst thing that could happen," Chris said.

"How so?"

"Think about it. How you are right now makes it difficult because Danielle has feelings for you. We all know that. I thought she had feelings for me too, but they really couldn't go anywhere, not with what she felt for you always getting in the way. But we all know you and Danielle have no future together. I don't think even you would like it to end up like *The Ghost and Mrs. Muir*."

Walt frowned. "*The Ghost and Mrs. Muir?*"

"It's an old movie. About a—"

"Yes," Walt interrupted. "Danielle has mentioned it before. But I've never seen it. What do you mean I wouldn't like it to end up like *The Ghost and Mrs. Muir?*"

"In the movie, they fall in love. But as you well know, not much future in that. When the ghost realizes he is interfering with her finding true love, he leaves. Well, he doesn't actually leave. In the

THE GHOST AND THE DOPPELGANGER

movie he just makes it so she can no longer see him—she even forgets him."

"Does she find true love?" Walt asked.

"No. In the movie she never falls in love again. But when she dies, he's there waiting for her. They walk off together into the clouds. At least, I think the scene had clouds." Chris shrugged.

"So she lived the rest of her life without love?" Walt asked.

"I suppose she had the love of her children and friends. But falling in love—no. She lived alone."

"I don't want that for Danielle."

"That's why I don't want you to just disappear now. Danielle is not going to forget you like in the movie, and your leaving will just make it more difficult for her. Whatever she feels for you will be magnified. If she isn't in love with you now, she'll have herself believing it, making it impossible for her to move on."

"Why will me alive be the better option for you?" Walt asked.

"Because then you and I will have a level playing field. I can't compete with the ghost of a man who is just out of Danielle's reach. There is too much romance and the allure of forbidden love."

"You think if I take Clint's offer, Danielle will end up choosing you over me?" Walt asked.

Chris studied Walt a moment and then said, "I have no idea. But at least I'll have more of a chance than I do now. And who knows, maybe once you get a taste of life again, you'll want to move on and see the world and leave Danielle here."

Walt smiled and shook his head. "Not a chance. I think you know how I feel about Danielle. It's not going to change."

Chris's eyes twinkled as he met Walt's gaze. "Game on, friend."

THIRTY-FOUR

A fter Danielle's shower, she wandered back downstairs, wearing her fleece pajama bottoms and a T-shirt. By her damp hair, Walt could tell she had also shampooed. When she walked into the living room, she glanced around.

"Did Chris go home?" she asked.

"Yes. He just left a few minutes ago." Walt took note of Danielle's bare feet. "You're going to catch a cold."

"I couldn't find my slippers," Danielle told him. She took a seat on the sofa and pulled her feet up with her. "What are you going to do?"

Before he answered the question, motion from the open doorway caught her attention. Her slippers floated into the room and to the sofa. She laughed.

"Thanks, Walt. Where were they?"

"You washed them, remember? They were in the dryer."

Grabbing the fuzzy shoes from the air, she slipped them on her feet. "Thanks. But back to my question. Are you going to do it?"

He took a seat across from her and watched as she adjusted her now slippered feet on the sofa to get comfortable. "What do you think I should do?"

"I'm just afraid that Clint will change his mind at the last minute, and you'll be forced to move on."

"Perhaps that will be for the best," Walt said softly. "For all of us."

Danielle shook her head. "Not for me. I know it's selfish of me, but I like having you here. And if you could have a second chance at life—that would be even better. But what terrifies me is not knowing."

"What do you mean, not knowing?" Walt asked.

Danielle's gaze met Walt's. "We both know you have a limited time between when you leave Marlow House and when you have to move on to the next level. If you don't get to the hospital within that time frame, then you won't be able to accept Clint's offer even if he wants you to."

"I won't have a problem getting there in time, you know that."

"I'm thinking of me," Danielle told him.

Walt frowned. "What do you mean?"

"If I don't go with you, I won't know for sure if it's you or Clint. Clint could easily pretend to be you."

"Danielle, surely you would instinctively know if it was me or not."

Her eyes still meeting his, she shook her head again. "No, Walt. When someone wants something bad enough, they're willing to believe anything. I'm not sure my mind won't play tricks on me. That I might ignore and make excuses, wanting to believe."

"You want me to do this, don't you?" Walt whispered.

"If you mean if I want it to work—more than anything in the world."

Walt smiled. "There is a way to be sure it's me."

"I suppose I could leave first," Danielle suggested. "Get there before you leave Marlow House, give me a head start, so to speak." Danielle considered her suggestion a moment and then groaned. "But what if something happened along the way? Maybe I get a flat tire or get stuck in the elevator of the hospital, or maybe when I get there, they won't let me in the hospital room."

Walt laughed and shook his head. "Danielle, all you need to do is remember something that only you and I know."

"Such as?"

Walt considered his suggestion a moment and then smiled. "Do you remember when we first met, and you were trying to explain to me that I was dead?"

"Of course," she said in a soft voice.

207

"You wanted me to know the year."

"I remember, I went and got my purse and—"

Walt placed a finger across his lips, silencing Danielle. "Just remember that, Danielle. Only you and I know. You never told Lily?"

Danielle shook her head. "No. No one."

They were interrupted when Marie suddenly appeared.

"Is it true? Is it really true?" Marie asked.

"Depends on what you're talking about," Walt said with a chuckle.

Marie began pacing the room while wringing her hands. "That annoying cousin of yours is really giving you his body? Do you believe him?"

"It's a chance at life, Marie. No guarantees," Walt told her.

Marie stopped pacing and faced Walt. "Now you sound like Eva. She told me all about it, and she kept saying no guarantees, free will, blah, blah, blah. I don't know why things can't be more orderly, more certain."

"Do you think I should take Clint's offer?" Walt asked Marie.

She studied him a moment and then let out a sigh. "It wasn't right what happened to you back then. You were cheated out of your future. And if Clint is foolish enough to give it all up, I say why waste a perfectly good body? As for me personally, I rather get the short end of the stick no matter how it turns out."

"Why do you say that?" Danielle asked.

"I've become rather fond of Walt. I'll miss our talks. If he takes over Clint's body or Clint changes his mind and Walt is forced to move on, I won't see Walt again until we both move on. Actually, I'll see him, he just won't be able to see or hear me. And seeing how things work around here, there doesn't seem to be a guarantee in that." Marie flopped down on an empty chair and let out another sigh.

"There is always a dream hop," Walt reminded her. "You could bring me into one once I'm alive again, and we could have a nice visit."

Marie let out a snort. "I'm not nearly as good at those as you are. Heavens, the last few times I tried with Adam, nothing. The best trick I seemed to have mastered these days is turning off Adam's computer."

Danielle didn't ask Marie why she would turn Adam's computer off, and if she didn't have other things on her mind, she might have given it more consideration.

Sitting in the chair next to Marie, Walt leaned back, rested his elbows on the chair's arms, brought his hands together and absently steepled his fingers. "If I do this, I will miss communicating with Sadie and Max as I do now…and being able to see and hear you and Eva."

"I don't suppose conversing with two stubborn spirits who refuse to move on is worth forfeiting a chance of life," Marie begrudgingly admitted. "I won't lie; I'll miss our talks. But I think you should do this. You have to at least try."

Walt stood up. "Then I need to go have a serious conversation with two dear friends." Walt vanished.

"Where did he go?" Marie asked.

"I think he went to go talk to Sadie and Max."

SADIE LIFTED her head and began wagging her tail when Walt appeared in the parlor. The movement of her wiggling butt attached to the wagging tail woke Max, who yawned lazily, showing off pointy feline teeth.

"I should scold you for being on the sofa," Walt said good-naturedly as he sat down on the sofa's arm.

Sadie cocked her head at Walt. Max, who was now awake, sat up and looked in Walt's direction.

"I'm not sure I can explain this. But you know my cousin? The one who looks like me?"

Sadie let out a little growl, and Max began grooming.

Walt chuckled. "I know you don't care for him." Walt went on to explain—as best as he could so they would understand what might be happening. He wanted them to know that if Clint returned to Marlow House and stayed, that it would really be him. Sadie and Max needed to understand whatever line of communication they now shared would end. He also wanted them to know that it didn't mean he no longer cared about them.

In his explanation, Walt spoke the words out loud, as he always did when speaking to Max and Sadie. But he knew it was not the words they understood. Max and Sadie understood Walt's spoken words no better than what they managed to pick up from Ian or

Danielle. It was the mental telepathy—although Walt wasn't sure that was the correct terminology—between him and the animals that allowed them to convey their thoughts to each other.

Eva interrupted Walt's conversation with Sadie and Max, her transparent vision appearing in the middle of the room, sparkling light gently swirling around her as she fully materialized. Glitter rained down from the ceiling for a brief moment while she appeared to be standing in a spotlight.

"Walt, if you're going to do this, you need to stop dillydallying. I'm hearing there's a disgruntled new spirit roaming the halls of the hospital. He is not happy about being dead. If he stumbles across Clint's body, there is no telling what he might do."

"Would he even know something like that is possible?" Walt asked.

"It's about survival, Walt. Sometimes that is instinctive. You need to hurry."

THIRTY-FIVE

W alt found Danielle still in the living room with Marie.

"Marie, can I speak to Danielle alone for a moment?" Walt asked. "Eva is in the parlor if you want to go in there."

Marie glanced from Walt to Danielle, then back to Walt. She arched her brow and made a harrumph sound before disappearing.

"It has to be now," Walt told Danielle when they were alone.

"When you asked Ian to leave Sadie for the night, I knew you were going to try. You're really going to do this, aren't you?"

"Before Clint made his offer, I imagined I could stay here indefinitely—let things continue as they are," he told her. "But once Clint opened that door, I began seeing things differently. The more I considered it, the more I wanted it. Ironically, when Heather casually mentioned the possibility, I dismissed it. No, I take that back. I didn't just dismiss it. The entire concept felt foreign and in some way repugnant."

"It doesn't now?"

"No. I wish I could explain, but I can't find the adequate words to convey what I'm feeling. I just know this is something I need to do —or at least try."

"And if he changes his mind at the last minute?"

Walt smiled sadly. "Then he changes his mind, and I accept the fact it's truly time for me to be moving on in my journey."

Danielle blinked, coating her lashes in unshed tears.

"If I don't come back, be happy, Danielle."

Walt vanished.

"Come back to me, Walt," she whispered to the empty room, no longer fighting back the tears.

DANIELLE STOOD in the living room, tears running down her face, when she remembered Eva and Marie were probably still in the parlor.

"Why didn't I think of it before?" Wiping tears from her face, she ran from the living room and found Eva and Marie sitting in the parlor.

"Quick," she told them. "Go down to the hospital. Walt just left."

"Yes, dear," Marie said with a smile. "He just popped in and said goodbye."

"You have to go with him. You need to make sure Clint doesn't change his mind!" Danielle insisted.

Eva smiled sympathetically. "It doesn't work that way, Danielle. Clint has the right to change his mind. That's how it has to be, at least if Walt doesn't wish to suffer future consequences when he gets back on our side again."

"Yes, yes, I understand that. What I meant is watch and let me know what happens."

"I'm sure we'll find out soon enough." Eva made no attempt to get up from her place on the sofa. Next to her Max slept soundly.

"Eva, I just need to know that when Clint finally wakes up, who will it be? Walt or Clint?"

"Or that other guy," Marie interjected.

Danielle frowned at Marie. "What other guy?"

Eva shrugged. "A poor man passed away this afternoon. It was a simple procedure; I suspect there will be a lawsuit. He shouldn't have died."

"What are you talking about?" Danielle found herself about to hyperventilate. If Eva didn't get her glittered self off the sofa and down to the hospital to see what was going on, Danielle would need to find a paper bag to breathe into.

"Eva was just telling me about the man who died during surgery today. He wasn't pleased at the outcome, and if he happens across Clint's uninhabited body, he might be compelled to jump in."

Danielle groaned. "Please, Eva…Marie…one of you…before it's over…go down to the hospital and watch so we'll at least know who it really is when Clint finally wakes up."

Eva smiled at Danielle. "I've done what the Universe asked of me, and now it's up to Walt. Don't worry, Danielle, because worry never solved anything."

Danielle might have continued arguing with the two spirits, but they vanished the next moment.

Sadie, who was no longer napping on the sofa, was now curled up under the parlor window. At the spirits' sudden departure, she lifted her head and let out a bark. Max continued to sleep.

WALT KNEW the hospital was where it had been during his lifetime. Technically, it was not the same hospital. That building had been torn down decades earlier and replaced with the modern one now standing in its place. For a moment he regretted leaving Marlow House so quickly, especially knowing he had a limited time in which to inhabit Clint's body before he would be forced to continue on in his after-death journey.

He should have taken a moment to ask Danielle for directions to Clint's hospital room. Walt couldn't waste time looking for his cousin, and he wouldn't be able to ask anyone for directions. Relief washed over him when he entered the front lobby and noticed a sign pointing the way to the intensive care unit. Knowing that was where Clint was, he continued on his way.

Walt discovered his cousin—spirit and body—in the third patient room in the ICU. Clint's spirit-self sat on the chair next to the bed.

Clint looked up at him and smiled. "I guess this means you intend to accept my offer."

"If you are still offering." Walt moved closer to the hospital bed.

"I understand that I can change my mind. I don't have to give my body to you."

Walt nodded. "True. It has to be totally voluntary on your part."

Clint smiled and leaned back in his chair. "And you came all this way knowing I could change my mind? Knowing you couldn't return to Marlow House—to Danielle?"

"Why would you change your mind?" Walt asked. "You said yourself there was nothing more for you here."

"True." Clint nodded. "My life as Clint Marlow doesn't offer me much. But a life as Walt Marlow—that's different."

"Walt Marlow is dead."

Clint laughed. "Obviously. I'm just thinking of Danielle Boatman and all that money she's inherited from you. The way she looks at you. The way you look at her. Some people have to choose between love and money...other people get both. I suppose I have to make a choice."

Walt frowned. "What are you talking about?"

"Love or money? What do I want most? Choose love and move on with Stephanie, or choose money and stay here as Walt Marlow?"

"Danielle would know it's you and not me."

"Are you so sure? I can be convincing." Clint smiled.

"There are things you don't know that I do."

"You mean like, *Walt, what is my favorite ice cream? What is my favorite color?*"

Suppressing his anger, Walt muttered, "Something like that."

"Often people suffer amnesia when waking up after a head wound and trauma. Who's to say that won't happen to me? If I wake up not knowing who I am, do you think Danielle will assume I'm not you? What do you think she would do?"

DANIELLE WALKED Sadie across the street without a flashlight. Overhead was less than a half moon. She hadn't bothered calling Lily or Ian and letting them know she was coming. She could see their light on in the living room window, so she knew they were still up.

"I thought Walt wanted her to spend the night," Lily asked when she opened the front door and Sadie ran into the house. Lily held the door open for Danielle, who followed the dog inside.

"He's gone, Lily," Danielle said dully.

After shutting the front door, Lily took a closer look at Danielle. She noticed her red-rimmed eyes and tear-streaked cheeks.

"Come, Ian is in the living room." Lily grabbed Danielle by the arm and led her down the entry hall.

"Walt wanted you to leave Sadie so he could say goodbye," Danielle told them after she greeted Ian. She and Lily sat side by side on the sofa while Ian remained in the chair facing them, Sadie now curled up by his feet.

"I suspected that's why Walt wanted Sadie to stay," Ian said.

"Why are you so sad?" Lily asked. "This is exciting! Goodness, you act like Walt's leaving forever!"

"If Clint changes his mind, that's exactly what will happen. I won't see Walt again. Well, not until I die, anyway."

Lily reached out to Danielle and clutched her hand. "Have faith, Dani. Have faith."

AFTER DANIELLE RETURNED to Marlow House Friday evening, she stood in the middle of the entry hall and looked up the staircase. The house felt excruciatingly empty. She realized this was the first time she had ever been in the house without Walt.

"No, that's not exactly true," she reminded herself. She remembered the brief time after finding the Missing Thorndike when she believed Walt had moved on. Yet he hadn't. Instead, he had made some sort of bargain with the Universe, allowing him to stay—at least until he left Marlow House again.

Emotionally exhausted, Danielle wandered through the rooms on the first floor, locking windows, any exterior doors, and turning off room lights. When she returned to the entry hall, the only visible light came from the night-lights plugged into random sockets throughout the first floor and a bit of moonlight slipping in the front window.

"Max?" Danielle called out.

There was no response.

"Max!" she shouted a little louder.

A moment later she heard a meow from the direction of the parlor. Looking that way, Danielle watched as Max sauntered leisurely toward her. When he reached her side, she leaned down and picked him up.

"This house feels so empty without him, Max."

She wasn't sure the cat understood, but he began to purr, making no effort to jump from her arms.

With a sigh, she continued to hold him while making her way up the staircase. Her left hand clutched the railing while her right hand held on tightly to the not so lightweight bundle of purring fur. Step by step, she made her way upstairs. Once on the second floor, she set Max on the landing and then went from room to room. Most of the lights were already out, yet she felt compelled to check each room.

Instead of going to her bedroom, she headed up the attic stairs, Max trailing behind her. The attic light was turned off, yet moonlight made its way through the attic window. Standing at the doorway, she looked in the darkened room. The silhouette of Walt's spotting scope stood silently by the window. The attic, like the rest of the house, felt utterly abandoned.

Taking in a fortifying breath, she stepped into the attic. Max had already made his way into the room, not waiting for her, and had jumped up on the windowsill to look outside. His tail swished back and forth while he looked out into the night.

Danielle wandered to the sofa and sat down. For the first time since moving into Marlow House, she was a little afraid. The house seemed bigger somehow—emptier—and a little spooky.

Danielle began to laugh. "A normal person would be terrified living in a house with a ghost. But I find it scary living in a house without one."

A few minutes later she stood up. "Come on, Max. Let's go to bed."

When Max made no effort to follow Danielle, she walked to the window, scooped him up in her arms, and took him with her. He mildly protested, but she refused to put him down. Normally, she would have let him wander the house at night, yet she didn't want to be alone.

Once she entered her bedroom, she shut the door, locked it, and set Max on the floor. He let out a meow in protest, pawing on the door.

"Really, Max? You can't just sleep in here with me tonight?"

Stubbornly, Max sat at the closed bedroom door, his front paws pounding it like a drum. With a sigh, Danielle acquiesced and opened the door slightly. Max slipped out into the dark hallway, his black tail swishing behind him.

Danielle closed the door again and locked it. She walked to her bed and pulled down her bedspread and then the top sheet and blanket. She climbed into the bed. Once under the covers, she scooted to the left side and then looked to the empty side of her bed. Whatever happened, she realized in that moment she would never again see Walt's spirit—clad in a three-piece suit—lounging casually on the bed while they discussed the day's events.

Danielle rolled over, her back to the empty side of the bed. Pulling herself into a fetal position and clutching a pillow, she began to cry.

THIRTY-SIX

D anielle woke Saturday morning to the sound of pawing on her bedroom door. Sitting up in bed, she wiped sleep from her eyes and yawned. The pawing continued. Stumbling out of bed, she made her way to the door and opened it. Max rushed into the room and leapt onto her mattress, making himself comfortable in the midst of her rumpled sheets and blankets.

Combing her fingers through her hair, she looked down at Max and shook her head. "Seriously? You ditch me all night, and now you expect to take over my bed?"

No meow came from Max. Instead, he started to groom himself.

Rolling her eyes, Danielle grabbed her cellphone from the night-stand and sat on the edge of her bed.

"You can stay there, Max. No one is in the house. Who'll know that I didn't make my bed this morning?" Danielle said as she dialed the hospital. A moment later someone answered, and she asked to be transferred to the ICU.

"I'm calling to find out if there is any change in one of your patients...Clint Marlow...Umm, I'm his sister...Yes, the one who visited him...Really? None?"

When Danielle got off the phone a few minutes later, she groaned and flopped back on the bed. Looking up to the ceiling, her head a few inches from the cat, she said, "Max, he's still uncon-scious. Why isn't he awake?"

While she still held her phone, it began to ring. Not bothering to sit back up, she answered the call. It was Lily.

"I thought he'd be awake," Lily said after Danielle told her about the morning call with the hospital.

"I didn't tell you last night, but Marie and Eva told me something rather unsettling." Danielle sat up on the bed.

"What's that?" Lily asked.

"Apparently someone died during surgery yesterday at the hospital, and his spirit was wandering the halls—very upset about being dead."

"What's this have to do with Walt?" Lily asked.

"If he got to Clint before Walt did, he might jump into the body like Tagg did poor Kent. That could explain why he hasn't woken up."

"I don't understand."

"If a spirit does something like that, they're normally confused. Once in the body, he might not really understand what's going on."

"Dani, last night you were paranoid about Clint changing his mind, and this morning you seem convinced a complete stranger hijacked the body."

"So?"

"So, I can't believe how negative and paranoid you are being about all this. There could be countless reasons why Walt hasn't woken up yet. And I say Walt because I have faith this is going to work. Walt deserves this second chance."

"But, Lily—"

"No buts, Dani. Sadly, people die every day in hospitals, for one reason or another, and most of those folks aren't too thrilled about being dead. And there are often comatose people in hospitals. But Eva told you it was very rare for a spirit to hijack a body. If that was the case, no one would be in comas for a very long time. There would be spirits lining up to jump on in."

"It doesn't work that way—"

"Maybe it doesn't work that way exactly, but I'm not that far off, and remember, I was once one of those wandering spirits misplaced from my body—and so was Chris—and neither of us got hijacked. Stop looking for the worst."

Danielle groaned. "You're right. I don't know what's wrong with me. I should be excited for the possibility, but I'm terrified I'll never see Walt again—at least not in this world."

"It's because you're in love with him, Dani."

Danielle did not respond.

"Think positive, girl," Lily went on. "Get yourself down to that hospital, and wake Walt up. If you'll recall, I didn't wake up until you were by my bedside cheering me on."

"You're right, Lily. You didn't wake up immediately."

Danielle could feel Lily's grin through the phone.

"So you go down there, Dani, because Walt needs to come home."

WHEN DANIELLE WALKED into Clint's hospital room forty minutes later, she didn't detect any lingering spirits. Slowly approaching the bed, she looked down at the still body. She didn't know if that was Walt—or had Walt's spirit been forced to move on? Was it Clint's spirit or the man who had died in the hospital who now inhabited the body? Or was it possible it was still an empty vessel and Clint was wandering elsewhere while Walt perhaps had not reached the hospital in time?

Danielle groaned at all the possibilities. Pulling the chair closer to the bed, she sat down and leaned toward the unconscious man.

"Walt, is that you?" Danielle whispered. "If it is, please wake up. It's time to wake up."

She glanced around the room. There was no sign of Clint. *Is he with Stephanie now?* she wondered. *Or did Clint change his mind and reclaim his body?*

Remembering Lily telling her to be more positive, she reached out and took the man's hand in hers. It felt cool. Pressing her finger along his wrist, she felt a pulse. Again holding his hand, she squeezed it tightly.

"Walt, please come back to me. Wake up," she whispered.

STEPHANIE MOUNTIFIELD'S mother had died when she was just fifteen, leaving her father, Barry Mountifield, to raise his emotional and challenging teenage daughter. Since she was an only child, he tended to spoil her, and she relished her position as a daddy's girl.

However, when Stephanie went off to college and Barry began

dating again, the daddy's girl was not thrilled when her father introduced her to the woman he intended to marry. Stephanie did not make his courtship a smooth ride. In spite of her selfish antics, she found herself with a stepmother she resented. Stephanie retaliated by moving from Texas to California, where she met Clint Marlow. Like her father had once spoiled her, Clint was willing to step up and fill the gap left by her once doting dad. Once again she was someone's princess, a role she savored.

Barry Mountifield loved his daughter in spite of her self-absorbed ways. He blamed himself for her faults, understanding in retrospect that he had been overcompensating after losing his first wife, and he hadn't done Stephanie any favors by spoiling her.

Since she had moved to California, he had only seen her once or twice a year—something he now deeply regretted. One thing he was grateful for was Clint Marlow. While he didn't know the man well, he knew he had loved his daughter, and she had adored him.

A parent should never outlive a child, he told himself for the hundredth time. He hadn't received the news of her death until the day before. It had taken the authorities that long to track him down. Much to his current wife's protest, he insisted on making this trip alone. Stephanie had been his little girl, and while he loved his wife, he knew his daughter had hated the woman he had married. Barry didn't want her by his side when seeing his beloved daughter for the last time.

He knew Stephanie and Clint had been engaged, and he knew if they had gone through with the marriage before the accident, it would be Clint's place to make Stephanie's final arrangements, not his. What he hadn't known prior to learning of her death was his daughter's plans to go to France with her fiancé. According to the police, they had found one-way tickets to Paris in Stephanie's purse. It hurt knowing she had not told him of her plans.

After making arrangements for Stephanie to be cremated—her urn would be buried at her mother's cemetery plot in Texas—Barry headed for the hospital to see Clint. He knew his almost son-in-law had no family, and he knew how much his daughter had loved him. Barry vowed his final act for his daughter would be to look out for the man she loved, since Clint had no one else to look out for him.

"I'm here to see Clint Marlow," Barry told the nurse at the ICU.

"Are you a family member?" the nurse asked.

"My name is Barry Mountifield. Clint would have been my son-in-law."

The nurse gasped. "Oh dear, it was your daughter who was killed in the accident?"

Barry nodded. "Yes. The police told me Clint was in some sort of coma. I was hoping there has been an improvement."

The nurse shook her head. "No. I'm afraid there hasn't been any change. His vitals are good, but he hasn't come to yet."

"Can I see him?"

"Yes. He's in room C. His sister is in with him now, but once she leaves, you can go in," the nurse explained.

Barry frowned. "Who?"

"Mr. Marlow's sister." The nurse smiled.

"Mr. Marlow doesn't have a sister," Barry snapped. He looked over the nurse to the doors leading to the patient rooms in the ICU, trying to figure out which one was room C.

"I'm sure he does," the nurse stammered. "She's visited him several times and seems very concerned."

"I don't know who she is, but she is not his sister, and I don't care how concerned she might be. Do you always let strangers in to see your vulnerable patients?" Not waiting for the nurse to answer, Barry marched past the nurses' station and headed to the open doorway of room C. The now frazzled nurse got up from her desk and hurried after him.

When Barry charged into the room, he found an attractive young brunette sitting beside Clint, holding his hand. Startled by the intrusion, the woman looked up at Barry while still clutching the unconscious man's hand.

"Who are you?" Barry demanded.

The woman blinked in confusion and looked from Barry to the nurse, who had just entered the room.

"Excuse me," the nurse said nervously, walking past Barry and to the bedside, where she quickly checked the monitors, as if worried the mystery woman might have done something malicious to the unconscious man.

"Yes?" the brunette asked.

"I was under the impression you were Mr. Marlow's sister. But it seems…you aren't?"

The woman smiled sheepishly and then gently set Clint's hand onto the bed. She stood up and faced Barry and the nurse.

"I'm not his sister, exactly." She smiled.

"Who in the hell are you?" Barry roared.

She blinked her eyes in response and then asked, "Who are you?"

"I'm Barry Mountifield. Clint was to be my son-in-law."

The woman cringed and then walked forward and extended her hand. "I'm so sorry for your loss, Mr. Mountifield. My name is Danielle Boatman. Your daughter and Clint were guests at my bed and breakfast."

"That doesn't explain why you're lying about being Clint's sister."

When Barry refused to accept Danielle's hand, she drew it back to her side. She looked from Barry to the nurse trying not to cringe. "I'm sorry about that. But Mr. Marlow didn't seem to have anyone here. And since he was a guest of ours—and he is the distant cousin of Walt Marlow..."

"Walt who?" Barry frowned.

"I'm sorry, you really need to leave," the nurse told Danielle.

With a sigh, Danielle turned from the pair and headed out of the room, yet not before giving a parting look to the unconscious man in the hospital bed.

WHEN DANIELLE STEPPED out into the hospital hallway, she heard a man call, "Wait!"

Pausing, she turned and watched as Barry Mountifield rushed in her direction.

"You never said, who is Walt Marlow?" Barry asked.

"My bed and breakfast is Marlow House; it was built by Walt Marlow's grandfather. Walt inherited the house, and when he died, he left it to my great-aunt's mother, and my great-aunt left the property to me. Walt and Clint are distant cousins. Clint and your daughter checked out of Marlow House before their accident. When I heard he was here and didn't seem to have any family to look in on him, well, I just figured I needed to. In some way, I felt we were family, but explaining all that to the nursing staff was a little complicated, so I lied...and said I was his sister." *It was mostly true,* Danielle thought.

Barry digested what Danielle had told her. He seemed to relax slightly. With a nod he said, "Okay, Ms...Boatman, is it?"

"Yes, but you can call me Danielle." She smiled sweetly.

"Ms. Boatman, thank you for your concern, but I'm here now, and I will take care of Clint's needs. There is no reason to concern yourself further."

Barry turned abruptly from Danielle and headed back to the ICU, not waiting for her response.

THIRTY-SEVEN

Danielle didn't head home after leaving the hospital; the only one there was Max, and he wasn't a great listener. She was reluctant to stop at Lily and Ian's, not wanting to hear Lily give her another *be-optimistic* pep talk. For a brief moment she considered stopping at Chris's, but she knew how he still felt about her, and it didn't seem particularly cool crying on some guy's shoulder about another guy—especially when the one loaning you a shoulder had feelings for you.

Heather was an option, but knowing her, Danielle figured Heather would start throwing together a mixture of essential oils and insisting they make the nurses diffuse it in the ICU. Danielle didn't think that was going to happen considering the nurse at the ICU had told her it was best if she didn't come back.

The only person she could talk to about the current situation—and who might actually be able to help—was Police Chief MacDonald. She remembered him saying he was working today in spite of the fact it was Saturday. Remembering that, she drove to the police station.

"He hasn't come to," Danielle announced when she walked into Chief MacDonald's office later that morning. The chief looked up from his desk and gestured for her to come in and close the door. The previous night she had called him to let him know Walt had left Marlow House and why.

"I know. I spoke to the ICU a few minutes ago. I understand your little deception was uncovered." He picked up the cup of coffee from his desk and took a sip.

"They told me not to come back." Danielle sat down on a chair facing the desk and dropped her purse to the floor. "So I need you to keep checking on him for me."

As he set the cup back on the desk, he asked, "You want some coffee?"

Danielle shook her head. "No, thanks. I'm jumpy enough without more caffeine."

He noticed her flushed complexion and the way she nervously jiggled her right leg. She wasn't kidding about being jumpy. "Take a deep breath, Danielle. Relax. Everything is going to be okay."

"Is it? Do you know who was there to see Clint this morning?" she asked.

"Stephanie's father," he answered.

Danielle frowned. "How did you know?"

"He stopped in the office this morning."

"You could have warned me," Danielle grumbled.

"Sorry. I was going to call you. I wasn't even sure he was going to stop at the hospital. From what he told me, he barely knows Clint, and he knew he was still unconscious."

"I feel sorry for the man, he lost his daughter. But sheesh, he was pretty snotty to me about visiting Clint." Danielle slumped back in the chair.

The chief arched his brow. "Clint or Walt?"

Danielle shook her head. "I don't know. I didn't see any spirits at the hospital this morning. So I have no clue who the man in the bed really is."

"If it is Walt, then it may be a little awkward if Mr. Mountifield sticks around to see him," the chief told her.

Danielle shrugged. "I'm starting to wonder if this was all a crazy idea. Maybe listening to a glitter-happy ghost was our first mistake."

The chief frowned. "Glitter happy?"

"You know, Eva."

The chief continued to frown.

Danielle laughed. "Sorry. I guess you don't know. Unless Evan told you."

"Told me what?"

"Eva Thorndike. Let's just say, her spirit-self is rather dramatic, which is not surprising considering who she was when she was alive. When she makes her appearance, she has a tendency to toss glitter around."

"Glitter?"

Danielle chuckled. "It's not actually glitter. Thank god. I'd hate to clean up that mess. But it looks like glitter." Danielle shrugged. "Anyway, Eva convinced Walt this was all meant to be."

"And you don't think it was?"

"I don't know. I just know Marlow House feels so empty right now. Oh, trust me, I really want this second chance for Walt." *I also want it for me*, Danielle silently told herself. "But now, with Walt gone, I'm wondering if it was an insane idea. It all happened so fast. And if it does work, will there be problems, like with Stephanie's father?"

"I imagine he's going home in a few days. He told me he was from Texas."

"Will there be more Mr. Mountifields?"

"Danielle, we already went over all this when Walt was deciding. There isn't anything you can do now but wait. Getting all worked up isn't going to help anyone, least of all you."

Danielle let out a sigh and leaned back in the chair. "You're right."

A knock came at the office door. Danielle sat back up straight and glanced over her shoulder as the chief told whoever it was to come in. The door opened. In walked Officer Brian Henderson.

"I just wanted to let you know I was going home…" Brian said to the chief before noticing Danielle sitting in the chair. He looked to her and smiled. "Hey, Danielle, out goofing around now that you don't have guests for a few weeks?"

"How did you know that?" she asked.

Brian walked into the office and sat down in the chair next to Danielle. "I ran into Joanne the other day. She told me you were taking a break from guests for a few weeks. Terrible what happened to Marlow and his girlfriend. I understand he's still in a coma?"

Danielle nodded. "Yes."

"Having a party?" Joe Morelli asked from the now open doorway.

Danielle glanced to Joe. Unlike Brian, he was not wearing his uniform.

"What are you doing here?" Brian asked when Joe walked into the office. "I didn't think you were working today?"

"I'm not. But I think I left my jacket in the lunch room. Came to pick it up." He glanced over to the chief and nodded a hello before looking back to Danielle. "How are you doing, Danielle?"

"We were just talking about what she's going to do now that she has all this time on her hands," Brian told him.

Joe arched his brows at her. "Time?"

"Yeah, she's taken a break from the B and B business," Brian told him.

"Good for you." Joe smiled. "I can understand that. Your last guest was a major jerk."

"Joe, one of those guests is now dead," Danielle scolded.

"I didn't say she was a jerk. And it's tragic what happened to her. But you have to admit, I bet you were relieved when they left. That guy was a creep."

"He's now in a coma in the hospital, with a broken leg, and when he comes to, he's going to have to deal with the loss of his fiancée," Danielle snapped.

"Or not," the chief muttered to himself, thinking that if it was Walt now in the body, he doubted he would spend much time thinking of Stephanie.

"I spoke to one of my friends in the ICU. I was curious to see how he was doing," Brian said as he looked at Danielle. "She told me his only visitor was his sister."

"Sister?" Joe asked.

Brian nodded. "I happen to know Clint Marlow doesn't have any siblings." He chuckled, still watching Danielle, who shifted nervously in her chair.

Joe frowned. "I don't get it?"

"It was you, Danielle? Wasn't it? I didn't tell my friend Marlow doesn't have a sister, but I did ask her to describe her. Sounded a lot like you."

Joe turned to Danielle and frowned. "Did you tell them you were his sister?"

Danielle shrugged. "They only let family in ICU. I wanted to check on him; what's the big deal?"

"You don't really want to get involved with this guy," Joe told her.

"Who's to say I'm getting involved with him?" The moment the words were out of her mouth, Danielle glanced over to the chief. They were both thinking the same thing: *just wait for Joe's reaction if it is Walt who wakes up in the hospital and then goes back to Marlow House with Danielle.*

"It's just that the guy is obviously going to need some place to recuperate after he finally gets out of the coma and leaves the hospital. He doesn't have any place to go. I could see him looking to you, expecting you to put him up since he's a Marlow," Joe told her.

"You see, Danielle," Brian explained, "after the accident, we tried to locate a relative—a next of kin. What I found out was that he doesn't seem to have any family, and he had just sold his condo and quit his job before coming up to Oregon. By the plane tickets we found in his fiancée's purse, we have to assume they were planning to go to France for an extended trip. So Joe is right. He really doesn't have anywhere to go when he eventually gets out of the hospital."

"And you need to promise not to let yourself get involved," Joe told her.

Danielle frowned at Joe. "Excuse me?"

With a stern expression, Joe continued. "It's one thing to take Lily in and nurse her back to health; she is your best friend. But you barely know this guy other than knowing he's a distant cousin to Walt Marlow and a rude jerk. You don't need to get involved. And the fact you're telling the hospital you're his sister...well...that doesn't make me feel any better."

Danielle leaned down and grabbed her purse off the floor and then stood up abruptly. She glared at Joe. "I didn't realize it was my job to make you feel better. And if I decide to offer Clint Marlow a place to stay while he recuperates, then that is my business!"

Without another word, Danielle turned from Joe and marched from the office, ignoring Joe's plea for her to return.

"ARE YOU OKAY?" Chief MacDonald asked Danielle when he called her on the phone ten minutes later. She had just pulled into the side driveway of Marlow House and had parked her car when she answered the phone.

"Are you alone?" Danielle asked.

"Yes. Brian and Joe left a few minutes ago. Joe's kicking himself, believing you will probably invite Clint to stay with you just to spite him."

Danielle began to laugh. "I know, isn't it wonderful?"

"Excuse me?"

Danielle's laugh simmered to a chuckle. "This kind of works out perfectly. I kept wondering what I was going to tell people like Brian and Joe—or Adam—or even Kelly—if—when—Walt comes home. This is kind of perfect." She giggled.

"Perfect?"

"Yep. Think about it, Chief. I won't have to say anything. I'll let Joe tell everyone how it's all his fault and how I'm doing this to spite him."

"You have a point."

Danielle let out a sigh and then grabbed her keys from the ignition while holding her phone to her ear with her other hand. "There is just one problem."

"What's that?"

"I hope Kelly doesn't read too much into this. She gets a little sensitive when Joe tries to interject himself into my life."

THIRTY-EIGHT

On Sunday morning Lily walked over to Marlow House, entering through the side yard. Danielle hadn't shut the gate, yet she had locked the kitchen door. Lily didn't need to use her key. Danielle was just pouring herself a cup of coffee when she glanced out the kitchen window and spied Lily walking up to the house.

"Morning," Danielle greeted her as she opened the kitchen door.

"Have you heard anything?" Lily walked into the house and closed the door behind her. She helped herself to a cup of coffee and joined Danielle at the kitchen table.

"I spoke to the chief about fifteen minutes ago. He called the hospital for me and talked to someone he knows. He still hasn't woken up, and they're planning to move him out of the ICU this morning."

"Move him where?" Lily asked.

Danielle shook her head. "To another room temporarily. I guess he doesn't need to be in the ICU...and from what the chief says, they're looking for another place for him."

"Like a care facility?" Lily frowned.

"But this gets worse. Remember how I told you Stephanie's dad showed up?"

"Yeah, what about it?"

"According to the chief, Stephanie's father wants to take respon-

231

sibility for Clint and is trying to have him transported to a care facility in Texas."

"What? It's not even Clint!" Lily gasped.

"We don't really know who's in that hospital bed now. I thought it was bad enough that I couldn't get in to see him—but what if Stephanie's father manages to have him moved to Texas?"

"Can he do that? He's not even a family member."

Danielle shrugged. "The chief doesn't think so, not without some sort of power of attorney, since he isn't related to Clint. But we have no idea if maybe Clint gave him a power of attorney. After all, Clint doesn't have family, and he was crazy about Stephanie, and they were planning to get married. Maybe he considered her family his family."

Lily groaned and shook her head. "Why isn't Eva or Marie down at the hospital keeping an eye on him for you?"

"Because those two just took off after Walt did—and I haven't seen them since. I swear, you can never find a darn ghost when you need one!" Danielle grumbled.

"I'm sorry, Dani. But hopefully Stephanie's father won't be able to move Walt."

"If it is Walt, Lily."

"You need to stop being so pessimistic about this," Lily insisted.

Danielle fiddled with her coffee cup a moment and chewed her lower lip, silently considering Lily's statement. With a grimace, she finally looked up into her friend's face and said, "I know you're right. But it's so important to me, and I'm afraid. I'm so afraid, Lily."

THE ICU NURSE was just checking the comatose patient's vitals when she heard him moan. Startled, she leaned closer to the man, her face now just a few inches from his, and whispered urgently, "Mr. Marlow, can you hear me? Mr. Marlow?"

With great effort, the man turned his head on the pillow, now facing the insistent voice beckoning him. His eyes fluttered open, revealing vivid blue eyes. He blinked several times, licked his lips as if parched, and mumbled, "Where am I?"

The nurse began to cry, tears running down her face. "You are at the Frederickport Hospital, and I'm so happy you're awake!"

"WELCOME BACK, MR. MARLOW," the doctor said cheerfully, clipboard in hand. He stood at the bedside; a few feet away was the nurse, listening.

"How long have I been here?" the patient asked, his voice raspy.

The doctor glanced at the chart in his hand. "Four nights now. Can you tell me what you remember? Let's start with your name." The doctor smiled patiently.

"My name? Didn't you just call me Mr. Marlow?"

"I guess that's cheating a bit." The doctor chuckled good-naturedly. "How about you tell me your full name."

"My full name?" The man, still leaning back on the pillows, turned his head from side to side. "I don't know."

"Would you have remembered your last name if I hadn't said it?" the doctor asked.

"Is that my last name? Marlow?"

The doctor exchanged glances with the nurse and then looked back down at the patient. "Your full name is Walter Clint Marlow. Does that sound familiar to you?"

The man frowned. "I don't feel like a Walter."

"It's because you don't go by your first name," a voice said from the doorway. Both the nurse and the doctor turned to the newcomer.

"Mr. Mountifield, would you please stay out in the waiting room until I come for you?" the doctor asked.

Ignoring the doctor's request, Barry walked into the room and headed straight for the bed.

"But I can help." He looked at the patient. "Your name is Walter Clint Marlow, but you've always gone by your middle name. That's why you don't feel like a Walter."

The man in the bed stared at Barry for a moment and frowned. "Who are you?"

"I'm Stephanie's father, remember?"

"Mr. Mountifield, please, you really need to leave," the doctor insisted.

Without having to be told, the nurse hurried to Barry's side, took him by the arm, and gently ushered him from the room.

"I just wanted to help," Barry told her once he was back by the nurses' station.

"I understand that, Mr. Mountifield, but Mr. Marlow is in a fragile state. He doesn't remember anything right now."

"I'm sure he'll remember Stephanie!" he insisted.

"Yes, but he's just come out of his coma, and I don't think he's ready to deal with the loss of his fiancée. You may be able to get him to remember her, but do you really want to tell him in the next breath that she's gone? He needs time to adjust before he has to deal with the reality of what's happened to him. The poor man hasn't even been conscious for thirty minutes!"

Barry let out a sigh and nodded. "I see what you mean. Clint was absolutely crazy for my daughter. I could see it in how he looked at her. What now? What's going to happen to him?"

"We're still moving him to another room, out of the ICU, temporarily. But now that he's awake, he can decide where he wants to go when he leaves the hospital."

"How can he do that? He doesn't even know his name?"

The nurse patted his arm gently. "Let's give the man time, shall we?"

DANIELLE HAD PUT the word out to all her fellow mediums: *if you see Eva or Marie, tell them to come to Marlow House immediately*. She was sitting on the front porch swing, with Max by her side, when Chief MacDonald pulled up to the house. He wasn't in his squad car; it was Sunday, and she knew he had the day off. Eddie and Evan weren't with him.

"He's come out of the coma," the chief announced after he parked his car and walked up to Danielle.

She bolted out of the swing, leaving it swaying and dislodging Max, who jumped down, disgusted by her abrupt movement.

"Where is he?" Danielle asked MacDonald while Max wandered off to the side of the house and disappeared into the backyard.

"They moved him to another room. But they aren't letting him have any visitors right now aside from Stephanie's father. I guess he was there when he woke up."

"And? Did he say anything?"

"Like what? I'm Walt not Clint?"

"Of course not. But did he say anything? He must have said something."

In a solemn voice, MacDonald said, "He doesn't remember anything. He didn't know his name."

Danielle frowned. "Are you sure?"

"Unless he's not telling the truth, which is possible considering the circumstances." MacDonald sat down on the swing and Danielle joined him. "Apparently, after he woke up, one of the first questions the doctor asked him was his name. He didn't know who he was."

"When are they going to let him have visitors?"

The chief shook his head. "I don't know. Is it possible that it could be Walt, and he really doesn't know who he is?"

Danielle leaned back and looked out in the distance, seeing only her own thoughts. "I honestly don't know. I'd ask Eva, but she isn't here. I haven't seen her or Marie since Walt left. If I could clobber a ghost, I would."

The chief reached out and gave Danielle's denim-clad knee a pat. "On the upside, I don't think we have to worry about Stephanie's father moving Walt to Texas."

"Are you certain he still can't have visitors?" Danielle asked.

"That's what they told me."

Danielle shook her head. "Then if it is Walt, he really has amnesia."

"Why do you say that?" he asked.

"If they've moved him to a regular hospital room, they don't typically restrict visitors unless the patient says he doesn't want to see anyone. I don't see Walt requesting that, because then it makes it more difficult for me to get in there."

"I'll try to get in to see him. If I have to, I'll claim it's official business. I'm sure I can make up something; I've been hanging around you long enough," the chief said.

"CAN I GET YOU ANYTHING, Mr. Marlow?" the nurse asked after settling the patient in his new hospital room.

"No, thank you," he said politely, now sitting up in the hospital bed and glancing around the room. With the cast on his leg, it would be difficult to get out of bed without assistance.

"Do you think you're up to having company?" she asked. "There's someone in the waiting room who wants to see you."

"That's fine. It's better than just sitting here alone."

About ten minutes after the nurse left the room, his visitor arrived.

"It's you?" the patient said.

Hesitantly, the visitor walked to his bedside and smiled down at him. "I'm Barry Mountifield."

"Yes. I know who you are. You're Stephanie's father."

The man brightened. "You remember? You remember Stephanie?"

He shook his head. "No. I'm sorry, I don't. But you told me earlier you were her father. I heard one of the nurses talking; she said your daughter was killed in the accident I was in. I'm very sorry for your loss."

Barry frowned at his would-be son-in-law. "She was your fiancée. You were in love with her."

Again the man shook his head. "I'm sorry. I just don't remember."

"You need to remember her. I don't want you to forget Stephanie."

The man smiled sadly. "I'm sorry. I'm sure I eventually will. At least—I hope I do. It's strange not to remember anything—not even my name."

With a sigh, Barry pulled the chair closer to the bed and sat down. "I'm sorry. It's not your fault."

"Maybe you can tell me about Stephanie. What was she like?"

"She was the most adorable little girl—beautiful woman…" Tears glistened in Barry's eyes.

"You two were close?" he asked.

Barry sighed sadly. "We used to be. I'm afraid we weren't as close these last few years."

"I hope it wasn't anything I did."

"No." Barry shook his head. "I think you were good for her."

The patient leaned back against the pillows and silently listened as Barry told him all about his beloved daughter.

THIRTY-NINE

Chief MacDonald walked into Pier Café on Sunday afternoon and glanced around. He spied Ian sitting alone in a back booth. Without pause, he made his way to him.

"Hey, Chief," Ian greeted when MacDonald reached his booth and started to sit down.

"Thanks for meeting me here," the chief said.

"No problem. Where are your boys?" Ian opened the menu he had been holding.

"Their mother's parents are here for the weekend. They wanted the boys to stay with them for spring break, but since that side trip of ours to Seligman, they don't like staying away from home for more than one night." MacDonald picked up a menu from the end of the table. "So I invited their grandparents here for the weekend. I had to work yesterday anyway."

"Poor kids." Ian shook his head, remembering how stressful it had been for all their loved ones during the hijacking. It had been young Evan's tenacity and his ability to see ghosts that had ultimately saved them all.

"I suppose you heard Walt—or Clint—or whoever it is over there—has come out of the coma."

Ian let out a snort and shook his head. He looked up at the chief. "How do you get used to this?"

The chief frowned. "Used to what?"

237

"I thought it was a stretch to believe Lily about ghosts—but this thing with Walt and Clint—that thing with Tagg and Kent." Ian cringed at the idea.

"I guess nothing really surprises me anymore." The chief shrugged.

They were interrupted when Carla walked up to the table, her now pink hair streaked with purple, reminding Ian of an Easter egg, which seemed fitting for the season.

"Hey, guys, what can I get you?"

"The cheeseburger combo," the chief told her, tossing the menu to the end of the table.

"Same here. But no fries," Ian told her.

"Then it's not a combo," Carla mumbled as she scribbled their order on a pad of paper. She then paused and looked to them. "Hey, I heard from a friend of mine that that Marlow guy woke up from the coma, but he doesn't know who he is."

"Word travels fast," the chief grumbled.

"The guy is super hot," Carla went on. "Blue eyes to die for. But kind of a jerk."

"I sort of feel sorry for Walt if this works," MacDonald said after Carla took their drink orders and walked away. "His cousin didn't leave a great impression."

"No, he didn't. So what did you want to talk to me about?" Ian asked.

"Where's Lily? Does she know you're meeting me?"

Ian shook his head. "No. She thinks I'm at home, working. She took Sadie over to Marlow House to keep Danielle company. It's driving Danielle crazy not to be able to go to the hospital."

"They're not restricting his visitors anymore. Apparently he told the nurses he would like to have visitors, said it might help him to start remembering. So she could see him."

"Does Danielle know this?"

The chief shook his head. "Not yet. She knew I was going to try to get in to see him. I called the hospital to find out what room he's in; that's when I found out they aren't restricting his visitors anymore. I know I should tell Danielle so she could go down there, but I wanted to see him first. I'm a little concerned for her. What if Clint did change his mind and that's not Walt? If Danielle isn't sure it isn't Walt, you know she'll invite him back to Marlow House."

"Now you're sounding like Joe."

MacDonald arched his brows. "You heard about that?"

"From Kelly. I guess Joe came home last night ranting about how Danielle is probably going to invite Clint to stay with her."

"What did Kelly think about it all?"

"Aside from not being thrilled her boyfriend gets a little too involved in what Danielle does in her personal life—she actually agreed with him. She wasn't happy it bothered Joe, but she shares his opinion that Danielle seems to make poor life choices."

MacDonald sighed. "I suppose from their perspective it looks that way. And it's not that I think Danielle is a pushover, but in this case I think she's vulnerable. Not that I'm going to try to stop her from seeing him. But I'd at least like to see him first and then prepare her—warn her if necessary."

"So why did you want to see me?" Ian asked.

MacDonald shrugged and said, "I suppose for moral support. I don't want both Lily and Danielle jumping all over me when they find out Danielle could have seen him this afternoon."

"You keep saying *him*."

"Because I don't know what to call him. I don't know if it's Walt or Clint—and that's the problem."

"Or that other guy Eva told them about," Ian suggested. "The one who died during surgery."

MacDonald cringed. "Oh please, I don't even want to consider that scenario."

WHEN CHIEF MACDONALD arrived at the door to Clint Marlow's hospital room, he heard voices inside—two men's voices. He recognized them both. One was Clint's, and the other was Barry Mountifield's. Instead of going into the room, he remained in the hallway, listening.

"I appreciate the offer, Barry," MacDonald heard Clint say—*or is it Walt?*

"You are more than welcome to come, stay as long as you need. It's going to be hard getting around with that cast, and you're not up to looking for a place to stay—or going back to work."

"If I was planning a trip to Paris, I'm sure I have some money somewhere that will allow me to rent a room while I get back on both my feet again. And while I appreciate the offer, I would rather stay on the west coast. It seems that's where I'm from. If I want to get my memory back, I need to be near familiar surroundings."

"Does this mean you're going back to California?" Barry asked.

"I suspect I may eventually do that. I'm just going to play it by ear for now."

"I want you to know, if you need anything, all you have to do is ask."

"Thank you, Barry. I appreciate that. I'm sorry I'm not going to be able to make Stephanie's service. I know I don't remember her, but it doesn't seem right that I miss it."

"I understand."

MacDonald got the feeling Mountifield was preparing to leave, and he didn't want to be caught listening at the door, so he cleared his throat and walked into the hospital room. Upon his entrance, both men looked in his direction.

"Chief MacDonald," Barry greeted him, "I was just saying goodbye to Clint."

"When are you going back to Texas?" MacDonald glanced around the room. There were two hospital beds. One was empty.

"I have a flight late tomorrow afternoon. I'm picking up Stephanie's ashes in the morning and taking them with me." He glanced to his would-be son-in-law and smiled. "I was trying to convince Clint to come home with me."

A few more words were exchanged before Barry said his final goodbye and left the hospital room. Just as he stepped into the hallway, a nurse wheeled a new patient into the room, heading for the empty hospital bed.

"You have a roomie, Mr. Marlow," the nurse said cheerfully. "This is Mr. Carter. Mr. Carter, this is Mr. Marlow." The strawberry blond man in the wheelchair wore a hospital gown and looked to be in his forties. The two patients exchanged a brief hello before Mr. Marlow turned his attention back to the chief, and Mr. Carter started asking his nurse questions.

With a nod to the door, MacDonald said, "He seems like a nice man."

"Barry? Yes, he does. So tell me, do I know you?"

Mr. Carter stopped talking and looked over to his roommate's bed.

MacDonald stepped closer to the hospital bed, hoping for an element of privacy. The next moment the nurse said her goodbyes and left the room. Her absence allowed Mr. Carter to focus his entire attention on what was being said at the next bed. His curiosity was not lost on the two other men in the room.

"As for your question, yes, we've met before. I'm Edward MacDonald. I'm the Frederickport police chief."

"Please don't tell me I have a problem with the law." He smiled when asking the question.

"Not that I'm aware of." The chief smiled back. "Can you remember anything more?"

"No. They said my name is Walter, but Barry told me I go by Clint. I don't really feel like a Walter. But frankly, I don't feel like a Clint either. So please, you can call me Walt."

The chief perked up. "Walt?"

"Yes. Walter is my first name, after all. But Walt doesn't sound as formal. Don't you think?"

"Okay, Walt it is."

"So tell me, how do we know each other?" Walt asked.

"I'm a good friend of Danielle Boatman," the chief told him.

"Danielle Boatman? Who is that?"

"She owns Marlow House Bed and Breakfast."

"Interesting. They tell me my last name is Marlow. Am I connected to the bed and breakfast in any way?"

"It once belonged to your distant cousin, Walt Marlow."

"Really? Same name. How interesting." Walt smiled.

"Before your accident, you had been staying at the bed and breakfast."

"Really? You know, the hospital tells me I can leave tomorrow or the next day—yet they're a little reluctant to let me just walk out of here since I seem to be suffering from some sort of amnesia brought on by the accident." He then paused a moment and looked down at his cast and chuckled. "Although I doubt I'm going to do any actual walking for a while. That's why Barry wanted me to go with him. A generous offer, but he's a stranger to me. I think it would be better for me to leave the hospital and go somewhere familiar—like this inn you say I was staying at. It might help me get my memory back."

The chief arched his brow. "You want to stay at Marlow House?"

"If there is a vacancy. Do you think there's a vacancy? It really would be the perfect solution for me."

"Umm…how about I have Danielle Boatman come see you? You can discuss it with her."

"Danielle Boatman? She's the one who owns Marlow House?" Walt smiled.

The chief nodded. "Yes. I'll talk to her about it."

"Why, thank you, Chief MacDonald. I really appreciate your help."

"My name's Bud," Walt's roommate blurted after the chief said his final goodbyes and left the room.

"Hello, Bud, nice to meet you. I'm Walt."

"Do you have amnesia or something?"

Walt smiled. "It appears that way."

"You don't seem that upset about it."

Walt shrugged. "What's to be upset about? I'm alive, aren't I?"

"I suppose," Bud muttered. "You really stayed at Marlow House?"

"That's what they tell me."

"Dang, I wish you didn't have amnesia. I'd love to hear what it's really like there. I heard you say you wanted to stay there again, but you might want to reconsider that and stay someplace else. The Seahorse Motel is nice."

"What's wrong with Marlow House?"

"I heard it was haunted," Bud told him.

"Haunted? By who?" Walt asked.

Bud shrugged. "I'm not sure. I just know a lot of people have died in that place. You were lucky to get out alive. I sure wouldn't go back if I were you."

FORTY

Outside, the sun was setting. Danielle was inside, alone in the parlor. The house felt so empty. The chief had promised to call and let her know what was going on with Walt, yet she hadn't heard from him yet. She didn't believe calling the hospital was an option, certain they wouldn't tell her anything.

Debating if she should go into the kitchen and make herself a peanut butter sandwich or skip dinner altogether, she heard the doorbell ring. Standing up from the sofa, she walked to the window and peeked outside. Chris stood by the door with a brown paper sack in one hand and a pizza box in the other, his back to her. Danielle smiled.

"Did you bring dinner?" Danielle asked when she opened the door a few minutes later.

"I figured you might need some nourishment," Chris said as he walked into the entry and headed for the living room. Danielle closed the door and followed Chris.

They sat together on the sofa while Chris set the pizza box and sack on the coffee table.

"How did you know I hadn't had dinner yet?" Danielle asked as she opened the paper sack he had brought and pulled out two sodas and two napkins. She set the sodas on the coasters already sitting on the table and started to hand a napkin to Chris, yet paused, waiting while he opened the pizza box.

"Just a hunch." He accepted the napkin, set a slice of pizza on it, and then handed it back to Danielle, taking the other napkin from her.

"Pizza actually sounds pretty good," Danielle said as she leaned back on the sofa and took a bite.

Holding a napkin with a slice of pizza, Chris glanced around the room.

"Something wrong?" Danielle asked.

"It really does feel different in here. Strange not having Walt pop in and make some sarcastic crack to me."

"You have no idea," Danielle mumbled before taking another bite.

Chris turned on the sofa and faced Danielle, his uneaten pizza slice still in his hand. "How are you doing?"

"I've never been fond of living in limbo, and that's what this feels like. Ironically, that's sort of where Walt has been since his death—in limbo. I know he needed to do this, try this chance or move on. I suppose it was time, but it doesn't make it easier."

"You sound like he isn't coming back." Chris took his first bite while watching Danielle, waiting for her reply.

She shrugged. "The chief told me he has amnesia. I just find it hard to believe Walt would have amnesia. I know Tagg didn't when he took over Kent's body. But Kent did after he reclaimed it. Which makes me think maybe Clint changed his mind. And I can understand that. I can't fault him if he chose to stay and give life another try."

"Danielle, Kent didn't have amnesia when he returned to his body—he forgot things later. After he had settled back in. That's not what's happening here. Plus, if I was in Walt's position, when I woke up, I'd tell everyone I had amnesia too."

Danielle frowned. "What do you mean?"

"Seriously? Think about it. If Walt wakes up in Clint's body, he'll know very little about Clint's life—about the people Clint knew. A prime example is Stephanie's father. He didn't know who he was. Far easier for Walt to come out and claim to have amnesia so no one will expect him to know anything about Clint's life. Just makes sense. I'm surprised you didn't consider that."

Setting her napkin and pizza on the table, Danielle rubbed the heel of her right hand against her forehead and shook her head.

"You're right. I'm not thinking straight. All this happened so fast. But you are right; Walt claiming to have amnesia makes sense."

"Of course, it's also a tactic Clint might use if he wants you to take him in and believe he's Walt."

Danielle groaned and slumped back on the sofa. "You're killing me, Chris!"

"Sorry, kid. But I'm trying to look at it from all angles. Fact is, you don't know anything right now. It could go either way."

The doorbell rang. Chris offered to get it. He left the living room and a moment later returned with the chief, Lily, and Ian.

"Aw, how sweet, Chris is cheering you up with pizza." Lily said as she took a seat across from the sofa.

"More like making me crazy," Danielle grumbled.

"We need to talk to you," the chief announced.

Danielle looked from the chief to Ian, noting their serious expressions. She glanced back to Lily, who simply gave her a shrug.

"The hospital is letting him have visitors," the chief told her.

"Since when?" she asked.

With a sheepish smile the chief said, "Late this afternoon our patient told the hospital he wanted to see visitors. That was before I went to see him."

Danielle sat up straight. "Wait a minute…he could see visitors, and you went down to see him and didn't tell me? You didn't take me with you?"

"You knew I was going to see him," the chief reminded her.

"Yeah, because we figured you could get in and I couldn't. Before you went down there, did you know they had lifted the no-visitor restriction?" Danielle asked.

"The chief just wanted to get a feel for the situation before you went down there," Ian interjected.

Danielle looked from the chief to Ian and then to Lily.

Lily shrugged. "I just found out about it fifteen minutes ago. It seems they're trying to protect you. I suppose that's sweet, but kind of annoying too."

"Don't you want to know what the chief found out?" Ian asked.

Danielle let out a sigh and looked back to the chief. "What did you find out? Is it Walt?"

"He claims he has amnesia. However, he wants to be called Walt. He told me neither Clint nor Walter felt right," MacDonald told her.

Danielle groaned. "Amnesia? If he has amnesia, then how am I going to know for sure? He won't remember anything."

"The thing is, he may not have amnesia," the chief said.

"What do you mean?" Danielle frowned. "You just said he claimed to. Why would he lie to you about it?"

"Clint would lie if he's trying to get you to believe he's Walt," Chris noted.

"At this point, I'm not sure if it's Clint or Walt. And if it is Walt, I wouldn't have expected him to come out and tell me who he was when I was there earlier," the chief said. "Because we weren't alone in the hospital room. He has a roommate, one who seemed to be hanging on our every word. If it was Walt, he certainly couldn't tell me, not with Mr. Nosey listening in. Making up an amnesia story makes sense," MacDonald told her.

———

DANIELLE STOOD in the hallway outside Clint's hospital room, mustering the courage to go inside. Taking a deep breath, Danielle stepped into the hospital room, forcing a smile, while her heart raced. In the farthest bed, the one by the window, a ginger-haired man with a ruddy complexion grinned in her direction.

In the bed closest to her was a familiar face. He smiled at her, his blue eyes twinkling. *They are Walt's eyes*, she thought. Yet then she remembered both the chief and Ian cautioning her—reminding her not to see things that weren't there—things she wanted to be there and might imagine.

He was sitting up in bed, the top of his hospital gown in view. It seemed odd attire for the Walt she knew. Sticking out from the covers was his left leg wrapped in a cast. It was no longer elevated as it had been in the ICU. His hair wasn't Walt's; it was too spiky and trendy. But those eyes—they looked at her in the same way Walt had looked at her countless times.

She took a hesitant step in his direction, her smile wavering, her heart still pounding wildly.

"Danielle," he said.

She wasn't sure if it was a statement or question. She knew the chief had told him she would be coming.

"Do you remember me?" she asked impulsively.

His eyes darted momentarily to the man in the next bed and

then back to Danielle. "Chief MacDonald said you might be coming."

"How are you feeling?" She knew the other patient's eyes were on her. He was listening, as he had been when the chief had visited earlier.

The man she wanted to be Walt put out his hand to her, as if extending a handshake in greeting. Danielle walked the rest of the way to the bed and accepted his hand. Instead of a handshake, he squeezed it gently and stared intently into her eyes. "Nice to meet you, Danielle Boatman. Please call me Walt."

Someday it would sound corny to her ears, describing how it felt like a bolt of lightning surging through her body as his hand held hers, refusing to let go. But lightning she felt, and the lump growing in her throat made it virtually impossible to breathe. He continued to hold her hand, not letting go. She didn't want him to.

Speechless, Danielle didn't know what to say—part of her wanted to ask the question, *is that you, Walt, is it really you?* But the man in the bed next to them continued to watch and listen, blatantly eavesdropping without shame. It seemed as if minutes were ticking away—minutes of excruciating silence—when it was actually only a few seconds. Danielle was getting to the point where she no longer cared and was prepared to blurt the question when another voice joined the room.

"Buddy, when Sandy told me you were in the hospital, I just couldn't believe it! Why didn't you tell me you were having surgery?" The question came from a petite young woman who rushed into the hospital room, ignoring Danielle. She ran straight to Bud and threw her arms around him, a string of questions tumbling from her lips, one after another.

The man holding Danielle's hand took the opportunity to jerk her toward him. She practically fell onto the bed, yet her feet managed to remain firmly on the floor. Her face was just inches from his, and she could feel his warm breath.

"He chose love over money, Danielle," he whispered.

Danielle frowned. "What?"

"Clint, he chose love over money." He smiled up into her face, his blue eyes twinkling.

Danielle swallowed nervously. She felt his hand squeeze hers tighter, not letting go.

"It was a calendar, Danielle. That's what you showed me on the first day we met. You got it from your purse. The one you left so carelessly on my grandmother's cherry wood table." He smiled mischievously.

"Walt? It's really you?" Unshed tears glistened in her eyes.

Still holding her hand, Walt glanced over to his roommate. The woman was now sitting on the bed with Bud. The two were busy talking; neither party was paying attention to him or Danielle.

Walt looked back into Danielle's eyes. Pulling her hand to his lips, he quickly kissed it and then whispered, "I want to go home, Danielle. I want to go home with you."

THE GHOST OF SECOND CHANCES

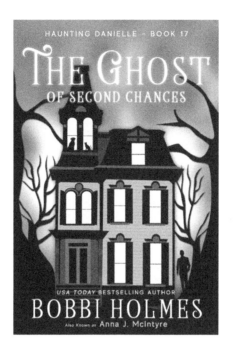

RETURN TO MARLOW HOUSE IN

THE GHOST OF SECOND CHANCES

HAUNTING DANIELLE, BOOK 17

When Clint Marlow's partner in crime is found murdered in the basement of Marlow House, Clint is the likely suspect. The only problem, Clint is dead. But that doesn't matter to the FBI agents investigating the case. Clint looks alive to them.

Meanwhile, Danielle's housemate Walt is coming to terms with his new reality, which is complicated with the FBI underfoot. Fortunately for Walt, he still has a few paranormal tricks up his sleeve.

NON-FICTION BY

BOBBI ANN JOHNSON HOLMES

HAVASU PALMS, A HOSTILE TAKEOVER
WHERE THE ROAD ENDS, RECIPES & REMEMBRANCES
MOTHERHOOD, A BOOK OF POETRY
THE STORY OF THE CHRISTMAS VILLAGE

Made in United States
North Haven, CT
27 April 2022

18634025R00157